THE SIEGE OF DARABAD

First published in Great Britain by Black Apollo Press, 2010

Copyright © Haig Tahta 2010

A CIP catalogue record of this book is available at the British Library.

ISBN: 9781900355704

The Siege of Darabad

HAIG TAHTA

For my good friends
Roly & Audrey and for all
their support over the years

Haig

BLACK
APOLLO
PRESS

To the memory of my friend Ronnie with whom I explored the Krak des Chevaliers and who accompanied me on my first visit to woo my future wife, the mother of my three children.

CONTENTS

PROLOGUE

The Siege of Darabad is a work of fiction. Darabad, as described, does not exist, but it is typical of a small town in the province of Bihar at the time. Many of the events portrayed happened in one form or another somewhere in British North India during that fateful year of 1857, the hundredth anniversary of the Battle of Plassey which had created British India in the first place. The individuals playing their part in the drama of the siege are also fictional.

The background however, and the characters and events outside the fictional district of Shantapur are factual. They represent a part of the historical baggage of almost every small boy brought up in any English school before the cultural revolution of the sixties. This historical background as portrayed ignores the impact of political correctness in all its forms, both the correctness that is and remains necessary and that which is merely part of a changing fashion. It is no use deploring some of the opinions and attitudes of the characters – that is how it was in 1857.

As the most cursory military research would show the 66th and 68th Sepoy Regiments of the Bengal army did not then exist, though, once again, they are representative of the many that did. The Nawab of Jagpur is also an imaginary character, although again the problems that he faced were duplicated throughout North India in that year and had to be faced by many such rulers.

Finally, while the characters involved in the siege at Darabad are entirely fictional, they are inspired by a work of strictly historical research carried out by the late Sir Ronald Lindsay, about a minor incident during the mutiny which took place at the town of Arrah in the province of Bihar. This concerned a historical situation where a party of Europeans, with the support of a detachment of Sikhs, were besieged in a building much like that at Darabad.

The judgements throughout and the argument of the epilogue are my responsibility alone.

THE PEOPLE OF DARABAD

The British officials:

Arthur Drummond	the Judge
Henrietta Drummond	his wife
George Grant	the senior magistrate
James Henty	the civil surgeon
Azimullah Hassan	the deputy collector
Henry Johnson	the Assistant magistrate

The Railway employees:

John Tate	thes enior Railway manager
Harriet Tate	his wife
Conrad Tate	their twelve-year-old son
Chloe Tate	their three-year-old daughter
Paul Kelly	the chief engineer
'Dickie' Derounian	the sale manager

Some civilians:

Marietta Postern	wife of Ensign James Postern
Alphonsine da Costa	mother of Marietta
Ali	Derounian's cookboy
Dr. Bannerjee	Tutor to Conrad and Ali

Jagpur

Haidar Presaud	a merchant from Patna
Saridar Khan	the Nawab of Jagpur

PART I

The Storm Approaches

May 1857

"Harriet, my dear, Conrad is twelve. He's a lively boy and could go far given a decent chance. But he has to be given that chance to compete in the world we live in. He has to be sent back to England to one of those crammers or prep schools or whatever, to enable him to get into a good public-school. It's already very late. Everyone we know have already sent their sons back – most of them even before they were eight years old."

John Tate sat on the hard upright cane chair opposite his wife stretched out on a sofa, both sipping dark Indian tea, in his case without any milk or sugar. It was after dinner. There was a welcome breeze ruffling the long muslin drapes that covered the open doors and windows. The children were in bed and the couple were sitting comfortably together in the large high-ceilinged sitting room of their house half a mile out from the centre of the town of Darabad.

Their discussion was on a problem that faced all the British in India. Harriet was arguing passionately and with real conviction. However this was 1857 after all and she was aware that however liberal her husband may be there was a limit beyond which she could not go.

"John, I…"

"For God's sake, my dear, you must see that he is running round wild here – playing with Indian boys, roaming the countryside, always exploring in the native town, and what his education…"

"Well that may all be so, but he is learning a good deal more than he would be if he was sent to some hopeless boarding school in some remote part of the English countryside. His maths grounding under Dr. Bannerjee is far superior I'm quite sure to anything he might have been achieving in some uncaring establishment deep in the Surrey or Sussex rural backwater. I myself give him an understanding of history and literature far better than anything he could be getting back at home and..."

"*There*, Harriet, *there*... you said it – 'at home'. That is the whole point. Unless he goes back and lives there he will never think of England as 'home' – backwater countryside or not."

"John, John – for all children, home is where their parents live, not some remote idealised..."

"Come, you know very well what I mean. You must see that in the long run it would be wrong for Conrad to think of Darabad as his home. Sooner or later we are going to leave this country and..."

"Are you saying we, as in the family, or we, as the English."

"Both probably – but certainly in this context I am referring to the family."

There was a short silence between them and then Harriet said sadly –

"John, those places to which you want to send Conrad are second-rate. Harsh unfeeling discipline – no visits – no letters – no special days for the children like birthdays – no love."

"But that is what boys have to learn to cope with."

"Ultimately, John, the choice is this. You and almost everyone else here in British India have decided to sacrifice the emotional security of their children, particularly the boys, for the sake of their material prospects. I cannot agree that that is the right priority."

John Tate looked at his wife affectionately and remained silent for a short time as he sipped his tea. John was the only son of a Dorsetshire farmer, the youngest in a family with four elder sisters, the last-born of whom was already ten years older than himself. He had been used all his life to having unstinting love extended to him by all these older women and girls. Confronted with the arrival after so many years of a somewhat delicate baby boy, his sisters had doted on him, each in their own way competing to take on the role of the mother who had died in this last unexpected childbirth.

The farm, tucked up on a hillside facing south running down towards the sea in the distance some miles away, was small and easy to manage. It was a modest holding – an apple and plum tree orchard, fields for the sheep, a few cows and some well maintained vegetable plots. The whole farm was worked fairly easily by his father with only occasionally the necessity of a helping hand by a local itinerant farm labourer.

It became clear from quite an early stage that John was not destined to take over the running of the farm when he grew up. He received as good an education as was possible in the circumstances with all the encouragement of his four robust and cheerful sisters and with the somewhat grudging approval of his father.

From the age of eight John had become fascinated by hearing and reading about the emerging railways and the development of the steam engine. The Middleton railway had already been running for more than six years before John was born in 1818, so that by 1826, when he was eight years old, the railways were no longer a complete novelty, and knowledge about them was available even in the depths of the English countryside.

So it was that John Tate had taken up engineering as a career and had moved specifically into railway engineering. In May 1845, when John was still only 26 years-old, the East India Railway Company was founded. A year later John had been accepted by that Company as an employee, had married Harriet, and almost immediately after the marriage had sailed to Calcutta where he soon became one of the senior engineers working on the new railway line the Company was building. This line was ultimately destined to connect Calcutta with Delhi and the North-Western provinces. The couple's first-born son Conrad, the subject of this important discussion, was born in Calcutta soon after their arrival in 1845 and was now twelve years old.

John already knew when he married Harriet that she was an

unusually independent and strong-minded woman. It was what he wanted. He didn't like riding roughshod over anyone else's opinions or feelings, preferring to listen first and only insist after, if necessary. However, as the father of the family, he had to take final responsibility. He broke the comfortable silence, saying –

"Harriet, my dear, the fact is society currently requires boys to have a grounding in classical education if they are to succeed. A knowledge of Greek and Latin and their philosophical under-pinings is essential. So we have to see that he acquires that knowl-edge – knowledge he can only acquire back in England."

"Very well – I have to accept that, even though I think it is a lot of nonsense, but I..."

"Harriet, calm down, my dear. Look, we don't live in a vacuum. I am not saying you are entirely wrong, but if the world respects classical learning and grants success to those who have mastered it – then we have to comply with that requirement to give our son his best chance in life. But my love it is not only that. You yourself, without thinking, used the words 'back home' just now. Conrad will only be able to think of England that way if we send him back when he is still at a formative age. I accept your point about loneliness, and that no care or attention by even the most sensitive of guardians can take the place of a parent – but he is now over eleven and will be able to cope."

"Oh, John, my love. Just as you humoured me in not sending Conrad away when he was only eight, I too will have to compro-mise. I agree that Conrad will have to leave us to go home – there I've used the word 'home' again – as soon as possible after the summer ends."

Harriet smiled at her husband. After Conrad, two more babies had been born but had died almost immediately. The couple however now had a little girl, already three years old, who was thriving in the charge of a good-natured *ayah*. Harriet's son had had no difficulty in accepting the arrival of a competitor for his mother's affection. He had been over eight years-old and the fact that the new baby was a little girl had helped. Either way, the birth of Chloe had reconciled Harriet to the inevitability of Conrad's return to England after his twelfth birthday.

Harriet was the only child of rather elderly parents who had married late. Her father was a carpenter and they had lived in a tiny stone terraced house in Lyme Regis in the beautiful county of Dorset. She, being an only child, had benefited from the fact that her jolly father, and somewhat severe mother, could afford to send her not only to school but also for further education. Accordingly, she had not had to go out to work at thirteen as had so many of her contemporaries. But the family was small, her parents both also having been only children, and thus as far as the future of Conrad was concerned she had had the additional problem of not knowing to whom she could entrust him in England.

She had easily persuaded John that the practice of sending six- or seven-year-old boys to live for years with total strangers was undesirable. Living with grandparents during school holidays was the usual solution, but in her case, her own parents, well into their sixties, would simply have been unable to cope. But sooner or later Conrad would have to go. It would not be too difficult to arrange. There was, of course, no way they could afford for her to go with him to help settle him down before returning to India, which was the solution for some. He would have to be entrusted to a lady or family journeying back to England on leave, who would, at a cost, chaperone the boy and see him delivered safely.

Conrad, of course, was not consulted. However, after this last conversation on the first of May, Harriet started writing all the letters required to begin the process of organising all the necessary arrangements.

* * *

For the moment then, what constituted 'at home' for the young Conrad Tate? Darabad was a small ramshackle town striving to be more than an overgrown village, sitting right in the middle of the province of Bihar in Northern India. It lay about

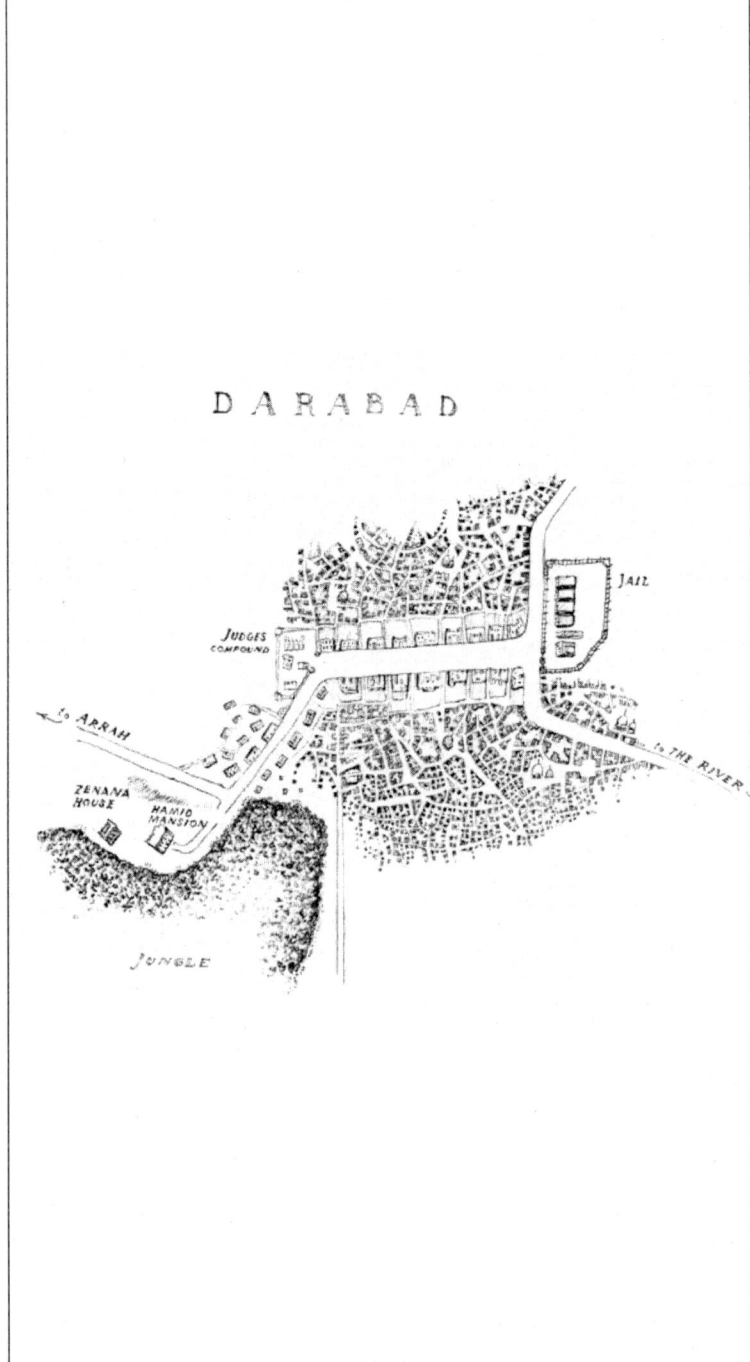

thirty miles south of the River Ganges. The town was neither on any major river, nor on any important trunk road. It had figured in no great historical epic and had never had any walls or forts. It commanded no important pass, nor was it of any strategic importance so far as the surrounding countryside was concerned. It was simply there.

The town had five Hindu temples of various types and sizes, and there was a new and imposing mosque on the road approaching the town from the east. The old imposing stone houses, which ran on each side down the main street, gave a solid, pleasing appearance if you stood looking directly at them. They had the usual balconies on the upper floor, and many of them had heavily latticed windows overlooking the street, where the ladies of the zenana could look out on the hustle of the street below without themselves being seen – a style well-known throughout the East, which reached its apogee of design and beauty in the principle cities of the Ottoman Empire.

This main street in question was very wide and on most days contained covered market stalls which ran all along it on both sides during the morning until midday. It was referred to, somewhat grandiloquently, as the Maidan.

Behind this line of houses, and the courtyards which they surrounded, lay the open drains and mud walls of the poorer inhabitants. Leading away from the main street, both north and south, in a confused jumble was a maze of hard-packed clay and dirt lanes through which the children ran screaming and shouting most of the day. This was the darker side of the town where the less fortunate members of the community lived, repro-duced and squabbled.

It was an area which had one redeeming feature – it was the only part of the whole town where the children, at least up to a certain age, played together with little attention to colour, caste or religion. From the age at which they were first let out to play in the streets and the surrounding fields until the age of about ten or eleven, they ran about the lanes, formed their groups and counter-groups, hated each other and loved each other, with no regard to their parent's ridiculous prejudices and inane religious taboos and ritual exclusivities. This freedom and the friendships made in the streets always came to an abrupt end with the onset of puberty and the strains and stresses of burgeoning sexuality, when they were all suddenly forced to become aware of their differences and of the overlay of religion, culture and custom which divided their parents.

So lay Darabad, brooding all summer under the burning North Indian sun, drowning for a short time in the rainy seasons, thinking only about itself all the year round. It was there – because it was there.

However two factors had recently changed this age-old mediocrity. Firstly, it had been chosen by an anonymous British administrator, working in a cramped East India Company office in Calcutta, to become the local headquarters for the surrounding rural district of Shantapur. Secondly and even more significantly, sited as it was right in the centre of the district and on the direct route to Delhi, it was now destined to become an important stop on the Calcutta to Delhi railway line being constructed by the newly formed East India Railway Company.

The line had already been opened between Calcutta and Raniganj. An average of 12,000 passengers a week were already travelling on the line. The third class fare was less than a half penny per mile and all the gloomy prophecies that the Indians would not use the new form of transport, due to caste prejudices and religious sensibilities, had been proved to be totally wrong.

This meant that in addition to the handful of British officials now stationed in the town there was also a significant group of railway employees preparing the ground for the arrival of the line. Under the overall supervision of John Tate, whose problems with his spirited wife have already been noted, there were in fact a further six others.

There was Paul Kelly who was the chief Engineer in charge of the slow construction of the preliminary works for the approaching railway line. He was in particular concerned with the erection of a large bridge across the river about five miles away. He had settled in Darabad with his wife Sylvia and would remain here until the railway arrived and stay on as it passed on for another twenty miles or so. He would then move to his next posting further down the new line. Paul was young, even by the standards of British India of the time and the couple had no children as yet.

Also in the employ of the East India Railway Company was a somewhat eccentric moustachioed bachelor – an Armenian from that community in Calcutta which provided so many employees of the railways. Known to the rest of the European community in Darabad as 'Dickie', his actual name was Dikran Derounian. He was the official Inspector of the Railways and was supposed to be evaluating the passenger custom likely to be available that could be expected from the Shantapur district. He was also required to deal with new contracts for all the possible freight traffic that could be found. A large booming voice, a propensity to envelop men whom he liked in Russian-style bear hugs, whilst insisting on the dying practice of bending to kiss ladies' hands, left his English colleagues somewhat at a loss. In the socially stratified hierarchy of the British in India, railway employees were in any case lower down the scale than government officials and the military. But in the person of 'Dickie' Derounian the stuffy side of the Raj had met its match. Insensitive to the snubs he occasionally encountered he boomed and roared his way through the little European society of Darabad.

Derounian had a young servant boy who helped in the house and acted as a cook. The age of this lad was not clear. Dickie said he was twelve – though it was not entirely clear as to how he knew this. Being small and wiry the boy looked younger. His name was Ali – just that – though he did not claim to be a Muslim, nor did Dickie appear to encourage him in any partic-ular religious observances – neither Christian nor Muslim. He had a very fair complexion and it was obvious that he was a Eurasian of some sort of mixed parentage. On his arrival in the town one of the first things Dickie had arranged was of course to get some bearers and servants for his house, but also to everyone's surprise to enrol young Ali with the one-on-one school run by the same Dr. Bannerjee who tutored Conrad.

Derounian became a frequent visitor to the Tate household

and it was fairly natural that Conrad soon struck up a friendship with the lively but diffident Ali, who though older was the less dominant of the pair. The two boys, when free in their separate times from having to attend on the good Dr. Bannerjee, would roam about the streets and fields of Darabad until they came to know the little town like the proverbial back of their hands. Ali would provide the bright ideas of where to go and what to do; where to find the best fishing; where to spy on grown-ups; while Conrad would provide the protection against the bigger boys. Some of these boys, catching the two friends together on the streets, would try to bully Ali, but would not dare to face up to a red-faced angry Conrad who would stand in front of Ali with his fists clenched. These stand-offs were fairly rare and it was never quite clear whether their street enemies held back because of Conrad's obvious healthy strength and relatively large size, or because of his angry red face when roused, or perhaps more likely because he was known to be the son of a British official of some kind.

The fact is that English boys over the age of nine were a rarity in the whole of India, never mind in the sleepy little town of Darabad with its very limited European population.

The wide main road of Darabad – the Maidan – with its picturesque stone houses ended at the west with the Judge's unwalled compound, inside which there were several small buildings dotted about the grounds as well as the Judge's own residence and the court house. At the other eastern extremity, the Maidan ended with the road narrowing and turning sharply to the left and right alongside a high wall enclosing the local jail. This was the main jail of the whole district and had about four hundred inmates. They were all undoubtedly the hardest and most violent cases not only of the Shantapur district but of the whole area south of Patna, the largest nearby town, which lay about forty miles away.

* * *

The four other junior railway employees in Darabad,

together with John Tate their superior and Paul Kelly his deputy, and Derounian were all of course inferior in rank and status to the civilian officers and their wives. However, the stiff and strict hierarchy, which pertained in all the major British stations throughout India, was not quite so rigid in Darabad. The number of Europeans both male and female were so much less than normal that perforce the ladies, normally so mindful of their status elsewhere, simply had to visit each other on fairly equal terms. Above all there were no military personnel of any kind applying their stiff rank-conscious taboos that applied in most of the other stations of British India.

The senior civil officer was the Judge – Arthur Drummond. Forty-two years old he was the oldest European in the town and lived within the unwalled compound at the west end of the Maidan. His wife Henrietta, a year or two younger than he, knew with the certainty of her class and background that she was the prima donna of the European ladies of the town. She was a deeply pious and committed Christian, who believed that the ignorant superstitions of Islam and the Hindu pantheon amounted simply to paganism. It seemed clear to her that the Prophet's trip to heaven and back to have the Book dictated to him, or the animalistic fantasies of the Hindu Gods were irrational and illogical – whereas the purity and logic of her own faith, the birth of her own God-prophet from a virgin, the fact that he walked on water, his trip to the skies in the company of the Devil and the raising of the dead, were all so much more rational.

There was no church in Darabad, but Henrietta Drummond had arranged for a small building within the Judge's compound to be cleaned out, painted and used as a prayer meeting-house. This was merely one large room, with a raised platform at one end, used originally as a storehouse. Unfortunately, it all smacked a little of a socially unacceptable non-conformist chapel, but it was the best Henrietta could manage. It was not of course consecrated in any way. One day, she thought, as the town grew and if more Europeans, particularly British, arrived, then a proper church with a civilised Anglican vicar could be possible.

But meanwhile this room, shaped like a hall with its convenient platform at one end, would have to do.

Arthur Drummond was prepared to lead the small congregation, strictly conforming of course to the Anglican Book of Common Prayer. Arthur liked to hear the sound of his own voice, deep and sonorous, and considered himself particularly capable of reading aloud the more purple passages of the Old Testament. The more terrifying that this Jewish God thundered at his chosen people, the better Arthur enjoyed it.

The prayer-meeting took place on each Sunday morning. Almost all the Europeans in the town attended, whatever their private beliefs, with the exception of the two Catholics. Even Dickie Derounian turned up and somewhat to Henrietta's discomfiture would bring the young Ali with him. Both of them would stand at the back of the room, not sitting or kneeling throughout the proceedings. After the end of the ritual, everyone would gather outside and gossip a little. During the milder season Henrietta would arrange for servants to provide lemonade and cold water with a few titbits.

Conrad of course had to attend at these Sunday morning gatherings. He was not allowed to stand at the back with the Derounians but had to sit demurely between his mother and father. But once out into the grounds it was a different matter and he and Ali would scamper about, drink the lemonade and savour the flowers, trees and shrubs of the well-kept garden. Henrietta herself had given birth to five children but only the three boys had survived. They were all back in England and she had not seen them for over five years. They were now 11, 13 and 14 and each one of them lived desperately unhappy lives in three different second-rate English boarding-schools in the midlands, separated and passed from one relative to another during the short school holidays.

Even if Henrietta had been aware of how unhappy her three boys were she would have believed to the very depths of her soul that the experience was good for them. They would grow up believing in God, self-reliant and able to look after themselves. Above all they would know what it meant to be English. After all look at that Tate boy – running wild with only a Eurasian as a friend. All those carefree days of sunshine and blue skies – all this warm wallowing in nature – all that parental love and attention that he was receiving here in India – where would the moral backbone come from? Where would he ever find the stern resolve to run an Empire?

That stern resolve was present in abundance in the Senior Magistrate – George Grant. He was known to all either as 'GG.', or sometimes, but not to his face, as Grabber Grant. GG was thirty-five, which seemed to be the age of almost all the European males in the town. He ran the whole district of Shantapur with a firm hand and was generally accepted by all the Indians with whom he had any official dealings. They considered him to be just and incorruptible. He was a Haileybury product, and though he had had no military training of any sort he was the nearest thing in Darabad to a man with a military bent. He had never been the slightest bit unhappy at being sent home at a tender age to a boarding school which he had completely enjoyed. He was a courageous rider of considerable skill and a consummate sportsman. Like so many of the European males in the station he roamed the wilder parts of the countryside in search of game of one kind or another and was a good shot. Above all he had no doubts about his own 'correct' opinions, nor of the 'incorrect' ideas of others. On one memorable occasion when he had been arguing with John Tate about the moral justification of some punitive action that had been ordered by the Governor-General, he had said –

"After all Tate old fellow, great empires are not built or kept by seeing the other fella's point of view."

Grant lived in a house surrounded by a large garden in the leafy suburbs to the west side of the town beyond the Judge's compound. He was a bachelor and had swarms of servants to look after all his domestic needs. He spent much of his time on horseback travelling through the district and sorting out the many administrative tasks which required attention. There was no British Senior Collector in Darabad at this time; but a wealthy local Muslim merchant – Azimullah Hassan – with a house on the

Maidan had been appointed as Deputy Collector. He had turned a ground floor room in his house into the official Collector's office. Grant would often go there when he was in Darabad and sit with the old man with whom he shared some of the concerns inevitable in managing the district. A Senior Collector was always just about to be appointed, but nothing had transpired for months.

Grant, short-tempered though he was and insensitive to the feelings of others, nevertheless had the knack of getting on with most Indians. This was in sharp contrast to the liberal John Tate who always ended up more stiff and awkward in his relations with the locals. John, aware of his shortcomings in that respect, left all the necessary details of dealing with the Indian employees of the Railway Company to Derounian. Dickie simply cheerfully shouted at the top of his lungs at everyone, white and black alike, and no one worried or got upset in any way.

The Deputy Collector Azimullah Hassan was a wily, some might say even devious, old man. In an environment where all the males seemed to be in their mid-thirties, he stood out as being over sixty. Wracked with bouts of arthritis, rare in that climate, he would sometimes be bent over almost double as he hobbled about. He was married, though no one ever saw his principal wife or any of the women in the zenana. In contrast to the Drummonds he had had no sons, but a plethora of daughters now mostly married and living in other households. He had been an efficient Deputy Collector, though he had not had to carry out many of the administrative tasks required from most Collectors. He was concerned only with the administration of the Revenue collection while the other usual tasks of a Collector had fallen to Grant to carry out.

Grant himself believed that Azimullah Hassan ran a fairly corrupt office. It was not so much a matter of financial greed as the peddling of social influence. The man had been appointed largely because he was so wealthy and thus the petty possibilities of a bit of extra cash would not be tempting. But the wielding of power, the ability to grant favours here and there, to friends or in-laws, was what Grant believed was going on. However, he was cheerfully prepared to overlook his suspicions whilst the revenue came in regularly and without the troubles and complaints necessitating police action which accompanied so much revenue collection elsewhere.

And so it was that life went on in the little town. The European ladies rode horses in the morning and drove about the station in the evenings, visiting each other in rotation, keeping even here the strict order of precedence. The men rode with their wives in the mornings when they were at home, returned home for the hot midday hours, and then occasionally worked from the end of the afternoon for the rest of the day. It was May 1857.

* * *

The presence in the little town of the large jail, containing about three or four hundred of the most violent prisoners gathered in from all over the district, added to the security worries born on the ample shoulders of George Grant. However it had little effect on the already turbulent character of the male inhabitants of Darabad. In the evenings, once everyone was back from whatever work they did, disputes and fights would break out in the maze of twisting streets of the old quarter erupting out from the seedy coffee and tea shops. The services of James Henty, the civil surgeon was in constant demand. He was always unstinting in his service in this respect. His training had been as a physician and when he first arrived in India his knowledge of surgery was fairly basic. But he had learned fast on the job and now sheer experience had made him superior in technical skill to most practitioners in London.

Both Conrad and Ali had to be back in their respective homes by 8.00pm at the very latest – Ali had to see to the meal for the Derounian household, while Conrad had to be washed and formally dressed for the evening meal whether his father was back or not. But the evening fights and disorder started immediately after sundown, and the boys were often still in the streets watching wide-eyed as the disputes began. They had no fear.

This was traditional India – no child would be deliberately harmed.

On several occasions they helped in carrying some wounded unfortunate to the house of Doctor Henty on the Maidan. Henty understood the vital importance of cleanliness in any medical operation involving surgery, minor or major. This was a good deal more than many a London Doctor. He would dismiss the riff-raff who had brought in the victim, but he was tolerant of the two boys if they were there. He would get them immediately to wash their hands carefully and would then allow them to help as he dressed wounds, stitched and cauterised. He never amputated even when he could see that there might be a risk of gangrene.

Conrad loved helping and learnt a lot just by watching Henty at work. Ali, on the other hand could not really stomach all the blood and moans, though he stood faithfully alongside his friend, occasionally going paler when the blood flowed too freely. James Henty was not married and had little interest in all the hunting, shooting and riding of the other Europeans in the station. This left him a rather isolated and lonely figure. No one called him 'Jim' or even 'James'. He was Dr. Henty to all, although he too was the same age of thirty-five matching all the rest of the men. Perhaps as a result of this slight isolation he came to enjoy the enthusiastic curiosity of the two boys who eventually scampered in and out of his house without any inhibitions or any invitation.

Yet in the midst of all this almost warlike turbulence of the local Biharis, Europeans remained entirely unmolested throughout Darabad. The ladies of the station frequently travelled alone by palenkeen dak, not only to visit each other in the town, but even throughout the district. Harriet did often worry about how Conrad was growing up, particularly as it was largely her insistence which had kept him in India. She would urge old Dr. Bannerjee to be firm in his teaching methods with the boy. But she never worried for a moment about his being out and away from the home during the early evenings. There was a certainty that children of the Raj would not be deliberately harmed or abused. But it was not only children of the Raj; Dickie Derounian too was never concerned about Ali wandering in the lanes of the old quarter. Children living in the slums of mid-Victorian London were far more likely to meet with vicious violence than anywhere in India.

But then as May came to an end, the rumours began. The story that first broke in the little European community was that the 3rd Bengal Cavalry, or was it the 13th, situated in the garrison town of Meerut about forty miles north of Delhi had mutinied. The next news, flashed from one house to another, was that the Cavalry regiment had not only mutinied but had killed all their officers English and Indian alike. Furthermore, it was claimed that they were then joined by the infantry regiments in the garrison who had gone on the rampage killing every European they could lay their hands on, not only the men but also all the women and children that they could find. It was rumoured that they had then fled to Delhi where they had proclaimed the decrepit old King of Delhi – the last of the Moghal dynasty – as Emperor.

Mutinies in the Sepoy army had of course occurred all over India many times before and at first it appeared that this was similar. The Europeans, meeting on Sundays in the Judge's compound, discussed, dissected and pondered over every bit of information and gossip that they could glean, but there was no immediate anxiety.

It was the 24th May, another Sunday and two weeks exactly after the actual outbreak at Meerut, that the Europeans were gathered in the grounds of the Judge's compound after the little service conducted by Arthur and Henrietta ended. The service – Henrietta refused to call it a prayer meeting – was better attended than usual, even including one of the Catholic ladies. As all the participants filed out into the bright sunshine of the Drummond garden, there was an atmosphere of enthusiastic and volatile excitement. The less people actually knew of what was going on, the more they tended excitedly to make up uncor-roborated stories. There was no fear. Their life in Darabad was so boring and routine that the first reaction of many of them to the news was a quickening of the senses and an exhilaration of the mind.

This deadening routine and the extremes of boredom was one of the least appreciated aspects of what they were about to experience for most of these young English males destined to come out to India. Educated in the muscular Christianity of the more second-rate, cheap and tawdry of the minor public schools, brought up with heady tales of power and glory in administrating the Indian Empire, they were simply not prepared for the sheer boredom that they often had to face.

Most of these men, both the government servants and even the busier railway employees would rise early in the morning, go for a walk or a ride as the sun arose, have his morning bath and a breakfast and then make his way to his office or place of work where he would work in a desultory leisurely manner until returning home for lunch and a siesta in the heat of the afternoon. The only leisure activity would be a drive with his wife in the early evening – always the same route – and then back home for dinner and an early bed.

So it was that the events at Meerut, as news of them filtered slowly in, did at least have the effect of being a welcome break from all that deadening routine, and accordingly did not immediately give rise to any real fear.

"My dear Mrs. Tate," said the stiff, straight-backed Henrietta Drummond as they all stood and chatted outside the meeting-house on that Sunday, "it's all just another storm in a teacup. I've been aware of at least five different mutinies, dotted all over India, during my time, in this country."

"But isn't this one a bit different? You know what worries me a little is that it appears to have broken out in Meerut of all places. That town is after all the only garrison town outside Calcutta which has a sizable force of British regulars – and yet it was just there that these awful events seem to have taken place."

"Well – all the more reason for us not to worry," replied Henrietta rather haughtily. "Once they have got over the initial shock – our troops will chase straight after them and retake Delhi in a few hours. I wouldn't be surprised if that hasn't already happened and we will hear about it soon."

At this point in the conversation, a young girl moved up to join them. She was Marietta Postern. She was married to a British officer stationed at the moment in Cawnpore and attached there to the staff of General Wheeler. She lived here in Darabad with her mother – one Alphonsine da Costa - in a large house on the Maidan near the jail. Alphonsine was, or claimed to be Portuguese, but all the British ladies of the station believed and volubly affirmed to each other that she was Eurasian – the product possibly of the union of a Portuguese soldier and an Indian woman - a Princess of course! In any case she was certainly a Catholic and so equally to be despised and ignored. However, her stunningly beautiful daughter, the sixteen-year-old Marietta, was the wife of Ensign Postern – an impeccably English army officer – and perforce had to be accepted by Henrietta and the rest of them.

"Madame Drummond, I have today heard that houses in the cantonment at Meerut were burned and that women and even children were hunted down and murdered. Could this be true?"

Both Harriet and Henrietta turned immediately to the young girl. Henrietta said quickly –

"Nonsense, my dear girl. Simply nonsense."

Harriet too quickly said, somewhat more kindly –

"It's out of the question – Mrs. Postern. You can believe how much or how little you like about all these other rumours floating about – but that one surely is rubbish. I don't doubt that some houses were burnt, perhaps some perished in the flames. But Sepoys hunting and cutting down children. No, no forget it."

"But, mother heard that..."

At this Henrietta actually sniffed. How do people actually 'sniff' in contempt thought Harriet? But Henrietta did and went on to say –

"My dear girl – just forget it. I would add that it is in any case our duty to ignore all this incipient panic. I'm certain that your dear husband would want you to remain completely cool and calm and show an example to the natives."

Harriet tried to reduce the rather abrupt and patronising

nature of this remark by smiling at the young girl – but the little group broke up in any event as Henrietta moved away to talk to Dr. Henty.

Day after day, as the news filtering through became progressively worse, the Europeans in Darabad began to move from excitement to apprehension. They were aware that they lived in the midst of a turbulent and violent population, amongst whom there were many families who had sons, brothers or husbands in the Sepoy regiments of the Raj. In addition there were about 400 hard-core prisoners in the largest jail in the district, guarded by local najeebs who, it was felt, were scarcely better than the badmashes they were supposed to be guarding.

Harriet Tate had felt the same preliminary excitement as everyone else when the news first broke and again like everyone began to feel apprehension as the news worsened and it became clear that for some reason or another the British regulars in Meerut had not intervened and that Delhi remained in the hands of the rebels. Of course she went on as before – it was after all the only thing one could do. Craving some comfort from her husband she said–

"John, my darling, the news seems to be getting worse. What are we to think? Should we be doing something – taking some sort of family decisions?"

"I don't think so at the moment – we can only sit and wait. I have heard that there have certainly been more mutinies – but they all tend to mutiny and then go off to join the original mutineers in Delhi. However, while we don't need to run anywhere, we do need to curtail our usual activities a bit. Make sure that you are ready to pick up Chloe at any moment. I will have a word with Conrad. He must limit himself to our compound for a time."

But John Tate was a good deal more anxious than he showed. He spoke sharply to Conrad, though doing little to enforce his command.

Then on the 8th June, a letter arrived addressed to Arthur Drummond the Judge. It had been sent by William Taylor the

British High Commissioner in Patna. It stated rather baldly that an outbreak among the native troops stationed nearby in Dinapore was feared and was now believed to be imminent.

* * *

After receiving the letter from Patna, Drummond sent a message to all the European males in the town informing them that he had received a message to the effect that that there was a possibility of an immediate outbreak of mutiny by the sepoy troops nearby. At the same time, he issued an invitation to all to whom he wrote to gather as early as possible the next morning in his compound to consider the position.

So it was that on the 9th June a meeting of virtually the whole of the European male population of the town took place in that same little building in the Judge's compound that was used as a chapel on Sundays. Drummond welcomed everyone in his cold and formal manner as if he was chairing a parish meeting to decide how the church roof should be repaired. The meeting was large, consisting not only of all the British officials, but also the railway employees and a number of non-British merchants in the town and two Indigo planters who had houses on the Maidan. Drummond read out the short letter and then said –

"Well, there you have it, gentlemen. We now know that all the rumours that we have been hearing about events in Delhi are basically true. We are therefore facing a real crisis. Despite the presence in Dinapore of 600 or more British soldiers of the 10th regiment, the native troops – I believe they amount to four regiments – are supposedly just about to mutiny."

A voice from the back called out –

"Is it known, sir, why the large British garrison in Meerut did not immediately follow the mutineers and drive them out of Delhi? It is after all the only place in North India outside Calcutta where British soldiers outnumbered natives."

"A good question, sir," called out George Grant. "It is not in fact known at the moment, but there will no doubt be questions asked about that, for while Delhi remains in the hands of those blackguards, more regiments are likely to waver in their loyalty."

As the meeting continued Grant began to take a more dominant role, a role that the relatively elderly Arthur Drummond was prepared to give him. In these critical circumstances, throughout the rest of India, it was the military – the professional soldiers – who tended to take over. The civilians in all these stations naturally turned to them for advice and leadership as the crisis became one involving security. But here in Darabad there were no soldiers. The more forceful and energetic of the civilians accordingly came to the forefront. But even George Grant was unable to arrive at any clear conclusion as to what should now be done.

The meeting dragged on for most of the early morning but in the end only one firm collective decision was made. This purely male assembly decided that all the European women and their children should be despatched to Dinapore at once. There was general agreement that once arrived there the presence of the British regulars of the 10th regiment should surely ensure their safety.

Once that decision, which seemed to be so eminently sensible to all those assembled males, was reached, Grant took over again. He suggested that rather than trying to escort all the women and children over the forty or so miles of turbulent countryside, moving slowly by carriage and oxcart, it would be safer if the group went to the nearby river only five miles away. This was fully navigable and ran into the Ganges to the north which then went on to Dinapore. The party could travel comfortably and safely on boats. He undertook to provide ample boat accommodation for everyone by first light the following morning.

Further decisions following naturally on from this one were then taken. Men were deputed to help families not present; lists of those leaving were to be prepared; arrangements for the necessary conveyances to take the party the five miles to the Syed Ghat where Grant's boats would be waiting, were agreed. Finally one or two of the men, armed of course, were deputed to accompany the women and children on the boats going down to the Ganges and on to Dinapore.

No decision was reached as to what the rest of the men in the station would do. However, the last words at the meeting, spoken somewhat loudly and truculently by George Grant, were –

"Look, gentlemen, if we all disperse and leave the town, think of the effect on the natives. Quite apart from the loss of prestige, we lose everything we have built up, the place will turn into complete anarchy. I certainly intend to stay and continue my work here as calmly as I can, and I expect all the government officials at least to stay here with me and carry on the administration."

Apart from George Grant himself who was now in a state of high excitement with his energy bubbling over, the rest of the men at the meeting appeared to be fairly calm. Somehow, as far as they could see nothing much had changed. There were no soldiers of any kind in Darabad – neither British officers, nor native sepoys. The population, though turbulent and violent as usual, were not acting any differently than before. So while they moved to carry out such decisions as affected them there was a sense of unreality in all they were doing.

As the men filed out into the heat of the late morning sunshine, Derounian approached John Tate and quietly informed him that all the railway employees had asked for a meeting to be held at Tate's house. John, who had said nothing at the meeting, looked round and saw indeed that a group consisting of Paul Kelly and the four other European employees were standing together at one side looking at him expectantly. John nodded at Kelly and then he and Dickie walked off out of the compound and down the road going back to his house at the far end of the western suburbs. Kelly and the other four discreetly followed them.

The Tate house was set in the middle of a large open garden. It was the largest house and grounds after the Judge's compound and reflected the importance that the East India Railway Company gave to its senior staff in the town to which their new railway line was heading. There were no walls or fences round the large garden, which appeared like a park simply merging into the countryside beyond.

The house stood foursquare in the middle of the grounds facing directly to where the road from the town arrived and forked to each side and went on. Behind the house, straggling back towards the jungle, which started some hundred yards away, were the kitchens and the servants' quarters. Away to the other side, also a little back from the main house, was a somewhat unusual brick and stone building. This was in two stories, originally built as a zenana annex to the original mansion. The building was not currently in use except as a store house and as a wonderful space for Conrad and Ali to run about in when they were free. It did contain a large public room on the raised upper floor and John's first thought was to take his staff there for the meeting the need for which he could not see. But remembering the dusty uncleaned state of the room, he changed his mind and led them all into the house.

Harriet, who of course knew nothing of what had transpired that morning, welcomed them all in and busied the staff in getting refreshments for everyone. The sound of little Chloe crying from somewhere upstairs could be heard. John recalled that she had awoken this morning with a fever and a high temperature. A servant had been sent to ask Dr. Henty to call round as soon as possible, but John had left for the meeting before the servant had returned, nor did he have the time now to ask Harriet. He just had time to tell her of the decisions that had been taken at the meeting. They hurriedly talked together in the entrance hall outside the large and cool sitting room, into which Derounian, Kelly and the four other Europeans of the railway staff had been ushered.

"And did you agree with this decision?" said Harriet.

"Well I wasn't totally happy with the way it was pushed through, but yes, in the end I think it is the right thing to do."

"Look – there is no way that I am leaving here without you. It's ridiculous. Firstly I believe that it's all exaggerated and there is not much danger, but above all if there is danger then we should share it as a family. What am I expected to do in the middle of India if anything was to happen to you."

"But the children…"

"Mere survival without parents is…"

"That's enough, Harriet. I really have to stay and you and the children simply cannot do so. Look we haven't the time now I must go in and hear what they want – but you are simply going to have to get used to… Oh my God!!"

John who had been facing the open front door turned a little pale as he saw George Grant jump off his horse, handing the reins to one of the stable servants and come striding in through the front door.

"Hello John – er Mrs Tate…I heard that you were going to give a pep-talk to your staff following on the decisions that we made this morning. I thought I could help by sitting in and explaining the arrangements I have made for the boats. In particular I need to explain to you and to them that after you left various problems arose and it has now been decided that the women and children will leave this evening when it gets dark rather than early tomorrow morning."

John was nonplussed. Clearly what Grant was going to impart was important – indeed vital – information that everyone needed to know. However his staff had wanted a private meeting with him – he was not quite sure why – but they would clearly resent the arrival of GG. There was nothing much he could do about it, however, short of turning Grant out of his house which was quite impossible. After all if the worst came to the worst they could have the private meeting later. They duly turned and went into the sitting room, Grant muttering something formal and nodding at Harriet saying – "Mrs. Tate!"

Everyone stood as John and GG came into the room which was already getting hot as the windows were still wide open with the muslin drapes wavering in the breeze created by the punkah wallah who was patiently sitting outside and already at work.

John in some embarrassment explained that there had been a change of plan and that Mr. Grant had come to let them have some further information. For some reason everyone remained standing and John never invited them all to sit again.

Grant, a man used to taking control of any meeting whether he was the senior official present or not, explained the change of plan and the requirement that all the women and children had to be ready to leave this very evening. The boats would be at the Ghat by 8.00pm at the latest, so it was intended that the carriages would leave from the Judge's compound at about 7.00pm when the Maidan was likely to be quieter with less people about.

When he had finished, he replied to a question or two from those who had families. John was then just about to intervene and explain that they were going to have a railway staff meeting after he left, when Grant said somewhat brusquely before John could say a word –

"And I trust that all of you will be remaining here with us to keep everything going on as before."

There was a very long silence as Grant began to turn red with anger. A natural anxiety mixed in with the excitement he felt had been building up in George Grant all morning. He had had to calm people's nerves, he had had to make hurried arrangements for the provision of the boats, he knew he would have to go and vet the boatmen, and all this while trying to maintain a cool and carefree exterior. He was not therefore at his most equable and the long silence unnerved him and he began to lose his temper. Dickie Derounian had already told him quietly after the meeting in the Judge's compound had broken up that he himself would certainly be willing to stay and back up the officials – but now there he was, standing completely silent.

For his part Dickie, aware that several of the other staff with families to think of had asked for this meeting to test Tate's feelings on the situation, was not prepared to apply any pressure to his colleagues by declaring that he would be staying. Here they were, being forced by the irate magistrate requiring, demanding, an immediate commitment. Dickie was quite determined to stay with the government officers, but he was not prepared to play Grant's game and put his colleagues into a moral quandary by calling out ostentatiously that he would be staying. Accordingly he said nothing.

At last Grant, face red with anger turned and said –

"Mr. Tate – are you not going to give any firm instructions to your staff."

"No, George. I myself will be leaving to accompany my wife and children down to Dinapore, as she will not leave without me. I will, however, endeavour to return as soon as I have seen them safely settled. I will not order or even recommend anything to the rest of the railway staff, whether they be family men or bachelors. They must each make their own decision."

Grant now almost purple with rage walked to the door and turned and almost spitting said –

"So you are all going to flee are you – just the sort of attitude that is giving rise to all these mutinies in the first place. You have all just come out here to make more money. Being paid much more than you would be in the same job in England, you are under an obligation therefore to stick to and try to protect your employer's interests and property when they are in difficulties. As for you John, what the blazes do you mean by saying that you could not advise your subordinates to stay when you yourself intend leaving on the boats as your wife will not leave without you. It's an utter absurdity that a man should listen to his wife's whims in such a crisis. How the bloody hell can I persuade the general public here that there is no immediate cause for apprehension when they see the entire European community cravenly scuttling away at the first hint of trouble."

"George – please moderate your language. I have told you that I will return once my family are settled and I will repeat that openly to all of you. However, I remain adamant that I will not require any other member of my staff to remain if they do not want to. The East India Railway Company does not require martyrs in order to carry on its business. As for your taunting us that we come out for more pay and prospects than we would get in England – for what else do we all come out here for anyway – and that includes you administrators."

"I will not say that you are all cowards. I will however say that your proposed actions are cowardly ones."

With this last parting shot Grant strode out of the door and straight out of the house to where his horse was still being held by the syce.

There was a long silence again after he left. Then Dickie

Derounian said, quietly for him but still in a loud voice –

"The man is obviously and understandably under stress. I believe that this crass attempt to browbeat is totally counter-productive, but I would at last like to say that I myself do intend to stay. However, I have no family, no obligations of that sort. I will be happy to stay and carry on with the work we are doing, and I am happy also to cover any vital work of anyone else who chooses to leave as best I can, until the crisis is passed."

Derounian smiled at everyone, shook hands with Tate and walked out, followed by Kelly and the other four. Apart from Derounian no one else made any comment as to whether they were going or staying.

* * *

As soon as John had seen everyone to the door, he turned and returned to sit down alone in the sitting room. It was of course quite unclear as to what might or might not now take place in Darabad. But as he reflected, he felt little doubt that despite all the turbulence and propensity to excitable violence of the local Biharis it was unlikely that there would be any general uprising or anti-European or anti-Raj outbreaks here. However, he was not so sure about the Sepoy regiments in Dinapore and Ravelkhind. What would they do? John was now aware that most of the other mutineering regiments had immediately made their way to Delhi. The extraordinary failure of the British regulars stationed in Meerut to follow up and immediately recapture Delhi in the early days of the chaotic situation that had arisen there when the Meerut mutineers had first arrived in the town, had undoubtedly given an impetus to the whole movement. While Delhi remained occupied, it was a magnet for the largely unled mutineers whenever a new mutiny broke out.

John saw that Grant had certainly lost his temper and had said things that he would probably later regret, but Dickie had been right. He was under a lot of stress and the mores of the time being what they were that stress would be infinitely lessened once he got the women and the children away and out of his responsibility. John liked GG – rarely for the small British community they called each other John and George – but they had totally different outlooks on what was their function in India.

John sat on musing, knowing that Harriet would be bustling in shortly and wondering idly what was keeping her. Grant had told him in confidence earlier in the morning before the meeting had started that he had heard from one of his informants that the Sepoy regiments in Cawnpore, about two hundred miles away had mutinied five days or so before. There had been no massacre of the officers, and his information was that General Wheeler, the senior British commander together with his officers and the European and Eurasian population of the town had moved into some sort of entrenchment. The local zamindar there, the Maharajah of Bithor, known as the Nana Sahib, had, according to these reports, taken a neutral position and the mutineers had marched off like so many others to Delhi. John reflected that it was all part of a pattern and there seemed to be little reason why it would be any different here.

He did not have to wait much longer. Harriet at last came in. She did not burst in as she usually did as John was expecting. She walked in quietly, bent over the back of the chair and kissed the top of John's head, before going round and subsiding wearily into the sofa opposite. John sat up sharply, there appeared to be tears in her eyes.

"John, my darling, I am afraid we are not going to argue or have the discussion for which I can see you are preparing yourself."

"Good heavens... What is it?"

"John, there is no more talk of your coming with me on the boats this evening. I will not be pressing you in any way as none of us are going anywhere. I have to..."

"What the devil are you saying! This is not a question of argument or discussion. With or without me you and the children are leaving tonight and I will not listen to..."

"Oh John...my dearest...wait a moment. Poor little Chloe is very sick. She has a high fever. Doctor Henty came this morning and brought some quinine which is relieving her poor little shivering body. But she is in a critical state. Henty said that her ultimate survival depends on her having complete rest and total care and attention over the next three or four days. He is not sure if it is just a virulent attack of dysentery or – Oh God John – it could be worse. He didn't actually say 'cholera' but that was…"

John, who had gone quite white, interrupted her springing up from his chair and going across to her as more tears oozed from her eyes. He lifted her out of the chair and held her tight as at last she gave way to weeping. This was India in 1857, the statistics were seared deep into the mind of most British parents. The chances of survival of European children below the age of five, if they went down with fevers or illnesses of this kind, was very low. John murmured into his wife's hair –

"I want to go to her."

Without a further word they went out together into the hall and up the stairs – but not hand in hand. There were the servants to think about after all.

Grant, left with the impression that John Tate was going with the ladies that evening, had put him in charge of the group. When he was hastily informed by messenger that neither John nor any of his family would be going he had to change his plans again. He rode down to where the new railway bridge was being constructed just further down from the Syed Ghat from where the boat party would be leaving that evening. Paul Kelly, in charge of the construction work was there on this side of the river supervising the arrival of some of the stout timbers which were being delivered by oxcart.

Grant rode up and dismounted. Paul stopped work and stared at him as he strode across. George Grant had a hasty temper and undoubtedly also often misunderstood and took exception to comments from his social equals, but he never harboured any kind of grudge. Indeed by the time of his arrival at the riverside, he had almost forgotten his bad temper of this morning and never thought for a moment that this man he had come to see might resent having been insulted only a little earlier.

"Ah Kelly – I'm glad I caught you on this side. Listen, I believe that your wife is among the party leaving this evening from the Syed Ghat. I need someone to be in command of the Guard boat leading the group to Dinapore. You have the necessary rifle. Could you do it?

"I thought that you intended John Tate to be in command."

"Yes...well for one reason and another he can't do it so I..."

"Well what about Drummond he is the senior..."

"Kelly, I really haven't got the time to discuss one name after another. Can you do it? You shoot well if it becomes necessary I know. There will be four boats including your lead boat, and you leave from, the ghat at 9.00 or 10.00 at the latest."

Paul, unlike John, did not like Grant. Like his colleague Dickie he too had been intending to stay on in Darabad once his wife was safe. However at the time of the meeting at the Tate house, he became determined not to bend to Grant's imperious demands in what he saw as sheer bullying. Now, here again, the brusque and hectoring tone almost led him to refuse. But then, he immediately realised the purely personal and trivial aspect of such an attitude on his part.

"Very well – Mr. Grant, I'll be there. If you are returning to town I wonder if you could get one of your men to find Mr. Derounian and ask him to come and relieve me here as soon as he can, as all this timber has to be properly stacked and covered before the evening. Once I can get away from here I should also be able to relieve you of the task of getting everyone to the carriages."

"Fine – the carriages will be gathered in the Judge's compound. I suggest that you don't leave there in convoy before it gets dark and the market in the Maidan closes."

With that Grant nodded and rode off.

That evening the European wives and their children gathered as discreetly as possible in the Judge's compound at the western end of the maidan. It was of course quite impossible for the coming exodus to be kept secret. Most of the women arrived with their Indian staff bringing along their baggage. Ayah's in charge of the infants also came along carrying their memsahib's babies as they had done ever since the baby in question was born.

In the grounds of the compound, as the dark deepened, there was surprising little confusion and certainly no panic of any kind. Grant had always been aware that the women were bound to clamour for at least one or two of their servants, particularly the indispensable Ayahs, to accompany them. Certainly he knew that there could be no question of separating the infants from any Ayah prepared to go with them. Kelly accordingly found that there was adequate transport available to take the party to the Syed Ghat at the river four miles away, though he managed to draw the line at including in the party most of the male servants who had brought the baggage, making an exception only if they professed to be Christians.

It was a sweet balmy evening, neither too hot nor humid. The clinking of the bells on the oxcarts – the neighing of the horses – the soft murmurs of people talking not cheerfully but also not anxiously – all made for a calm atmosphere. Henrietta Drummond was at her commanding best in this sort of environment. She moved round in the approaching dark, calming fractious little boys by her overwhelming presence and hustling them into the carriages next to their distracted mothers all with a baby or two. She herself was not leaving despite the enormous pressure put on her by both Arthur and by Grant. Henrietta had a very clear idea of where her duty lay. As the senior memsahib on the station, now without any young children of her own to think of, it was clear to her that she had to stand firmly by her husband, who as the senior Government official in the town obviously had to stay.

Henrietta's idea of duty was not just a matter of high muscular Christian morality; nor was it based on any convoluted theory of Imperial values; nor was there any conscious idea of racial superiority. She simply instinctively knew that 'order' of any kind was better for everyone rather than 'anarchy'. This principle, one that needed to be applied so emphatically in the Nursery, applied also for her in Society. If any political radical could have the temerity to suggest to her that the 'order' which she so extolled benefited only her own class, she would not of course have even deigned to reply. However, she would already have been able to point out that all around her, as the power of the Raj wavered and in some places disappeared altogether, it was the poor in the towns and the peasants in their defenceless villages, who suffered the most from the anarchic conditions. The release of violent prisoners from the jails resulted in

brigand gangs that arose and roamed the countryside. They did not prey on the rich landowners with their bodyguards but on the defenceless peasants.

Whatever her motives, her stiff arrogant certainty was just the right note in the evening exodus. Once full darkness arrived at about seven o'clock, Paul Kelly sent off the three oxcarts first and deputed one or two of the husbands milling about to accompany them on horseback, The carts would arrive, even at their slow pace, well before the deadline of nine. The horse carriages moving much faster would not set out before eight. The maidan was already clear of the market stalls, and the sweepers and cleaners employed by the town were already at work clearing up.

An hour later the horse drawn carriages, now led by Paul himself, pulled slowly out of the compound gates and into the Maidan. There were a few knots of interested Indian spectators who had emerged from each side of the main road. But there were no comments or demonstration of any kind as they silently watched the passing carriages. The soft Indian night with that lingering smell of jasmine blossom, frangipani and excreta hung over the town as all the European women and children finally abandoned Darabad.

* * *

By the end of that evening of the 9th June, therefore, it would appear that, apart from Henrietta Drummond and Harriet Tate, no European women remained in Darabad. But this was not true, for still in the district but temporarily absent that day was Marietta Postern. The sixteen-year-old girl, daughter of Alphonsine da Costa with whom she had been living, the wife of Ensign Postern at present serving with General Wheeler in Cawnpore, had not left the town with the rest.

Mrs. da Costa had certainly left on one of the last carriages. Paul had ticked her off on his lists and had assumed that Marietta was with her or had left earlier on one of the ox-carts. No one on that balmy evening had noticed her absence. No one, that is, except Alphonsine herself of course.

The circumstances which gave rise to Marietta's failure to join the departing women and children always remained a bit of a mystery to the rest of Darabad. Her actions and particularly those of her mother would undoubtedly have given rise to a considerable scandal, if the developing events of the mutiny had not intervened and caused the incident to be largely forgotten.

The local zamindar – major landowner – of the district was a flamboyant character, Saridar Khan, who called himself the Nawab of Jagpur. Most of the zamindars throughout Bihar were aware that they held their estates largely at the indulgence of the British East India Company. They accordingly were careful to remain loyal, at least outwardly, to the British interest and above all to the forces of law and order without which of course they would not be able to collect their rents. But the portly Saridar Khan was a little different. Although he was just literate, he was not very bright. He was keen on all sorts of sports and indulged, in particular, in hunting almost every day. Though he did absolutely nothing for them except to take and spend their rents, he was on the whole popular with the local people.

He was by this time already into his fifties. Like so many of the local aristocracy he was tolerant in his religious attitudes. Although a Hindu, unlike his earlier Timurid ancestors, it was he who had constructed one of the mosques in Darabad as an offering for one of his wives, a Muslim. But he had also built a beautiful small temple in Patna. It was not so much tolerance as indifference – he simply could not understand the fanatical zeal of the committed religious. But what with building religious temples all over the place and indulging in expensive and luxurious hunts he was currently heading straight for bankruptcy.

Saridar Khan had been fit and lithe as a young man, but he had become somewhat portly, more from good living rather than from any lack of exercise. He had never sported a beard and was clean-shaven except for a carefully nurtured moustache which curled up at the ends. He had several wives, but in the course of one of his visits to Darabad, in a reception given in his honour, he had come across the heavily scented and made-up Alphonsine, with her stunningly beautiful fourteen-year-old daughter Marietta in tow. The good Nawab had been deeply smitten by the charms of the young girl and for some weeks after, he became a frequent visitor to the house of the widow da Costa and took the two women out in his carriage for evening drives into the countryside. Costly presents were showered on Alphonsine, but it was Marietta who had to sit next to the Nawab. It was clear that the shallow Alphonsine thought that she had made a conquest and believed that the attentions of this middle-aged man were for her. This odd *ménage-a-trois* might have gone on fairly innocently, if it was not that it was suddenly made clear to Alphonsine that the Nawab's gallantry and attentions were aimed at the underage Marietta and not at her.

It was brought to her attention by her neighbour, Azimullah Hassan, the deputy Collector, who called upon her one evening. He, of course, brought with him his unmarried sister, who could not speak English but who was necessary for the sake of propriety. After the necessary whole hour of formal compliments the old man finally got round to his self-appointed mission.

"Madame, the honourable Saridar Khan is I believe a man of great goodness and integrity, I'm sure. I see him often here in your gracious and hospitable company."

Alphonsine may have been shallow, with dubious morals and not at all clever, but she was sharp at this sort of complimentary nuance and replied –

"Certainly, very attentive but always the height of correct behaviour of course."

" Ah, yes indeed, but madame, as an old friend I must warn

you that the youthful age of your beautiful daughter – not underage for us of course but certainly so for all your friends in the European community – is causing some adverse comment and could give you trouble in..."

"My daughter! My daughter! What do you mean?"

"Madame, the good Nawab's desire is well-known and I do think that..."

"My daughter – oh God I see. I thank you my good friend. I will certainly take heed of your kind warning."

With that Alphonsine ushered her guests out, although not of course without at least another fifteen minutes of mutual compliments and good wishes.

Within the next week Marietta had been packed off to a finishing school in Calcutta that specialised in a mild form of education in those all-important subjects of polite conversation, deportment, dancing and social skills for young ladies of the British and Anglo-Indian community. This was a strictly chaperoned establishment whose main purpose was to provide young unattached ladies for the dances and parties at which all the young men pouring off the ships from England would be present, looking, often without realising it themselves, for brides.

In the more tolerant and enlightened eighteenth century, many of these young men would have taken Indian mistresses and indeed wives, and they would often thereby create lasting and caring relationships, with loved and happy children. But the arrival of all those 'driven' missionaries; the spread of the prejudices of all that muscular Christianity; the hypocrisy of the racist attitudes in the second-rate minor public schools; the stuffy morality of the newly-enfranchised English middle classes; all combined to frown upon those liaisons. These were the days before the advent of the so-called 'fishing fleet' of ladies coming out to India and the young men had somehow to be considered, hence the growth of these ladies' finishing schools in Calcutta.

And it was there that the young James Postern, commissioned and fresh out of Haileybury, himself only eighteen, filled with visions of high glory in an exotic setting, met the lovely still only fifteen-year-old Marietta at one of the balls and parties arranged by all these schools. He was totally bowled over, and Marietta too, hitherto only on the fringes of the British community, fell for this impeccably English officer. The consent of Alphonsine for this underage marriage arrived by special messenger. Within a further two months, as the mild winter of 1856 turned to the spring of 1857, the young Postern received his first posting, which was to join General Wheeler's staff in Cawnpore. It was hurriedly arranged that when her new husband left to go to Cawnpore Marietta would return temporarily to Darabad, to live with her mother. The young James Postern was to settle down in his new posting and arrange to pick up his wife within a few months, after organising accommodation and sorting out the position with his immediate superiors.

So it was that the young Marietta, still just under sixteen, was back in Darabad at the beginning of the year. Only a week after her return the ardent Saridar Khan was back revisiting the da Costa household. Neither Azimullah Hassan living next door, nor indeed any of the other residents of the little town were ever sure quite how this came about, But it seems clear enough that the acquisitive Alphonsine had encouraged him to resume his attentions. She hankered after the expensive presents, and the gracious drives into the countryside, She also believed that now that Marietta was married she could manage the situation to her own advantage.

Alphonsine had not of course been present at the meeting that had taken place on this particular day – the 9th June – in the Judge's compound and was unaware in the morning of the decisions that had been taken. It so happened that that morning the amorous Nawab in the impeccable company of his oldest wife, Savida Begum, had called as previously arranged to take Marietta with them to a grand hunt that had been organised near his hunting lodge in woods about seven miles south of the town. She would be returning in the evening. Rich presents had been showered on the complacent Alphonsine and the Nawab had duly left with Marietta and his wife. An hour later Alphonsine heard that all the women in the town were due to leave the next morning, which was the original decision.

Whatever possessed her to act as she did? What exactly was she expecting from the attentions of the Nawab who was not in any case nearly as rich as she thought? She was certainly aware that if her acceptance, indeed even encouragement, of the attentions of Saridar Khan to her daughter now the wife of an English officer was to come out she would be deeply condemned and ostracised, So it was that believing that Marietta would be back during the evening she came out with the first lie which inexorably led to all the others as the day progressed. She explained that Marietta was visiting some distant relative in the district but would be back for the next morning's departure.

As the day progressed Alphonsine got into more and more of an irrational panic as the news came through that the group were all going to leave this very evening and not the next morning. The atmosphere of the coming departure of all the other European women began to affect her until she was simply not thinking straight. When it became clear as darkness fell that Marietta was not going to be back in time, she left instructions with her servants to tell Marietta to join them all at the Syed Ghat by 9.00pm – after all she reasoned she would be returning in the Nawab's fast and comfortable carriage, and it should not be too difficult to arrange for the carriage to drive on to the river rendezvous.

But then when she arrived at the Judge's compound with her important belongings carried by her bearer, her guilty thoughts began to shatter whatever composure she had. First she began to fear that after all Marietta might not return at all this evening and with that thought came a flood of guilt at what she appeared to have encouraged, and that was followed by a realisation of how all this would appear to all those around her. So it was that when everyone boarded the boats at nine o'clock and Marietta was still not there and no one had noticed, it was too late for Alphonsine to say anything. She reconciled the position in her mind by the thought that Marietta would either not return at all and thus be under the full protection of the Nawab, or would in fact return when she could no doubt come on to Dinapore overland with his help. She was bordering on a state of helpless folly.

Meanwhile the more lurid and guilty imaginings of the feckless Alphonsine were completely wide of the mark. The sensual Saridar Khan was indeed much taken by the charms of the lively young Marietta, but his wife kept a close eye the whole time, and in any case when it came to the pinch the Nawab's love of hunting overrode his waning sexual desires. The day's sport was hard and energetic and the hunt had not ended until after dark. The young Marietta, innocent in some ways, was nevertheless a great deal cleverer than her mother. Backed firmly by Savida Begum she stoutly resisted all suggestions that she might like to stay the night at the Lodge as it was so late. She also managed to persuade him that she could safely return alone in his carriage, accompanied only by one of the Nawab's elderly sisters. However, once that was decided, there seemed to be no reason for any great hurry and Marietta enjoyed a leisurely evening meal with Savida Begum and the ladies of the zenana, before returning to Darabad.

She did not therefore get home until after 10.00pm. She arrived to discover that her mother and all the other women in the station had already left. The Nawab's carriage with the elderly sister already asleep in it had turned and left immediately. Marietta absorbed all the news blurted out by the anxious servants – but all she did was to laugh out loud. She was exhausted and went straight to bed with the thought that she would sort it all out the following day. So it was that Marietta Postern was the third European woman left in Darabad that day.

* * *

Over the next few days after the departure of all the women and children, despite the exhortations of GG, most of the European non-official males also made their way away from the station. They departed in ones and twos on horseback or in their carriages. It was not exactly a panic exodus – just a slippage away. Grant blustered and rode around speaking sharply to all, claiming that the only way eventually to stop the contagion of mutiny spreading was to make certain that regular administration calmly continued. However, most of the merchants and other non-officials, including most of the railway staff who had been at John Tate's house that day of the 9th June, made it clear that they considered it to be utter madness to remain in this isolated outpost, surrounded by a possibly hostile population and without a single British soldier for miles.

As they drifted away riding through an increasingly lawless countryside, not one was harried or hindered in any way, and all arrived intact except perhaps for their dignity when they arrived in Dinapore. Meanwhile in Darabad the Europeans left in the town met regularly every morning in the Judge's compound. Grant as the Senior Magistrate would start by giving the latest news and this would be followed by a short report from anyone who had anything to say, before they all then departed to their various administrative functions. Arthur Drummond would walk across to his duties as the Judge in the local Law Court also in the compound near the entrance. Grant would be off to his innumerable tasks not only in the town but roaming far and wide in the surrounding countryside settling disputes of one kind or another; Tate to railway business of one kind or another; Derounian to the supervision of the work for the approaching railway line – not that Dickie had any idea about engineering, but he would bellow and shout and wave his arms about and at least make sure that there was no pilfering of railway property.

On the 12th June, early in the morning a grinning Paul Kelly rode back into Darabad and joined the morning meeting to a great welcome. Everyone was irrationally heartened by the return of the young Kelly and gathered round him shaking his hand and clearly all delighted, though shaking hands was as far as these quintessentially English gentlemen could go. Derounian was not so repressed however and almost suffocated poor Paul in a great bear-hug. It was almost as if Paul constituted a one-man relief force. He was able to report on the safe arrival of the boats and all their passengers and to their warm welcome by the British commander at Dinapore. But then the conversation turned to what he had been able to find out about what was happening in the rest of India.

"Well, as far as I can see the news is a mixture of good and bad. First the good news is that it appears that there is no trouble at all of any kind either in the Madras or Bombay presidencies. However, the situation here in the Bengal presidency is different. Despite the rumours, we have in fact failed to recapture Delhi, and day by day there are more mutinies."

"What the hell is the British garrison in Meerut doing?"

"Nothing as far as anyone in Dinapore can tell. In any event there is not a single British soldier between Dinapore here and Meerut and we all understand that the countryside is slipping into chaos and anarchy."

"Hang on Kelly – what about Cawnpore, that's between us and Delhi."

"Well I'm afraid that there too the news is bad. The Nana Sahib, after assuring General Wheeler of his goodwill to the Raj, has now turned tail and is, I heard, in the process of leading the mutinous sepoy regiments off to Delhi. In any case apart from their senior officers there are no ordinary British soldiers there."

"And the Europeans in the city?"

"They've all gone into an entrenched position prepared by General Wheeler. We understood that if you include the officers of the mutinied sepoy regiments, and the European and the Eurasian civilians of the town and the loyal natives they number almost a thousand. However it is fortunate that the sepoys appear to have gone off to Delhi as most of that thousand are women and children."

At this point the discussion became more subdued. So far everyone had been firing questions at Paul randomly from all sides and one could hardly tell who was the questioner, but now this calmed down. This was no longer the large company that had been present at that first meeting of the 9th June. This assembly in fact consisted of only eight people. In attendance were Arthur Drummond, the Judge, and his wife Henrietta who refused to be left aside on the grounds of gender, as was George Grant, the senior magistrate and James Henty the civil surgeon. John Tate was there but not Harriet, who was at home with the sickening Chloe who was barely clinging onto life. Then there was of course the booming presence of Dickie Derounian and now at last Paul Kelly himself, arriving just in time to prevent Dickie from taking the works for the new line in the completely wrong direction.

Johnson, the assistant magistrate was also present, nodding his head sagely, as always, at whatever his superior GG might say. He, too, spent his days dealing with the myriad of problems that arose not only in Darabad itself but also in the surrounding district. His method was always to travel with a small makeshift tent and a folding table and canvas chair all carried by his two assistants who would set them up outside each village that they visited. Sitting behind the desk, smoking his interminable pipe, he would dispense a rough justice and settle disputes without the back-up of a single policeman or soldier.

Despite these officers' endless wanderings and innumerable discussions day after day about water rights, village boundaries, irrigation problems, disputes about cows and every other possible animal species, nevertheless only a tiny proportion of the vast number of villagers throughout India ever saw him or any other British official in all their life.

The gatherings outside the meeting house in the Judge's grounds now took place every day. Sitting outside on the grass still being watered daily would be Conrad and Ali. John needed to take Conrad away from the sick-room atmosphere of the house and he could not let him go to Bannerjee's residence in the old town for his schooling till later in the morning. Bannerjee always claimed that he had important religious duties, puja, to perform and could not undertake to receive Conrad before 10.00am. The reality was that he liked lying on his charpoy in the early hours reading while it was still cool. That way, however, when it got hot as the morning progressed, getting irritated, he would take it out on Conrad whenever he got his sums or his recitation of the English poets wrong.

Derounian had decided that Ali was to have an education as well, and he had arranged for Ali also to attend Bannerjee. Ali and Conrad had never met for these lessons before as Bannerjee came to Conrad's house for tutorials in the late afternoon, while Ali went to Bannerjee in the early morning. But of course the two boys in their wanderings round the lanes of the little town had compared notes. Most of the irritation caused to the Hindu babu was as a result of mischief concocted by the two in tandem. But, with Chloe's illness and the fear of cholera, Bannerjee ceased coming to the Tate house and John perforce had to arrange for Conrad to go to him for lessons after 10.00am. Bannerjee accordingly now gleefully had two sets of fees for the one period he taught – strictly between 10.00 in the morning and ending no later than 1.00 midday.

This was a time when boys in England over eight years old were regularly beaten for the most minor transgressions or any failure in learning their lessons. The fussy and pedantic Dr. Hari Bannerjee was of course far too superior to indulge in anything like that, though he did stoop to the occasional clip across the ear or a rap on the knuckles with his ruler when particularly irritated or provoked by the two boys. But even in the environment of this little classroom there was discrimination, as this fairly mild punishment would almost always fall on the hapless Ali rather than the younger but stronger Conrad. If challenged, Bannerjee would undoubtedly claim that it was because Ali was the older and ought to know better. Nevertheless, it was almost always Conrad in fact who was the main instigator of such minor and harmless mischief that the two boys ever got up to.

What exactly the title of 'Doctor' referred to no one ever knew, nor did anyone ever have the temerity or bad manners to ask this high-caste Brahmin gentleman, with his tiny spectacles and rolled-up black umbrella to what it actually referred. He was simply always called 'Dr. Bannerjee' and that was that.

So it was that during these tense days Ali and Conrad met each morning in the Judge's compound. They would lie on the grass, still cool in the early morning, until John and Dickie came out and went to their work. They would then go together to Banarjee's house for their lessons. Ali would leave at midday to go home to prepare lunch. Conrad would stay a further hour devoted to the more abstruse rules of English grammar and literary style, before trudging home just ahead of the worst heat of the day.

It was on the same day that Paul Kelly returned that the group gathered in the meeting room first got round to discussing the matter of the young Marietta Postern. Marietta herself had made no attempt whatsoever during the days following the departure of her mother to take herself off to join the others in Dinapore. Her continued presence in the town soon became known, though not the reasons behind it of course. Grant, who was already annoyed that neither Henrietta Drummond nor Harriet Tate had left, was quite certain that Marietta had to be packed off, escorted by one of the men. In his efficient way he immediately began making arrangements for a carriage to be ordered and prepared. He then approached Johnson with the request that he should accompany the troublesome female. He neither consulted Marietta nor anyone else.

Marietta was only sixteen. Married woman or not surely she would have to do what she was told and that was that. Nothing in mid-Victorian India with its myriad of servants always padding around, could ever be entirely secret. So as the days passed, tales of her improper visit for a whole day alone to the Nawab of Jagpur began to filter through to what was left of the European community. Henrietta was shocked, though her mental strictures were all against Alphonsine – what could you expect - a Eurasian and a Catholic! She urged GG to get rid of the young girl as quickly as possible, and he of course was ready and had already made the preliminary arrangements. But Marietta, even though only sixteen was no longer just Marietta da Costa, but was Mrs. James Postern, the wife of an English officer. She had uninhibitedly enjoyed her day at the hunt with Saridar Khan and his wives. Nothing improper of any kind had taken place and she had been flattered to have been an honoured guest at an all-Indian event. When she got home she had found the freedom from her mother's presence very agreeable. The servants were overjoyed at her return, as the dilemma, which faced so many servants of fleeing Europeans as to what they should do, was removed at a stroke.

"But, my dear Mrs Postern – you can't live alone in the house. What would your husband say if we didn't make sure you were looked after? Come, come, I have made adequate arrangements for you to leave in the company of..."

"Mr. Grant, my mother has left ample means for me to remain here in ease and comfort. The servants are loyal and well paid and I..."

"Madame, it would be totally improper for you to remain here without any male support."

"Mr. Grant, the home of my mother's good friend Azimullah Hassan, is right next door. His sister lives there too and he has welcomed me and invited me to come to his house at any time that I might feel any disquiet of any kind."

As it happened this statement by Marietta was completely untrue, but she knew that if ever the Magistrate thought of checking up on it, the laws of hospitality and etiquette would make it quite impossible for either Azimullah himself or his sister ever to deny that any such invitation had been proffered.

At this point the increasingly irritated Grant almost shouted out at the stubborn girl – '...but you silly girl they are natives' - just stopping himself in time. No, no, Grant mentally censured himself. Azimullah was after all the deputy Collector and the girl was the wife of a British officer. He calmed himself down and went back to all the reasoned arguments that required her to leave. But Marietta herself was now in full flow and in command of her situation. She pointed out how the countryside between here and Dinapore was already becoming increasingly dangerous. She stood on her dignity as the wife of a British Army officer. She was to her own surprise enjoying herself in this discussion with a man whom she had always previously held in awe. Once Grant realised that he had met his match, he saluted and left.

However, he felt that he had to make the position as clear as possible and so immediately went next door to visit Azimullah Hassan, who was after all one of his own officials. There he rather brusquely cut short all the long and flowery compliments that were threatened by the old man and said after the good man could come out with only a few meagre and quite insufficient sentences of welcome and good wishes –

"Azimullah Hassan, my old friend, I understand that you know that Mrs. Postern has not left the town with all the other European ladies."

"Yes, Sahib, I…"

"I understand furthermore that you have already indicated that you and your sister would be happy to help her and take her in if any danger was to arise."

"Er … well … umm… I…" said the old man nodding amicably at Grant but not actually saying anything or even mentioning that his sister had in fact left that morning for a long planned visit to relatives in the countryside.

Grant was of course far too impatient to wait for the man to come out with whatever he was saying, and stood and said –

"Thank you sir. As you can see our work of administration is proceeding and I expect you to continue your duties as far as you can in these difficult times. We must all keep a calm and united front. I leave Mrs. Postern as part of your responsibility if any danger looms. If I hear of anything I will of course let you know at once."

Grant then took his leave as Azimullah Hassan sat on, contemplating what he could possibly ever do if any major problem did indeed arise, or if any mutineers arrived in Darabad.

The very next day sixty Sikh policemen sent by William Taylor from Dinapore arrived with instructions to remove the eight lakhs of rupees stored in the little town's treasury. They trotted in – commandeered a cart – and trotted out and away, leaving only about seventy thousand rupees.

* * *

As the days passed in a mixture of tension and even more boredom the government officials went on with their duties as serenely as they could manage. George Grant became even more a hive of activity, as if the more he did the further he kept at bay that dread word – anarchy. He recruited more men into the town's small native police force. He consulted with the local village headmen. Above all he arranged for a nightly patrol of all the European men who remained. At first he tried to avoid using the services of Arthur Drummond, who, already in his late forties, was by far the oldest European in town. However Drummond insisted on taking his part. With the return of Kelly there were still about twelve Europeans left in Darabad, but as each day passed one or two more slipped away.

Each night two would stay up and patrol for about six hours from about 11.00pm until the sun came up early in the morning. They were of course all armed but it was never clear what their function was. For Grant any activity was useful in itself – if the phrase had then been fashionable he would have called it 'showing the flag' – but most of them would have had no idea what to do if they saw any criminal activity. As it happened, if anything there was even less petty crime in the town than usual.

The news, filtering through to the little community continued to be bad as one by one more of the small military stations between Dinapore and Delhi came out in mutiny. The event was almost always the same. The sepoy regiments, usually led by the cavalry, would erupt in a furious mutiny. They would then murder their British officers, murders largely instigated by the few ringleaders who saw this as the best way to force the ordinary soldiers into realising that they could no longer turn back. These British officers, often right up to the very last moment, refused to believe that their own men, men whom they somewhat arrogantly believed that they knew well, would succumb to the contagion of neighbouring mutinous regiments which were obviously not as well officered as their own.

The mutineering sepoys, lacking any clear leaders and in the main having no great political agenda would then march off, usually in good order, to Delhi. Some of course would simply melt away to their own villages. However, having been tricked into taking that final irrevocable step of murdering their officers, they were aware of the possibility of fearful retribution and they thought of Delhi and the pathetic symbol of the feeble Bahadur

Shah as a haven – someone who by his very presence would legit-imise their actions. They certainly had no idea of being part of any great political movement. The idea that the high-caste Hindus, who constituted the bulk of the Bengali regiments, had risen up and murdered their officers simply in order to replace the British Raj with the old Muslim Raj was ridiculous.

The trouble was that once that first step was taken – the shooting of the haughty young man fresh out from England galloping up on horseback to deal with the 'dratted disturbance', and who thought that he already knew 'his' men – the sepoys realized there could be no turning back. They were, despite their high caste, fairly simple men, well-respected in their home villages, who had become confused by the change that they sensed in their British officers. The old enlightened and tolerant eighteenth century attitudes of those earlier British officers who often took the trouble to learn their language and to respect their customs, had changed to the arrogant racist superiorities of the mid-Victorian products of the new minor public schools.

The old British army comprising younger sons of the landed aristocracy leading the dregs of the lower classes, was changing. The Victorian middle class began sending their own sons to those second-rate boarding schools, hotbeds of racial and class arrogance, allowing them to opt for a previously despised military career. This new breed of officer never thought for a moment of learning the language, or getting to know the culture, of the men they commanded.

Then, there were now the meddling missionaries peddling their superior certainties about a God born from a human virgin, a God who could raise other humans from the dead. And what was the nature of this God/Man – divine or human or a subtle mixture of both? The arguments were endless. The old East India Company had throughout the eighteenth century imposed an absolute ban on allowing entry to any Christian missionaries throughout all the lands which they controlled. But as the British Parliament increasingly interfered in Indian affairs so the removal of that ban was one of the first changes that were made.

Of course none of these simple sepoys were aware of all these subtleties. What they were aware of, or thought that they were aware of, is that these same missionaries and indeed some of their own senior officers wanted them to abandon their own beliefs, which these Christians thought were so irrational and full of superstitions.

Gods with six arms and animal heads in one of the native religions; a prophet who went up to heaven and had a holy book dictated to him for another. How primitive when compared to a God/Man, born of a human woman who somehow remained a virgin, who walked on water and went up into the sky to be shown the world by the devil. Some of these missionaries may of course have had the sense to suggest that most of these gospel stories were symbolic and not intended to be taken literally, but without exception they were quite incapable of seeing that the same could be equally said about the local religions they so deplored and despised.

Meanwhile, after the Sikh police detachment left to return to Dinapore with the rupees from the treasury, life in the town settled back into routine. The officials going to their administrative tasks; the railway staff to their work on the approaching railway; Kelly down to the Syed Ghat every day, even on those days after he had trotted round the town on horseback all night on patrol. The trestle bridge over the river began to grow. Occasionally Kelly would meet the engineer working on the cuttings and embankments moving towards the river on the other side. He was stationed in Revelkhind some eight miles away. They would exchange news and rumours sitting in the shade of some tree when it was too hot.

Every morning there would be a short meeting, at which Henrietta was always present, before everyone departed to their various duties. Arthur would always read out in a deep and sonorous voice the prayer of the day before any general discussions started. Henrietta would demurely kneel – this was a chapel of sorts after all. The men would remain standing: Grant stiffly at attention ready to salute his God: John Tate in a sort of bent-forward republican attitude, respectful but somehow doubtful:

Derounian always with a cheerful smile on his face: Ali and Conrad surreptitiously holding hands and staring from the back: the others in various submissive poses. For everyone it was a good moment to think about the coming day.

It was about a week after the Sikh policemen had left that Johnson again raised the possibility of putting one of the buildings in the Judge's compound into a state of defence. Ali and Conrad had slipped out as they always did as soon as the little service ended. Johnson said –

"Gentlemen, don't you think that it would be a good idea if we now carried out what was suggested before – that is the building of some sort of fortification of one or other of the buildings here. All now seems to be quiet, but a mutiny or a rebellion of some kind or another is always a possibility in view of what we are hearing and at least if we have some sort of fortified building we could at least make a temporary stand if matters came to a head."

"I, myself must immediately repeat what I said before", said Arthur Drummond. "We are only a mere handful, none of us with any military experience whatsoever. The few hours we might withstand any concerted attack would not be worth the loss of prestige and dignity we would suffer now if the local population see us panicking and building flimsy defences."

"I don't agree, sir," said John Tate. "I do believe that if we do it discreetly, and without any great fuss, it would at least be a place to which we could all retire if the worst came to the worst."

"I'm sorry John", said Grant, "but the judge is quite right. This compound is where people come regularly to present petitions and see the Judge. We simply can't be seen digging ourselves some sort of entrenchments or fortifications. In any case these sort of things are only as strong as the number of people who can man them, and you know how few we are. It's a mere panic proposal."

None of the others offered any opinion, and Johnson himself, seeing what his superior felt, immediately back-tracked. The matter was dropped.

But that very evening when John Tate got home he reported

the whole discussion to Harriet, who said –

"Well my love I must say that I find the arguments of George fairly convincing for once, and if the Judge is clear that the compound itself, normally open to all, should not be used for any kind of defence, then I can't see what can be done. None of the other houses could possibly be made defensible. Those in the town are totally overlooked and crowded in, while those, like ours, outside the town, have huge open windows and verandahs and are surely quite indefensible."

"I agree with you my dear, but I was thinking of something else. Also I would say that Grant is quite wrong on one count for a start. If the regiments in Dinapore do mutiny, they could pass through here if they are on their way to Delhi, but with a bit of luck we will be bypassed, particularly if they see that attacking us could delay getting away to Delhi. By the way where is Conrad?"

"I think he's out with Ali – he'll be back well in time for supper."

"How is Chloe? I'll go up and see her after my bath. Perhaps I could read to her a bit – is she up to it?"

"Oh, John that would be marvellous. Dr. Henty came again this morning and said that the crisis is not yet passed. But if she hangs on the danger will pass in about a week. He doesn't believe in all this talk about impure air or miasma – he thinks it's all in the water. We have to boil every drop of water before she can take a sip. He also wants us to try to get her to drink at least two pints every day."

"Fine. I'm worried about Conrad. He is twelve to all intents and purposes and we should have sent him home at least two…"

"Oh John, not again we've been…"

"At least, my dear, he would have been away from all this looming danger."

"Well, John, you know that I was in the middle of dealing with it all when this lot broke out. But look, if we have to die we have to die. He's not in much danger here. The Indians, particularly the sepoys, don't kill children whatever the provocation."

But on this point the usually eminently sensible Harriet was wrong; terribly wrong.

* * *

John Tate may have had the reputation among the other British in the town of being a mite dominated by his outspoken wife, but it was always accepted that he had the courage of such convictions that he might have. He was, for instance, the only man in the station who could stand up to GG when Grant was in full flow of any idea. John could see the strength of the Judge's argument about using any building in the very public compound in the town as a defensive point. He also saw the difficulty in trying to fortify any of the grand or modest houses out here in the suburbs, including his own. But his eye was on the old zenana building at the far end of his own garden.

Tate's house was an old mansion that had once belonged to a wealthy Muslim gentleman who had a large family with several wives and female hangers-on of all kinds. The property was known as the Hamid Mansion. The road out from Darabad branched at the point where this eminently respectable merchant had converted into an elegant dwelling the old large stone house that had stood where the road forked. The house stood in large well-kept grounds, without any walls or fences separating them from the road. Almost like a park, dotted about with trees and clumps of shrubbery, the locals had become used to sitting on the land in the shade of the trees, and the Tates had done nothing to change or prevent this habit.

When John and Harriet had moved in, although not exactly overgrown the grounds were beginning to look a little shabby. The lush grass had not been properly maintained for some time. Both of them were keen on gardens and almost immediately two gardeners had been employed, the creeping jungle had been cut back, the grass watered and scythed and the place again took on the look of a well-kept park.

Away to one side and to the back of the house was an unusual stone building. Whilst aiming to be a rectangular structure of similar proportions to that of the Parthenon, the measurements had gone subtly wrong and in fact it was almost square and

rather ugly as a result. The building was on two floors, but the lower floor was like a half-cellar sunk into the ground. The rooms on this lower level had arched windows matching the lofty arches of the upper floor. However these windows, faced with wooden latticed work, were cut-off half way down by the earth which went right up to the woodwork. These basement rooms were accordingly dark and rather damp in the short rainy season, but were beautifully cool in the heat of the summer.

The upper floor, not really much more than six feet or so above the ground, had a series of large and high arches formed by very solid stone pillars holding up the roof and shading a veranda which ran round three sides of the building. The room in the centre of this upper floor – if comparing it with the Parthenon it would be the inner temple – was a dark shaded long empty room with openings rather than doors out into the veranda on each of the three sides.

The fourth side of this upper floor was totally bricked up to the roof, though below on the ground floor there were again the same half windows down to the ground with their wooden lattices. On this fourth side the park-like grounds only went on for a further ten yards or so up to where the grounds merged into fairly dense jungle.

An unusual building – pukka stone and brick – it had lain unused and mouldering for some years. Tate's immediate European predecessor had used the large upper room as a billiard room, and indeed there was still an old billiard table there with mouldering green baize, but no cues and only two balls one red and one white. Conrad and Ali needless to say were in and out of this building and had explored every nook and cranny. In the lower floor, in the corner room at the back facing the jungle, they had come across a brick drain leading from a covered hole in the corner of the floor and going away from the house. With one of them taking turns to keep guard they had spent several glorious afternoons burrowing their way through the tangle of roots and weeds that had pushed their way through the brick sides of the square drain. It was not deep, nor was it large enough for any adult to wriggle through – even Conrad had difficulty squeezing through, though the wiry Ali had no trouble. It ended about twenty yards away in the jungle at the rear of the building, coming out in the side of a bank just above a stream that ran through the jungle at the back.

The boys were not stupid – they made it a rule that one of them must always be outside calling down the drain and holding up a second candle. They never knew what it could possibly have been used for, though their imaginations came up with several ingenious and unlikely ideas. They were of course careful to close up the holes again at both ends, with leaves and loose earth covering the exit above the stream and with broken bricks over the entrance in the building.

Upstairs, their favourite game was to stand at each end of the billiard table and to send the two balls as hard as possible from each end down the middle. If they met with a resounding crash in the middle, the resulting chaos was most satisfactory as each ball swung wildly away, bouncing off the dying cushions in various wild directions. Conrad had already devised a complicated and arcane system of scoring points according to where the two balls finally ended up, which entailed the use of a ruler and a lot of shouting and argument.

It was only the next day after the meeting had decided against any communal attempt to create any kind of fortification in the Judge's compound that John Tate, who now had even more spare time on his hands than usual, decided to take steps of his own. On this first morning he hired a strong bullock cart pulled by two oxen, with a driver together with two day-labourers. Riding alongside, he set off to the Syed Ghat on the river.

There, he rode up to Kelly who was sitting under a tree by the side of the river reading a moth-eaten first volume of Gibbon's *Decline and Fall of the Roman Empire*, and dismounted.

"Hello Tate – my God, have you read this book?" said Kelly turning and holding up the book for John to squint at the title.

"No – though I have heard of it. Isn't it rather heavy going?" said John as he came up still holding the reins.

"Well to be honest, no. It is a surprisingly easy read, though

I suspect I miss a lot of the allusions to other events referred to in the classical world. But I never realised just how violently anti-Christian it is. Very exciting. It would make dear Henrietta apoplectic if she ever read it. You should try it – chapter 12 – or is it chapter 16 – I can't remember – real tub-thumping stuff. He is extraordinarily clear in his opinion that it was the advent of Christianity that was the direct cause of the collapse of the Empire of which he was so enamoured. You look tired John – what is it, and what's that cart doing?"

"Look Paul, I've decided to do something about a fortification of sorts against any temporary trouble.. I know the meeting decided against – but this is going to be in my own grounds well away from the town. It will be done largely by me with just a couple of helpers – those guys there."

"Hm! I don't know how Arthur or GG will take it – you heard what they said."

"Fine. I understand their points – but no one can object to my taking my own steps for the protection of my own family in my own grounds. You know that old building at the far end of my garden – the one that used to be used as a billiard room. Well it happens to be one of the only solidly built brick and stone build-ings outside the main town and I intend making it defensible if I can."

"Look John – Grant's right – defensible outposts can hold out against an enemy only if there are men available to fight from them, and in our case I…"

"Yes, yes I know all that, but everywhere else the mutineering sepoys have gone racing off to Delhi. It only needs to hold out for a few hours while any rebels pour through. It would certainly beat staying in the house and cowering under the beds or whatever."

"Very well, very well. I think that you're mad, but probably no madder than the rest of us staying on here in the first place. But what are you here for right now?"

"Ah…well… I've, er, come to collect materials."

Kelly looked hard at him and then across to where the work on the brick supports being constructed for the wooden trestle bridge was proceeding very slowly indeed. With a twinkle, John said-

"As senior supervising officer of the East India Railway Company, I have decided that some of the materials painstakingly gathered here are needed to repair and shore up railway company property in the town."

"Meaning of course your zenana house in the garden."

"Certainly. I may live there but it is Company property and needs to be looked after as much as this bridge needs to be built."

For a moment there was a short rather tense silence, then the two men grinned at each other and John Tate swung back into the saddle saying –

"Do any necessary paperwork Paul, and I'll sign."

He rode down to where the oxcart was waiting and directed it to the piles of new bricks waiting by the side of the river. It did not take long, even in the heat of the afternoon for the cart to be loaded with as much bricks and pieces of timber that the oxen could manage, and slowly the cart turned to make its way back to the town. John watched it go and went back to sit by Kelly who had ignored the whole proceeding and had returned to squinting at the tiny print of the Gibbon. In true Indian bureaucratic fashion, however, he had had the time to prepare on a piece of Company paper a formal receipt stating – 'that by order and authority of the presiding supervising officer of the East India Railway Company in the town of Darabad, one wagon-load of bricks type 2 had been set aside for the repair and maintenance of other Company property in the town.'

John signed this document with a flourish and Kelly carefully folded and placed it in his field bag. The afternoon wore on. John was in no hurry to get back to the lumbering cart which would take over an hour just to get to the outskirts of the town. In many ways also it was probably better for it to make its slow way through the town without him being in escort alongside.

"So what do you think, John, are we going to have to use this little toy fort of yours."

"Maybe – maybe – but in any case it could only be a temporary refuge. If the Dinapore regiments mutiny, it will be likely that they will only come through here if they were on the way to Delhi. Hopefully all we are talking about is one night of anxiety as they pass through."

"But listen John, I heard when I was in Dinapore after leaving the ladies, that the mutineers at Cawpore, led by that Nana Sahib chap, turned back when they were at first on the way to Delhi, and surrounded and attacked the entrenchments that old General Wheeler had constructed."

"You never said anything!"

"No, I didn't want to worry anyone, but it was pretty well confirmed by the time I left to come back here."

"Kelly, my dear fellow, we'll just have to hope that we are not in the middle of the first chapter of the Decline and Fall of the British Empire."

"Aha – and indeed if that is so, no doubt we will have every right to join Gibbon and blame all this religion nonsense – pig loathers – cow worshippers – and symbolic blood drinkers alike."

"My dear Paul, please don't let Arthur or Henrietta hear you say anything like that."

He struggled up from the ground and swung onto his horse as Kelly also rose, carefully putting away his precious Gibbon. Nodding at Tate, he strolled away to check on the desultory work going on at the river.

John trotted off and then went into a short gallop for the few miles into town. He had timed it well and arrived alongside the lumbering oxcart as it passed the Judge's compound and turned onto the road leading to the Hamid Mansion.

Conrad and Ali were roaming in the grounds when the wagon arrived. They ran to join the two workers as they carried the bricks carefully three or four at a time and piled them up at various places on the veranda, between the arches, as John directed. At first the boys tried taking them three at a time also, but soon they had to give up and carry only one. When the workmen were finished and the cart empty, John nodded and confirmed that they would need two more loads. He then gave instructions to the driver and the two labourers for the next two afternoons and paid them off for the day. He turned to Conrad and Ali and said-

"Thank you boys – you've been very useful. You can both join the oxcart tomorrow when it passes out of the town if you want. It won't be leaving until at least an hour after you finish with Dr. Bannerjee. Go and see the work going on at the river and come back with the next load. I'll be working here with this lot and you'll be able to help me, so don't get tired helping to load the cart at the river. Ali, you must get Mr. Derounian's permission of course."

* * *

Day by day the work at the zenana house in the grounds of the Hamid mansion went on. Brick walls in the open arches slowly rose between the pillars on the upper storey of the house. John had only a little mortar and not much expertise in using it, so he could use the mortar only thinly, with none at the bottom of the walls, where instead, he strengthened them by adding two more thicknesses of brick, tapering to one. These walls went up to the height of a man all round the building, leaving room at the top from where to shoot out.

Although well away from the town it was of course quite impossible to keep the construction quiet. However, the Judge's and GG's worries about the effect this might have on the local populace turned out to be unfounded. Chloe's health at last began to improve and Henty confirmed that she might have just turned the corner, though it would be best if she remained in bed in a darkened room. Accordingly at last Harriet had the leisure to begin to take an interest in John's construction. She arranged for all the lower storey rooms in the building to be cleaned and cleared of all the accumulated rubbish. Meanwhile these lower floor half windows had their lattice woodwork removed and were all entirely bricked up except for a generous loophole at the top on which a musket could be rested and fired. It was clear from the start that from the room behind the wall, sunk as it was into the ground, the embrasure at the top would be too high for anyone to stand comfortably and shoot out. So she arranged for a series of benches to be placed against the wall in each of the rooms to enable anyone standing on them to fire out.

It was Conrad and Ali, standing on one of these benches, using carefully collected branches as muskets to fire out at the clumps of women and children picnicking among the trees, who noted that the benches were flimsy and shook even under their own slight weight. They pointed this out to John who then arranged for the benches to be bolted to the floor. The next addition was sandbags, placed along the top of the walls and pushed up along the bottom. John had several dozen jute bags delivered and these were filled with sand brought from the works on the river. At first enthusiastically helped by the two boys, the filling of the bags was carried out, fairly reluctantly, by the house sweepers. They did at least keep at it, whereas the boys soon became bored and wandered away.

Then came the day about ten days after the work had started when GG finally rode over to see how the work was progressing. He and John strolled over from the house, and Grant said as they walked –

"Look here Tate, you know I consider this to be a complete waste of time and materials, but at least let's see what you have managed to do."

They strolled round looking critically at everything done so far. They then went down into the cool dark rooms of the lower storey, and into the centre room, which now contained a large supply of rice. There was also already a small quantity of beer and brandy. Deep in the darkest corner were two large pottery pitchers already filled with water and covered.

"Well – there you are," said Grant pointing at the water pitchers. "There is your first problem and your second. This place could not stand for more than an hour against any concerted attack if there are less than a dozen or so men defending it. On the other hand, if all the outlying indigo planters and other Europeans came in and joined us, there would then not be enough water for them to survive for very long even if they were enough to hold off the first attacks."

"George – surely we are only talking about a few hours – a

couple of days at the very most as any mutineers pass through on their way to Delhi. But look, I take your point. We sit on a high water-table here and I will look into the possibility of sinking a well from inside the building."

"You're completely mad, John – but well done! What you have been doing has got around, and if anything it has been good if nothing else for our morale."

* * *

On the other side of the equation as it were, matters had not been static. The sepoy garrison at Dinapore consisted of three long-standing regiments – the 7th, 8th and 40th native infantry, together with a newly formed regiment the 68th. This constituted a total force of almost 4,000 men. Also part of the garrison was a regiment of about 600 British soldiers. This latter was a formidable force, as not only did they have six large and modern cannon, they were also armed with the new Enfield rifle, so much deadlier and more accurate than the old muskets still used by the native infantry.

Mutinies had by now broken out in almost every military station between Dinapore and Meerut. West Bengal contained no troops of any kind, Sepoy or British. Accordingly between Calcutta on the one side and Delhi on the other the only sizable British force was these 600 men in the garrison of Dinapore.

The Europeans gathered in Darabad regularly received rumours that the Dinapore garrison had at last mutinied – but they all turned out to be false alarms. It was an odd and unexplained aspect of the mutinies that they were nearly always initiated first by the cavalry regiments and spread from them to the infantry. It was not a matter of caste, as both infantry and cavalry consisted equally of high-caste Brahmins. But time and again it was the cavalry that moved first; there was, however, no sepoy cavalry in Dinapore.

Like so many of the old generals of the East India Company, General Lloyd, in command at Dinapore, simply refused to believe that 'his' sepoys would revolt. They did in fact remain quiescent even when the treasury at Patna was removed and sent down the Ganges to Calcutta. But a ferment was building up in these regiments similar to all the others which had already mutinied. It was, as always a matter of leaders. Was there anyone ready to take command of any sort? Was anyone ready to persuade the ordinary soldier to defy authority – a barrack-room lawyer – a religious crackpot – an opportunist – even perhaps an idealist with a vision of a Moghul or a caste-Hindu Raj?

A catalyst had in fact at last emerged in the local situation. Haidar Presaud was a noted merchant in the town of Patna. He was also a small-scale local landowner, who had only a few months before been deprived of his holding by the local British Collector. It had been a complicated case involving four villages and a squabble between two zemindars as to which of them had the legal right to exploit the unfortunate villagers, collecting their rents and organising corruptly the taxes they had to pay. The crafty Haidar had lost the case and was quite sure that it had simply been a matter of not having expended enough bribery on his part. It had left him in a disturbed and agitated frame of mind.

The news of the mutiny in Meerut, the capture of Delhi by the mutineers, the breakdown of law and order all the way along the Great Trunk Road, all coupled with the soothsayers and astrologers forever going on about the hundredth anniversary of the Battle of Plassey, convinced him that the British Raj was clearly about to end. He was certainly not going to let the current circumstances pass him by. Fortunes were to be made – landholdings to be acquired – in revolutionary situations of this kind. This was surely not the moment to sit back and simply watch events unfold.

Haidar was a thin, nervously active man in his late thirties. Clean-shaven, he was tall with a permanent slight forward-leaning stoop and with bright eyes always restlessly darting about. He was a dealer in all sorts of spices including opium and the milder narcotics. Opium was of course a Company monopoly. Most of the extensive Indian opium production went on export to China, where successive British governments had in the sacred name of freedom of trade forced the tottering Chinese imperial government to allow the import of this major and lucrative East India Company product. The unfortunate Chinese regularly formed armed patrols of flimsy war-junks in a forlorn attempt to stop the pernicious trade, but in conflict after conflict the British forced them to withdraw.

The drug was of course not intended in any way for the Indian market, as the British were perfectly well aware of the terrible and debilitating effects of its consumption and were certainly not going to have it spreading in their empire. However, on the basis that there would always be some people, Europeans as well as Indians, who would try to get their hands on some opium, the Company had licensed some traders to buy and sell a small proportion locally. Haidar was one of those so licensed.

Haidar had access to the sepoy regiments in Dinapore and as June turned to July he became more and more involved with the small group of men, ordinary soldiers but including one or two non-commissioned officers, who were involved in thoughts of mutiny. What worried these men more than anything else was the rumours which implicated them in loss of caste. Quite unlike the underclass – Wellington's 'scum of the earth' – which constituted the bulk of the British army, the sepoys of the Bengal army were almost all high-caste Hindus, respected and looked-up to when they went home to their villages. Their fear of loss of caste and the terrible threat of untouchability was due to a whole raft of religious ideas. Ideas no different in principle as the belief that the red wine you drank and the unleavened bread you nibbled in your temple turned miraculously into the blood and body of your God. Transubstantiation was the fancy word for it. Even if you belonged to the sect that believed that this same wine and bread was only a symbolic ritual, it remained similar in essence to the belief system of these high-caste sepoys.

What horror then for these pious soldiers – oh dear, having to bite the wrong kind of grease – having your tin water-can touched by an untouchable – having to cross over water – having your food prepared by the wrong caste, or with the wrong incantations. Of course you simply had to take the most drastic steps, even if it might cost you your life.

Haidar Presaud listened to it all. He had not the least idea what the grease to be used on the new rifles was actually made of but nevertheless he confirmed to these simple men that certainly, yes, yes, the grease on the new cartridges must surely be made of a mixture of cow and pig fat. What made the added difference in this district was that he was also a personal acquaintance of the young Marietta's admirer, Saridar Khan, the Nawab of Jagpur.

The position of some of these small-scale nawabs in British India was not easy throughout the whole of this year that the Bengal sepoy regiments mutinied, went off to Delhi and died. In the first place it was quite clearly against their class interests to encourage anarchic conditions in the countryside. They could all see that simply to return to the dying days of the decrepit Mughal Empire made no sense at all. On the other hand that very decrepitude which had characterised the end of the Mughals had led to a situation where active and resolute men, in command of some troops, could and did carve out for themselves small principalities. So, if the British Raj was to collapse, the first of such resolute men on the scene would have the best pickings.

The hapless villagers, the great mass of the Indian people, were of course not consulted in any way, nor was it their welfare that was at stake. They were simply the spoils over which everyone who counted for anything were squabbling.

Saridar Khan owned and lived in a crumbling old ruin of a palace. He even commanded a minuscule army, clothed in an extraordinary uniform of clashing colours. He could no longer really afford to maintain these hundred or so men, armed with a most unusual collection of guns and daggers, but they remained, sitting about at the gates of the palace. They looked after the small bronze cannon which was their pride and joy, keeping it clean and shining and even polishing the small cannon balls that were sometimes shot out and hastily retrieved on state occasions. Their principal employment now was acting as beaters when the Nawab went hunting. It was one of the more endearing qualities of the jolly Nawab, and indeed of many of the Indian princely class, that despite the fact that he was almost bankrupt he could not bring himself to dismiss these old men who had served for decades, on the flimsy and transient basis of mere efficiency.

Haidar Presaud became the catalyst. As the weeks passed, he moved on a daily basis between the barracks at Dinapore, the small garrison at Ravelkhind, and the palace at Jagpur where the Nawab sat in his disintegrating home, biting his nails and wondering whether he had the courage to act as the wily Haidar kept suggesting. Haidar wanted him to take command of the sepoys if and when they finally decided to mutiny, with a view to carving out a principality for himself as the current Raj collapsed. In the end, like so many of the local notables having to choose one side or the other, it tended to come down to 'money.' Those who managed their estates well, who repaired their palaces or forts, who occasionally grudgingly provided a few rupees to help build a bridge here or a well there, stayed quiet and in support of the forces of that law and order which gave them such material comforts. Those few on the other hand who were squandering their fortune, who could not manage their estates, who had less and less to lose, joined the sepoys. Saridar Khan, with his lavish hunts and his excessive hospitality was almost bankrupt.

Not far from Jagpur in the small town of Ravelkhind was another sepoy garrison comprising the 66th Infantry regiment with a small contingent of British officers in command. Here also Haidar Presaud was active. This new regiment had many men who came from the surrounding district and Haidar had far less difficulty in persuading the native officers of this regiment to agree to follow the lead of Saridar, whom they knew and who had collected their rents for generations. But for the moment these men too hesitated. Nothing was likely to happen until the garrison at Dinapore rose, if they ever did.

Meanwhile, brick by brick and sandbag after sandbag the zenana house at the back of the Hamid Mansion began to take on the aspect of a little fort. George Grant, increasingly reconciled to the whole project, rode down regularly and made many practical suggestions. John, for instance, had not thought of the flat roof – but Grant showed that this was a good vantage point both for seeing what was going on around, but also for precision shooting if it ever came to that. So, more sandbags were brought up a ladder leading up through a trapdoor from the main central room. These were piled up against the low parapet wall, forming a low barrier from where people could crouch to observe or to fire. Above all as they strolled round the building GG pointed out that the jungle at the back of the building came alarmingly close. John agreed and two days later the growth was cleared back for at least a further ten yards by John's gardeners.

On the day that that clearance began Conrad and Ali arrived breathlessly from their class and watched to see how far back the cutting would go and whether their secret drain would be discovered. As it was the clearance went back just as far as the little stream, and the exit of the drain on the bank above the brook was never discovered. The jungle on the other side of the stream was left as it was.

Grant also wrote to the British Commissioner in Patna – William Taylor - who had sent the original fifty Sikh policemen to remove the bulk of the treasure in Darabad. GG was not the sort to moderate his words and he made it clear that he still thought that Tate's refusal to forbid the flight by the other railway engineers was a moral failing and that the 'runaways' were cowards. But he now gave the news of the building of the little fort, giving John Tate the full credit for an initiative which he now accepted was useful and well-considered. He also informed Taylor in the letter that not all the women and children had been evacuated and that there were now three ladies and two children left in the station.

The days passed.

* * *

The 23rd June 1857 was the centenary anniversary of the Battle of Plassey – the day that all the soothsayers and astrologers and other necromancy experts were predicting that British rule would end. It was certainly beginning to look as if that might indeed happen. A few days after that day passed news came to the little town of the massacre at Cawnpore. The Europeans there, under the leadership of General Wheeler had had to face the fact that the local Nawab – the Nana Sahib – had turned back from his original intention to lead the regiments which had mutinied to Delhi. It had been pointed out to him that taking the men to Delhi would result in his being completely side-lined, as, once there among all the Moghuls and their generals, with his men merged with all the others, he would be ignored. He agreed and had turned back, persuading the mutineers instead to attack the badly sited entrenchments set up by General Wheeler who had imagined that he would not be attacked.

By a somewhat devious stratagem the Nana Sahib persuaded the trusting Wheeler to abandon the rather flimsy entrenchment he had constructed, which was in any case not standing up well to the bombardment. The figures were not clear even then but there could have been almost a thousand crowded into the area – certainly a good deal more than five hundred. These consisted of those British army officers who had escaped the original outbreak by the sepoys, the European merchants and business-men of the town with all their wives and children and a large number of Eurasians with their wives and children, all of whom had fled into the entrenchment immediately on the outbreak of the mutiny.

General Wheeler, an old East India Company officer, was married to an Indian lady and had his three Eurasian daughters with him in the makeshift camp as well as his wife. He was persuaded, by a promise of safe conduct for all, to arrange for everyone to leave the entrenchments and march off to the river Ganges less than a mile away, where about forty boats would be awaiting to take them all away. On the day appointed for the exodus the whole ramshackle party moved out on foot and in a variety of carriages and made their slow cumbersome way to the riverbank. There down below, moored, but mostly stuck in the mud, they saw the leaky inadequate boats that had been provided. The group began slowly trying to get aboard, when at a signal the boatmen jumped out and ran for safety whereupon a murderous fire was directed at everyone, man, woman and child either already in the boats or struggling to get in.

The young eighteen-year-old Ensign Postern, who would never see his Marietta ever again, was one of the first to die. His death was followed closely after by that of General Wheeler and his Hindu lady wife. This massacre was completely intentional and carefully and deliberately executed. Only one boat got away. As the shooting died away, some sepoy cavalry rode down into the shallower parts of the water to despatch with the sword all those who had fallen or jumped out of the boats and who were still alive. The whole episode had been watched by the Nana Sahib and some of his wives. Pressed by the women, he ordered that the killing of the women and the children should stop. None of the inflamed soldiers took much notice, but eventually, since there were no European men left, the killing petered out and the surviving women and children were gathered together and lodged in a set of rooms in the Nana's palace known as the' bibigargh', surrounding a compound with a well in the middle.

Soon, with the addition of other children rounded up and brought in, there were about two hundred and fifty persons in the rooms. The Nana had no idea what to do with them, and meanwhile the first of the British relief columns, this one under the command of General Havelock, was approaching. Despite all the urgent and repeated objections of the Nana's wives, he and those who were advising him decided to kill them all. The mutineering sepoys, already rather disillusioned with the leader into whose hands they had fallen, refused to carry out the orders. The Bibigarh had been locked and they had been ordered to fire through the windows at the terrified women and children within. They did as they were told, but all, without exception, fired their muskets up at the roof and not a single European died.

Unable to decide what to do, the Nana or perhaps someone on his behalf, sent in five men with knives and butcher's cleaves and the doors were closed behind them. The killing and screaming went on for over an hour as it got dark, with the men coming out occasionally to get a new sword to replace a broken one. In the morning the bodies were dragged out and thrown down the large well in the middle of the courtyard. During the course of this part of the operation it was discovered that some of the many children were still alive, having been buried below the bodies of the dead adults. They were nevertheless thrown in onto the pile of dead bodies already in the well.

It was now the 16th July. General Havelock's relief force arrived in Cawnpore the next day The Nana Sahib had fled without the sepoys and without his wives. The British press of course went hysterical as soon as the news reached England. The papers reported all sorts of facts which were quite unproven and mostly untrue. They went on and on about rape, which had not occurred at all. Illustrations, drawn by people who had never left their desk in London appeared showing all these ladies, still looking remarkably clean and well dressed with their hands raised appealing heroically for mercy from the fate supposedly worse than death. Yet, even though there were many more children, ranging from babies to ten-year-olds, killed than women they were scarcely mentioned save to heighten the horror.

The news of this massacre arrived in Darabad on the 22nd July and from that moment on everyone left in the town knew that it would only be a matter of time before they would soon have to face something very similar, if on a smaller scale. There had been rumours almost on a daily basis of a mutiny at Dinapore and another at Revelkhind.

That night of the 22nd July was the worst night that John Tate had till then ever experienced. As he considered the news that was coming in of the tragic events in Cawnpore, he faced the thought that all his pathetic attempts at creating a fortification had simply fooled him into a terrible complacency. He was responsible for a wife and two children and hearing of the horrors of Cawnpore he felt a deep guilt that he had not acted more decisively to overrule Harriet's decision to remain in Darabad. John had been in India long enough to discount the hysterical stories of multiple rape – but the extraordinary news of the killing of the children left him in a state of real terror. His little fort was useless if it was not manned. John spent the whole night awake and in a state of despair.

But then on the very next day there was a chink of light. William Taylor, the commissioner in Patna, having read and pondered on GG's letter had decided to send some reinforcements. Thirty-four Sikh policemen, with a further six Ghurka volunteers rode into the town. They were commanded by a larger than life figure - an imposing giant of a man with a black beard, a flamboyant moustache, and an immaculate cream-coloured turban. This was Jemadar Baldour Singh whose voice when issuing commands was louder even than Dickie Derounian's.

This magnificent party rode into the town and down the Maidan, watched all the way by the curious townsfolk who were silent and made no comments or demonstrations of any kind. It was an incongruous group – the Sikhs almost all over six feet tall and looking very grand and rather serious. The six Nepalese Ghurkas riding at the back, very small with wide grins on their faces. The party rode straight into the judge's compound and dismounted. Here Henrietta was immediately in her element. Although no one in the town had any idea that they were coming, she soon had organised food, the fixing of accommodation and the immediate provision of water. George Grant was summoned and all at once for the first time a note of hope arose.

Two days later the sepoy garrison at Dinapore – the 7th, 8th, 40th and the new 68th Bengal infantry finally rose in rebellion. They did not murder their officers but marched out in fairly good order under their own officers. They were not hindered in any way by the 600-strong British garrison under General Lloyd. The three older regiments began to make their way to Delhi, but were held up along the way.

Haidar Presaud meanwhile had rushed round to the garrison lines as soon as he heard the news of the mutiny. He was unable to make any impression on the 7th, 8th and 40th. But he persuaded the officers of the 68th, over whom he had already established a considerable influence, to move to Revelkhind to join with the regiment there and invite the Nawab of Jagpur to lead them. This persuasion worked and unaccompanied by any of his family he left with the defecting 68th regiment.

That evening, the moment that the soldiers from Dinapore arrived, the 66th regiment at Revelkhind mutinied, murdering their few British officers who were, as happened so often and despite all the precedents, quite unprepared.

The next morning on the 26th July the two regiments set off for the Syed Ghat and the unfinished railway bridge over the River, heading for the little town of Darabad.

PART II

The Storm breaks.

July 1857

The 26th July was a Sunday. The Europeans left in Darabad gathered in the Judge's compound as usual early in the morning. The prayer service went on as it had done every Sunday since the emergency had started. On this Sunday, Marietta Postern made another appearance. Although not particularly devout, she had been brought up as a Catholic and retained her childhood loyalty in that respect. She had therefore only come once or twice before. She sat modestly at the back. Henrietta, who had always been a bit impatient with the problem that the young girl posed, made a point as the service ended, of walking back before she could leave, to pass on some words of comfort. Everyone was conscious that the terrible news of what had happened in Cawnpore meant that it was almost certain that her young husband had died.

As the meeting was breaking up and everyone came out into the sunshine, there was a clutter of hooves and a very dusty Dickie, followed closely by an equally begrimed Paul Kelly came galloping into the compound and right up to where everyone were strolling out of the little building.

"They're here," panted Derounian as he got rather ponderously off his horse.

"What – where – who," came a chorus.

Paul who had also dismounted a good deal more nimbly, stood on the shallow steps leading up to the porch, raised his hand and gave his story of what had just happened at the Syed Ghat.

"Dickie and I were up early this morning as we were going to prepare a report for the Directors as to how far the work on the bridge had progressed and when it would be ready for the arrival of the line from the other side. Yesterday we had had a word with Harry and his Bengali assistant – you know who – in charge on the other side of the river. They too had heard the usual rumour that the Dinapore sepoys had mutinied but as it was the fifth such report and as the Revelkhind garrison had not been mentioned they discounted it. However they did confirm that they would keep a lookout and if any sepoys appeared they would destroy the boats on their side, making it more difficult for anyone to cross. You all know how swollen and fast the river is running at the moment.

Well, we have no idea what could have happened – we'll probably never ever know. At about half past ten, or perhaps a bit later, as we were inspecting the works on our side we heard pandemonium breaking out on the other side of the river. Pouring down the bank and onto the boats, still completely intact, came hordes of sepoys in their red uniforms. What a sight! All our own native gangs disappeared like a shot into the woods behind. Dickie and I didn't hesitate much either. We saw the first three boats being rowed across, filled with soldiers and we got on horseback, grabbing only our rifles and rode here post-haste."

"We have more than just a few hours", boomed out the voice of Dickie. "I looked back when we reached the top of the Rajiv hill and they had already burnt all the outbuildings and were busy setting fire to all the timber standing ready for the bridge building. But there were only those three boats, and it will take them a long time to get everyone across."

"How many were they," called out a voice.

"I'm sorry, I really couldn't tell – but we saw lots still milling about on the other bank."

"Look everyone," said Grant, "There is no way that we can protect the town, even if they wanted to be protected. So we either all have to take to the roads, or we stay and face up to what is on its way."

"No – no – under no circumstances onto the roads," said the

Judge with many nods and agreement all round. "It was bad enough weeks ago, never mind now. It would be fatal to be caught out in the open. We've got Tate to thank for setting up his little fortification, we can hole out there for a short time. This lot are surely simply on their way to join the rest of them in Delhi. They'll do a bit of burning and pillage on the way, and I don't doubt that they'll have a crack at us. But we should be able to deal with it with the help of the Sikhs, if they stay loyal that is. Well done Tate – it should give us more than a few hours, but then they'll get fed up and move on."

There was no need to take a vote or get any consensus it was clear that all were in agreement.

"I reckon that we probably have most of the rest of the day," said GG " but I would suggest that everyone should think of a maximum of four hours to get down there. I will get hold of the Sikhs and Jemadar Baldour Singh and make sure that they are on board. Have you made any other arrangements, John, since we last met?"

"Well I put in more dry food yesterday when I saw the arrival of Jemadar Singh and his men. I've also put in two more pottery jars of water – oh, and I have marked out where the best point to dig a well would be."

"What about guns and ammunition," called out Kelly.

"The Sikhs have their own guns," said Grant, "but whether we need more or not we've got to clear out the stores in the magazine, if only to prevent the mutineers getting their hands on them. Dr. Henty, you've got a dogcart, can you manage to get the stuff we need down to the Tate fort?"

John, still probably the most anxious of all the men there, felt an excited thrill of satisfaction at the words 'the Tate fort'. He called out that he himself would immediately leave in order to bring Harriet and his children together with what else of value remained in the house into the zenana building – er, oh yes, into Tate's fort.

"I will arrange for as much bedding and mattresses as we have to be dragged round. Harriet and I will certainly organise some rooms, though most of the men will simply have to bunk down in the main central room and around the veranda."

The grand and imposing figure of the Sikh Jemadar – Baldour Singh – had by now sauntered across and joined the group round the newly arrived railway staff. He nodded his head at Tate's words and said –

"Sir, I haven't yet seen this so-called fortification – but it can't be worse than trying to defend anything here in this compound. I'll send a couple of my men down with you."

With that, John rode off followed by a couple of tall Sikhs. This turned out to be very useful as on his arrival at the Hamid mansion John found that all the servants had melted away already. Harriet said that she had had no idea how or when it had happened. One moment everything was normal – servants were padding about everywhere – the ayah was sitting in Chloe's darkened room – then the next moment when she looked around they had all disappeared, completely gone without a word or a sound. All, that is, with the exception of the ayah. But even she was waiting at the door of the nursery when Harriet hurried up the stairs on hearing her voice softly calling her

"I'm sorry memsahib. I'm sorry. I have to leave to join my husband in the town."

She joined her hands together, bowed and shuffled past and away as Harriet went in to the bedroom. Harriet reflected that she had not just abandoned her post without a word like the others, but had at least made sure that someone came to see to the little Chloe before she left.

John's arrival with the two burly Sikhs was very welcome to Harriet who of course had no idea what was happening. John organised the two men to collect sheets and mattresses and take them over to the zenana house and dump them in the billiard room. He and Harriet then went round picking up valuables and important documents and such last minute items that caught their eye. These were all put in piles by the back door and it became Conrad's job to carry them over to the zenana house and dump them in the lower floor corner room that Harriet had allocated for her family.

Everything was happening at once. Harriet took one last look round the house. She felt sure that one way or another she would never see it again. Then as she ran out, a carriage appeared and to her enormous surprise out stepped the stooped figure of the elderly deputy collector – Azimullah Hassan. Dumbfounded, she watched as he paid off the driver who wasted not a moment but turned his carriage and drove his feeble horse as fast as it would go to get back to the town.

John, who had also heard the arrival of a carriage, came hurrying up out of the house carrying more papers – all Railway Company material – and walked up to the old gentleman. There was no time for all the usual preamble necessary before Azimullah could ever bring himself to say anything significant and John immediately burst out –

"My dear Sir – this is not a good moment for calling. As you can see we are..."

But at this point the old gentleman raised his hand in a very concrete gesture and John's words drifted away into silence.

"Mr. Tate, sahib, I am not quite so stupid. This is not a social visit. I too have heard of the arrival of the sepoys on this side of the river. You can in fact scarcely fail to hear about it with Derounian sahib talking about it in what no doubt he considers to be at the bottom range of his considerable voice. I am the Deputy Collector – I have taken your salt and been fortunate in my employment with the Company. I am not about to turn my back on the Raj now that it is in a time of trouble. I intend to enter your..." here he hesitated for the first time but immediately continued, "your fortification. I will take my chances with the rest of you."

John really had no idea what to say at this juncture. It was improbable that the old gentleman would be in any real danger from the approaching sepoys. It was not likely that they would even be aware of his position as the Deputy Collector. In any case his age would surely protect him. However, if he pointed this out, it would be denigrating the man's gesture and implying that it was only an act of self-preservation that was motivating him, which in fact John did not think was the case. He ended up by saying nothing but simply nodding at the old man, and then nodding at Harriet. The old man followed Harriet down to the zenana house and then sat cross-legged on the grass by the steps calmly reading the one book he had brought with him as people passed up and down around him.

Back in the Judge's compound, order was coming out of the earlier chaos. Grant had already achieved what few of the others would have been capable of – he had made immediate friends with Baldour Singh, the Sikh Jemadar. They had organised exactly what needed to be taken from the town magazine and what was to be destroyed. The list of what was to be removed included all the gunpowder, the twenty Enfield rifles, and what ammunition for them that was available.

Dr. Henty arrived at the magazine with his dogcart as requested. Grant and Baldour Singh were already supervising and placing outside what they wanted to take, ready to be loaded. When Henty arrived they saw that already in the back of the cart were several unopened wooden cases and a large suitcase.

"My God! What are they? We can't take the family silver, James."

"Grant, you look to your job and I'll look to mine. The unopened cases constitute a current shipment of two dozen Port, two dozen Brandy and two dozen Sherry, recently delivered. The large open suitcase contains all my medical equipment and important stores, though I suppose in some ways the liquor might well have even more medicinal qualities. Now, sir, get on with loading your own toys."

Grant, who had had no direct military training nevertheless thought of all sorts of things which regular British officers might not have spotted or dealt with. The horses for instance. Cavalry officers would have moved heaven and earth to keep their horses nearby somehow. They would inevitably have become a hindrance to the defence of the little fort. Grant, however, arranged for the horses to be quietly delivered in batches of four or five to a cross-section of the town's drivers and horse traders. These men did not need to have the arrangement spelt out to them. If the Europeans were wiped out, they each gained four or five good strong horses for nothing. If the Europeans somehow survived, some or all of the horses would have to be returned, but even then it was likely that there would be some pecuniary benefit to cover expenses.

Arthur and Henrietta, with the young Marietta now in tow, were the next to leave their house and ride down to the Hamid mansion. They went in their own carriage and instructed their driver to take it back to the compound. Joining them and coming up alongside as they drove down came Dickie, with Ali riding on the same horse behind him clutching on to him tight.

At Tate's Fort, as it was increasingly being called, Harriet had begun to get practical matters under some sort of control. The lower floor of the zenana house had eight rooms, with four tiny store rooms in between, all grouped round the dark windowless centre room directly under the billiard room above. This dark room she had already designated as the kitchen and which now housed all the provisions and the four large pottery jars of fresh water. Grant had said, and John had agreed, that it would be dangerous for all the gunpowder and ammunition to be stored in the billiard room upstairs and so one of the eight small rooms below would have to be used as a magazine. One room – the middle room facing back to the jungle – had been marked by John as being where the well should be dug. That left six rooms – the four small corner rooms and two longer and larger rooms at each side.

Harriet had worked out the best arrangements, but the sudden last-minute arrival of Azimullah Hassan threw it all out. He himself insisted that he could rest in any corner anywhere. At this stage of course almost everyone was under the impression that they would have to remain only a day or two in these cramped quarters. However, even if only for a few days, some sort of allocation had to be made, and it was clear that that would be the task of the 'hostess'. Even in such perilous circumstances these people clung to a semblance of formal social order – it was both their weakness and their strength.

Harriet was quite clear in her own mind, there was to be no racial discrimination. It would not be just a question of leaving

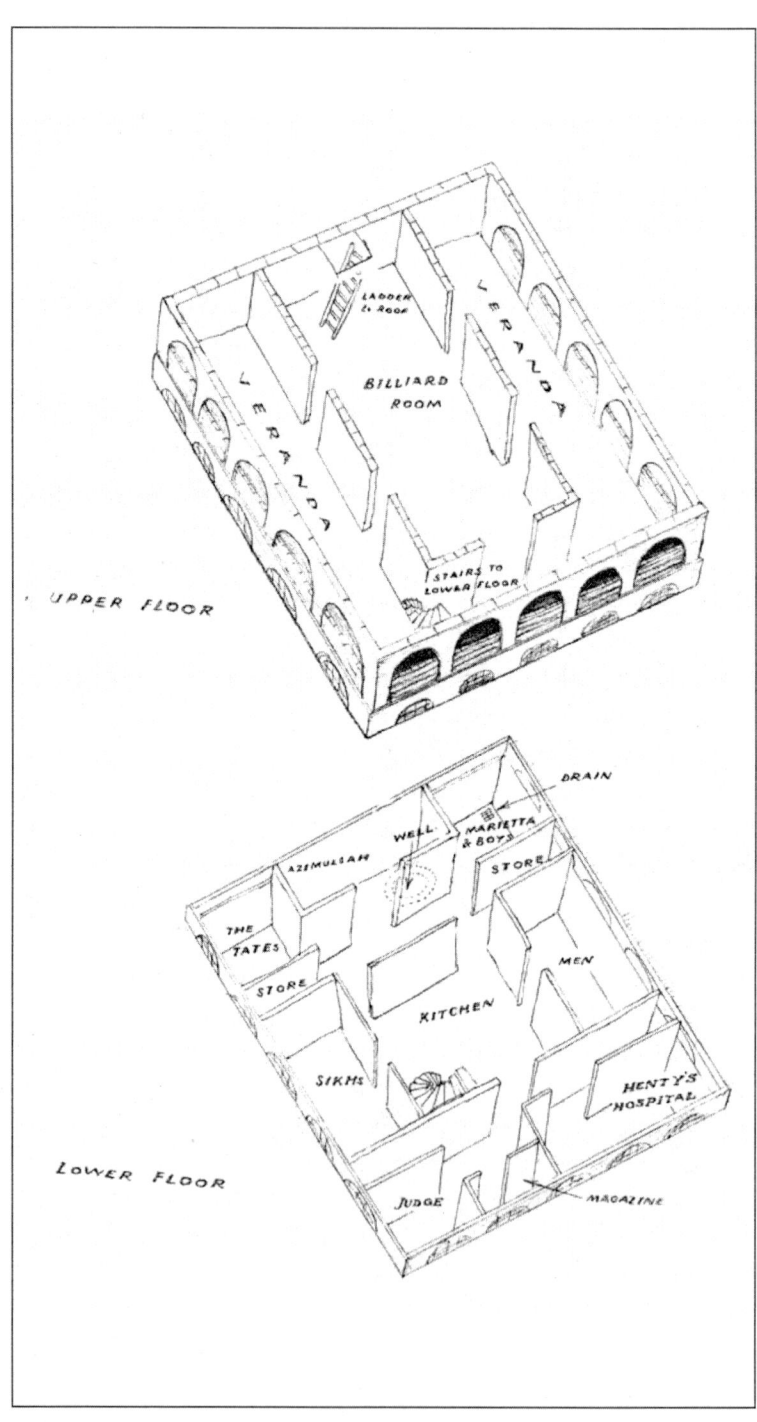

all the new arrivals, the Sikhs and the Ghurkas, to fend for themselves in the corridors and the billiard room while all the Europeans got rooms. It would be awkward but it would be controlled.

She decided that one of the two large side rooms would be for the European single men – Grant, Dickie, Paul Kelly and Johnson. The other would be for Baldour Singh and such of the Sikhs who might be exhausted and needed particular rest as chosen by the Jemadar. The two rooms in the middle of the smaller side of the building were also allocated – the one facing back towards the jungle was to be for the digging of the Well and soon came to be known as the Well Room. The other facing the front was to be the Magazine holding all the gunpowder and the arms and ammunition. That left the four small corner rooms. These would go to the families. The Tates and Chloe in one. The Judge and Henrietta in the other. Then one, the larger one, had to be allocated to Dr. Henty with a trestle table and an extra mattress to be used also as his hospital in the event of the inevitable medical emergencies.

This left the last corner room, coincidentally the one containing the hidden drain leading back to the jungle. In her mind she had allocated this to Marietta, who would however have to share in some way. Harriet's first reaction was to leave the two boys to bed down upstairs in the billiard room with the rest of the Sikhs and Ghurkas. But now there was the elderly Azimullah to consider. Also she suddenly didn't like the idea of the two boys being with all the soldiers – nor could she really leave the old man with them either. There could just be room in the Well Room for a tiny mattress. Then the thought of the horror likely to be caused to Azimullah if he was asked to share the little corner room with a woman decided her. The two boys would have to share a mattress in Marietta's room, while the old man could bed down in the Well room at least until the Well was dug.

As the afternoon wore on the rest of those destined to shelter in Tate's Fort came in, and the little fort began to fill. There were no complaints from anyone at Harriet's hasty arrangements.

Harriet herself took Marietta aside and explained her dilemma, and that she would have to share the little corner room with two twelve-year-old boys. Harriet was fairly embarrassed and totally failed to see that the young girl – she was after all herself only just sixteen – was delighted that she had not simply been lumped in with the Drummonds. Henrietta had spent the morning trying hard to be pleasant to the young widow, but there was always a constraint that prevented her from being entirely whole-hearted in putting Marietta at her ease, and the young girl felt it.

Baldour Singh, the Sikh jemadar, had with him two havildars, one for the Sikh force and one for the ghurkas. Once everyone had finally arrived and gathered in the zenana house, the three of them met with Grant and the other Europeans in the upper central room – the billiard room - and prepared a rota for the night watches. There was a general feeling that while a night attack would be unlikely it was a possibility and had to be taken into account. A tally was carefully drawn up of the available manpower and it was decided that at any one time there must always be at least two men on duty on each side of the building together with one on the roof and one 'officer' to liaise between them. This meant a detail of ten men. There were altogether 46 men available for night duty – 34 Sikhs, 6 Ghurkas, and 6 Europeans. There were in fact 7 Europeans but the roster only included 6 because, despite his strenuous objections, it was unanimously agreed that Dr. Henty should not be included on the roster so that he could always be available on a twenty-four hour basis for any medical emergency.

The question of what role the two boys should play was also discussed. Ali had been Dickie's cook since he was ten. It was decided that the boys between them should be in charge of the food, the kitchen and seeing that those on duty were fed – Ali doing the cooking and Conrad taking round the food to those on duty and unable to gather in one of the two rooms to eat.

As the afternoon wore on, everything remained quiet, but nothing was normal. Even in the heat of the afternoon there would usually be some locals sitting under the trees in the grounds, but on this day there was not a soul – the quiet was intense, even the birds and the trees appeared to be silent. Baldour Singh sought out John and suggested that this might be the moment for a concerted effort to be made to dig a well and use up the piles of bricks still lying about in the lower room – now to be called the kitchen. Taking short turns the men laboured hard – the digging being fairly easy, but the brickwork needed to keep up the sides being very difficult and time-consuming without mortar.

Soon the well was deep enough for fresh water, albeit rather muddy, to fill up at the bottom. Bricks were then placed at the bottom as well as the sides and by pulling up some water with a bucket it was seen to replenish slowly. The general rule was made that the water already stored by John in the large pottery cauldrons was to be used for drinking only. For all other purposes the well water had to be used.

By now it was evening. The first meal that was eaten in Tate's Fort, a mixture of Dhall and Chapatties, was prepared by Ali with Conrad's enthusiastic help and eaten slowly in turns round the large kitchen table. The evening was quiet, lit by a moon that was just coming up to the full. There were no alarms of any kind throughout the whole night.

The next morning on Monday the 27th came the first attack.

* * *

On that Sunday the 26th July the four regiments in Dinapore had duly rebelled. Here the British officers had been ready and had not been caught off-guard as in so many other garrisons, and consequently there had been no killings. Three of the regiments – the 7th, 8th and 40th - had retained their trained discipline and after the first few hours of chaos and discussion had paraded and eventually marched out in good order intending to make for Delhi following a route north of Darabad. As it happened they did not get far as they were held up near the river Soane by a spirited defence after which they dispersed as a group.

Haidar Presaud had rushed round to the sepoy barracks as

soon as he had heard the news of the mutiny, but he had failed
to persuade any of the men of those three regiments to remain
in the locality. Those who had families nearby did mostly melt
away and set off home, together with those who believed that the
mutiny was in any case a grievous mistake. But for most of the
sepoys, sticking with the regiment was their preferred and easiest
solution.

The native officers watched carefully for any move that
General Lloyd might make to prevent them leaving, sending
spies even in the middle of the chaos to keep an eye on the
British barracks. They were aware that he might hurry after
them with his formidable force of 600 British regulars, with their
Enfield rifles and their efficient cannon. But the General did
absolutely nothing, letting them leave without making any
attempt to harass them. It was to be the end of his military career,
but that did not help those who suffered from this neglect.

While Haidar Presaud was unable to make any impression on
the first three regiments, he had much more success on the
newly formed 68th regiment. Almost all the men of this regiment
came from villages dotted around Central Bihar and in particular the Shantapur District. In the febrile atmosphere of a
hurried meeting of the Jemadars and Havildars of this regiment,
Haidar persuaded them not simply to follow the other three
regiments but instead to make for Jagpur and the palace of
Saridar Khan. He assured them that the Nawab would be
prepared to lead them and in addition that the 66th regiment in
Revelkhind would also mutiny and join them to form the local
army.

What was the point, he argued, of marching half way across
India simply to be merged into whatever army was being formed
in Delhi. The British Raj was now finished and what was important was to be in at the start of the formation of the local powers
that would be taking over.

It had not been difficult to persuade the men, whose natural
inclination was to stay near their families in any case. The
regiment kept its cohesion and marched out immediately after
the first three, heading however due south to Revelkhind rather

then west to Delhi or south-east to Jagpur. Haidar, together with a small detachment on horseback, hurried off to Jagpur to make sure of Saridar Khan and to bring him and his 'army' to Revelkhind. All these men only knew of the Nawab of Jagpur as their local zamindar who collected their rent and saw that they paid their taxes. They talked of his army but had no idea that all it consisted of was about one hundred old men dressed in colourful but dirty uniforms, carrying old muskets which had not been cleaned or fired in years and whose only real function was to provide a slovenly guard of honour on state occasions.

The portly Saridar himself had not yet heard of any mutiny when Haidar Presaud, at the head of 100 impressive scarlet-coated sepoys of the British army cantered into the large dusty square in front of his crumbling old palace. The party came to a striking halt, with their British pennants and colours still proudly fluttering from their lances. Infantry regiment though the 68th was, they had good horses and they had been able to muster a good cross-section of riders to make an efficient cavalry detachment. The Nawab, watching discreetly from a first floor window saw Haidar and three sepoy officers dismount and walk across to the gates. These were not exactly open, but the wood was so rotted and the hinges so rusty that they could not be said to be closed either. The two guards supposedly on duty, sitting leaning back against the warm stones of the walls on either side of the entrance, rose rather languidly, had a few words with Haidar whom they recognised from previous visits and pushed the old doors that little more needed for ease of entrance, and then slumped back into their former somnolence exhausted by their efforts.

The Nawab hurried down to what was usually referred to as the Audience room and waited for Haidar to be shown in. He had understood immediately what it was all about. He recognised the insignia of the 68th, and if the 68th had mutinied then so had all the others in Dinapore. But what was he supposed to do about it? It was all so damn inconvenient.

The audience lasted over an hour. Over the last few weeks Haidar had already given the Nawab his arguments. The British

Raj was finished, it was now a matter of what would take its place. Some local zamindars would thrive in the new conditions; others, particularly those still clinging on to the foreign domination, would collapse. It behoved Saridar to be one of the ones who survived, indeed grew. Having command of two locally based regiments of infantry would give him inestimable advantages in the troubles that were certain to arise.

But Saridar Khan had his own arguments in his mind, which of course he did not intend mentioning to the domineering Presaud. Whilst he was at the moment almost bankrupt, his lifestyle remained pleasant and comfortable. He owned land and villages all over the district of Shantapur. He had a good income derived from all these villagers, and could leave to the British all the uncomfortable details of enforcing this exploitation. He would unquestionably have preferred if no mutiny of any kind had broken out. But one had and he was going to have to make a decision of some sort.

Standing behind him, as Haidar Pesaud talked away, the three native officers of the 68th who had accompanied him were becoming increasingly anxious. It was now clear that the wily Haidar had exaggerated the enthusiasm of the Nawab to lead them. Having seen the two guards at the gate of the palace they had also realised that the so-called army of the Nawab of Jagpur was unlikely to be of much help. But, from their point of view, the adherence of even this pathetic remnant of the old Moghal ruling class was vital in order to legitimise with some political point their otherwise futile mutiny. They had burnt their boats. While in their case no European officers had as yet been murdered, nevertheless British retribution if it ever arose would be brutal. If they were to retain any coherence at all as a body they needed a symbolic leader and this perspiring and uninspiring man was all they had.

The talk to an ominously silent Nawab had gone on long enough. The senior Jemadar pulled out his pistol, which was not in fact loaded, though it was clear to him that Saridar Khan would have no clue whether it was or not. He strode forward pushing the flustered Haidar to one side,

"Your Excellency – we do not have the time to discuss this matter any further. We must move on to Revelkhind before nightfall to join the men of the 66th regiment who have also rebelled. Your Excellency – as Nawab of Jagpur we offer you our allegiance, and you must accompany us with your army...er...retainers and take full command of your two regiments."

"But Jemadar sahib I have no military experience and..."

"Your Excellency – no military experience is necessary. What we need is political experience and political leadership."

"I cannot betray men whose salt I have..."

"Your Excellency, we cannot afford to waste any more time. I am sure you understand that we cannot afford to leave an army and a fortress behind us whose loyalty and adherence to our cause is suspect."

Saridar was not without an ironic sense of humour and the description of his palace and his hundred elderly retainers as a fortress and an army almost caused him to laugh out loud. Indeed he would have done so if the implied threat was not so obvious and he himself in direct physical danger. There was a short silence and then the other two officers drew their swords and each took a step to one side behind Haidar. The gesture was unmistakeable. It could just – but only just – be construed as the start of a military salute; but the threat was far clearer.

Presaud was equally nonplussed by this development. Suddenly to his chagrin his position appeared totally irrelevant. The men whom he thought he was manipulating, had in a very clear and positive way taken over the initiative. His motivation had always been the exercise of political and financial power after the current Raj disappeared. The principle motivation of the mutineers on the other hand was sheer survival, and for that they felt that they needed some political respectability to be attached to their desperate and rather thoughtless act of rebellion.

This left Saridar. He looked round for just one moment. There were witnesses – servants standing at the side of the shabby chamber. There was little doubt that a pistol and two swords had been brandished. Trying at one and the same time to smile at the four men in front of him and to scowl with pretended fury for the benefit of the servants at the sides, he finally said –

"Well gentlemen, you give me no choice, no choice at all. I must clearly go with you."

Then turning to the little group of servants he said –

"Prepare the state elephant. We are obliged to go with these gentlemen. Go!"

Then after all the servants had scurried off, he turned with a smile to the three sepoy officers and said –

"What have I to do with the British. I am your Nawab, let us by all means go to Revelkhind. My –er- army will remain here, but I will bring with me the state cannon of Jagpur with the men to man it. I believe you have no cannon so this will be an addition to your strength."

So it was that Saridar Khan, riding on the sole elephant left in the palace stable, preceded by some 100 infantrymen on horseback and followed by an increasingly irrelevant Haidar Presaud began a march to Revelkhind. The procession was trailed by one highly polished but rather small cannon, which was mounted on an oxcart and fussed over by five 'soldiers' of the Nawab's army.

Meanwhile the first news of the Dinapore mutiny together with the main body of the 68th had arrived at the barracks of the 66th regiment surprisingly quickly. By the late morning the 66th, which had been in a state of ferment for weeks, had mutinied and all four of the senior British officers had been murdered. There were no other Europeans anywhere nearby and the general consensus of these soldiers, or rather their leaders, was that they should make for Darabad on the other side of the River, which was eight miles away. Darabad was the headquarters of the local tax collection and contained the local treasury of the Raj. There was also the magazine known to contain guns of all sorts.

This regiment was not the slightest bit concerned about what the Nawab of Jagpur might or might not do. They too believed that the British Raj was finished, but they had no thought or concern at this stage as to what should take its place. For the moment their interests were entirely personal. The murder of their officers had sharpened their minds with the realisation that they were now committed – often the very reasoning of the ringleaders who contrived the killings in the first place.

The information that the Nawab of Jagpur might now be coming to join them gave the men at Revelkhind some comfort from the anxiety that pervaded the minds of most of them. About five hundred men set out, not in any order but straggling in groups, for the River and the Syed Ghat seven miles away. It was these five hundred who were spotted by Dickie and Paul Kelly. They had watched as the sepoys burnt the railway property on their side of the river and then grabbed the boats to row over to the Darabad side. There they set about demolishing and burning everything on that side including all the material waiting ready for the completion of the new bridge.

All had been confusion in Revelkhind that morning. There were plenty of examples throughout North India of sepoy regiments which maintained excellent discipline and who produced natural and talented officers who commanded their men in well-thought out campaigns against the returning British forces and those of their princely allies. But here all continued to be in disorder even after the five hundred had left.

It took Saridar on his lumbering and over-age elephant over four hours to get the ten miles from Jagpur to Revelkhind. Even then the oxcart carrying the bronze cannon had fallen behind. With him, of course, came the three native officers and Haidar Persaud.

On their arrival in Revelkhind a conference was called in the late afternoon. By then the crossing of the River at the Syed Ghat, unopposed, had been reported and inevitably the 'fait accompli' of the earlier decision of the leaders of the 66th to go and take over Darabad was accepted. It was agreed that the next day the remainder of the two regiments would join the first group, now ensconced on the other side of the River. The combined force would then make for Darabad and capture the town.

Just for a moment Saridar's mind went to the delectable Marietta and his trips to the town in a happier past. In the end, however, all he could think of as he sat listening to all his 'lieutenants' discussing what was the best course of action, was how he could possibly get out of having to accompany them at all. He already longed to be back in his comfortable old palace with one or another of his younger wives. There was not even any decent food available here. He sat and fiddled with his moustache and listened glumly as the talk turned to all the loot that was going to be available in the little town on the next day.

* * *

That first night when all the remaining Europeans had gathered in Tate's fort had passed without any incident at all. Conrad and Ali had together prepared the rather scratch meal eaten in rotation by everyone standing round the billiard table in the large upper room. However, this was the last time it would be used like that. With a great deal of effort the heavy table was manhandled into a corner, giving more room for men to lie down to sleep. Harriet pushed some of the many mattresses that had been brought into the building under the table to provide yet more sleeping space.

Ablutions too had not been forgotten. Two of the tiny store rooms alongside and in between the main rooms had been allocated for this modest but necessary function. A rough and ready pit had been dug in each. These were almost as deep as the well, though as far removed from it as possible. They were not lined with any bricks. At Henty's suggestion, the loose earth dug out for each pit together with the earth left from the digging of the well was left piled up to one side of the two little rooms together with a spade in each; the idea being that a spadeful of earth was to be thrown down every so often after use.

It was not perhaps very lady-like for Harriet to have busied herself with these matters, but it was supremely practical on her part and happened this way time and again in many stations throughout the course of the mutiny. Suddenly the 'little

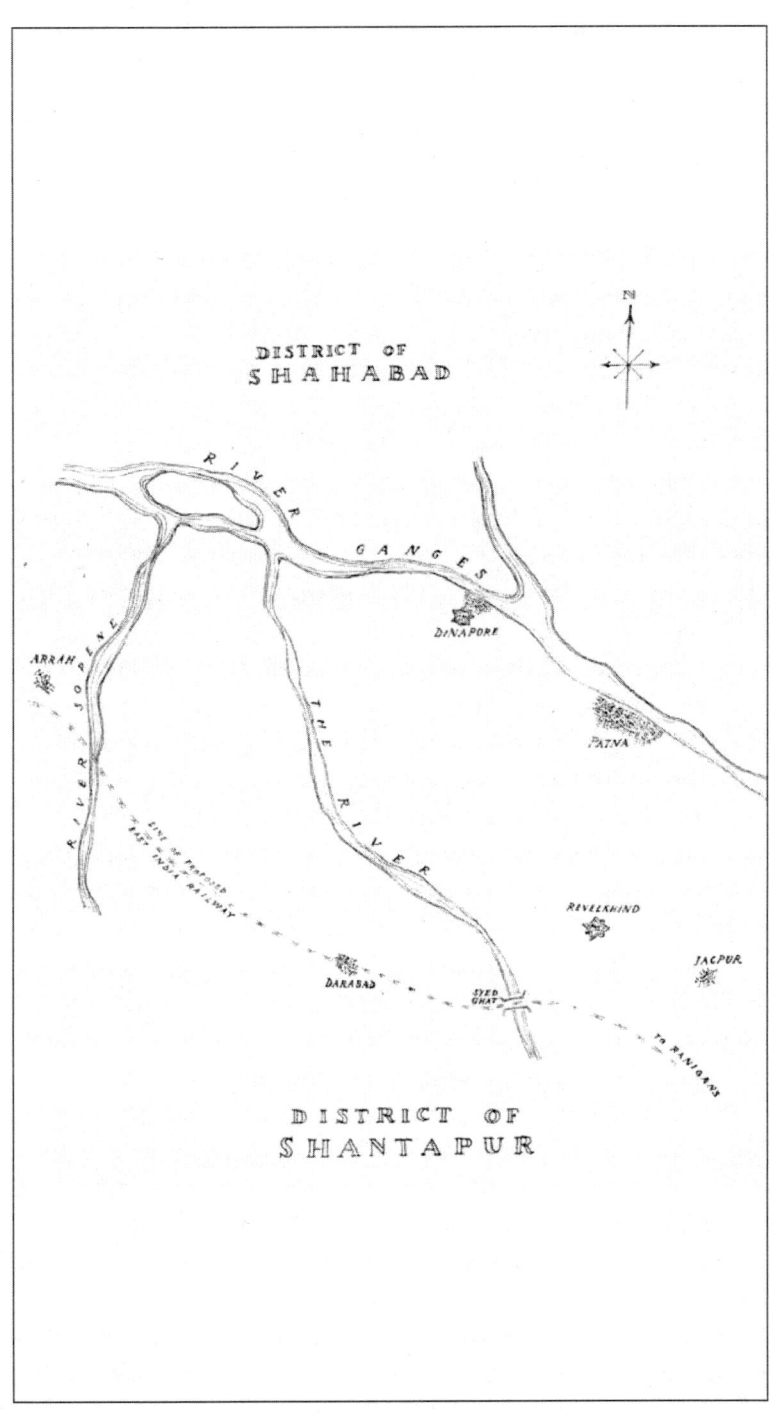

woman', normally placed firmly on a highly uncomfortable pedestal, too frail to go out into the hot Indian sun and kept from almost all useful activity, blossomed. They began carrying out all those vital practical tasks which the men, excited by all that thrilling masculine bustle of shooting guns, scarcely noticed and would have neglected.

Conrad, already in a state of enormous physical excitement had supposed that he was not going to be able to sleep a wink that night, though in fact he fell fast asleep the moment he lay down. Quite apart from the inherent excitement of the situation in which they all found themselves, there was for both boys the disturbing presence of the beautiful Marietta in their room. Both Conrad and Ali had begun to experience the stirrings of sexual desire, and both had had nocturnal dreams, though both would have died rather than discuss it with each other or with anyone else. Both of them were totally innocent, Ali even more than Conrad.

Ali appeared to have no parents at all. Conrad did have a mother who was well ahead of her time in this respect, but she had left it all, as normal, to her husband to deal with. John had indeed muttered a few nondescript remarks to the boy about not needing to feel any shame when he had been told by Harriet of the evidence on Conrad's bedsheets. But whereas in another age Harriet might have taken the bull by the horns and had it out with the boy herself, John was much more inhibited and hummed and hawed, ending up by giving no help of any kind. While Harriet may have been ahead of her times in many ways, there were some things absolutely taboo – and discussing these matters with her son was quite out of the question.

So Conrad remained uncertain as to what was happening to him in this respect, Nevertheless, both boys, wandering as they did all over the little town with so little privacy, certainly had more knowledge than those of an equivalent age and class in Europe. Marietta, meanwhile, a married woman who had consummated her hasty marriage and had lived with her husband for a few months before he had to leave, was nevertheless still a young girl. Not quite sixteen herself, she assumed that the two boys were even more innocent than they were and felt no shyness in going to bed in the same room – though she sternly commanded them both to turn their faces to the corner as she changed.

On the following morning – the 27th July – the whole garrison had risen early and completed their breakfast brought round by the boys, when the first sounds of the arrival of the mutineers were heard.

The two regiments – the 68th from Dinapore and the 66th from Revelkhind arrived in Darabad at about 9.00 in the morning as the sun was burning away the morning mist. They marched in on the road leading to the Syed Ghat in fairly good order. However this good order immediately collapsed when they arrived at the jail, Here there was no question of the jail guards holding out for even a second. The mutineers raced through the open gate and all the prison doors were unlocked. Out into the courtyard came all the prisoners, who had already been let out of their cells by the guards when they heard of the arrival of the sepoys. The majority of these convicts began ransacking those stone houses on the Maidan which were unoccupied, only just managing in some cases to be persuaded not to raid those still occupied by locals.

Following behind the two regimental columns came the hapless Saridar Khan on the state elephant of Jagpur. The Nawab made no attempt to stop anywhere near the jail, where all mayhem had been let loose, but moved on down the Maidan and stopped outside the house of Alphonsine da Costa. Helped down with some difficulty by his few elderly retainers, he summoned the da Costa servants still in the building, all of whom recognised him and welcomed him with relief. He indicated that he would be taking over the house for his own use during the next few days.

The officers of the two regiments joined the Nawab about an hour later in the company of Haidar Presaud and then followed a discussion of what was to be the next step. The rupees that had been left in the treasury building in the Judge's compound had by now been looted and commandeered by the officers. It was also clear by now that there were no Europeans left in the town. But interrogation of the servants had revealed the existence of the zenana house in the western suburbs, into which it was said all the Europeans had withdrawn. Nothing was known at this stage about the Sikhs or the Ghurkas. Without anyone at the conference actually ordering anything it was agreed that the men and the released jailbirds should be encouraged to go and root out those few people holed up in what sounded like a small outbuilding. No one had any idea of the existence of a fortification, however modest, and after passing out the word that the men should go and deal with the small group of Europeans in the far west of the town, they turned to discussing what should be done next.

Saridar Khan wanted the regiments to move on to Delhi while he returned to Jagpur. Haidar Presaud wanted the regiments to remain here in Darabad and to form the nucleus of an army of the new state of Jagpur. The mutineer officers really had no idea what they wanted to do, though they inclined towards a departure to Delhi as soon as this little pinprick of a building containing Europeans was extinguished. There certainly seemed to be no reason for the officers to oversee the taking of whatever it was that the Europeans were sheltering in. The buildings in the Judge's compound, the law courts and the meeting house, were by now all in flames.

So it was that without any specific commands or any military order or discipline some of the men of the two regiments, together with the 400 released convicts and a handful of unsavoury characters from the town rushed off down the road leading to the Hamid mansion.

The 47 men – 34 Sikhs, 6 Ghurkas and 7 Europeans – in the little garrison had heard the shouts and screams of the arriving mutineers and watched as the flames from the Judge's compound a quarter of a mile away had risen into the sky. They had immediately stood to with their rifles poking out from the embrasures and loopholes in the brick walls on both levels of the building – most facing forward towards where the mutineers were expected to arrive. Ali ran round clearing up and preparing tin cans of water. While afraid, he found that he was surprisingly calm. Conrad, on the other hand was exactly the opposite. He did not feel any fear at all but was hyper-excited and having to relieve himself rather frequently.

The three women prepared spare muskets and rifles and dealt with piling up additional ammunition. Dr. Henty arranged for Marietta to attend with him in his makeshift hospital room. They all waited in a state of tension looking out at the deserted park all around them.

Then, with screams and yells, and a spate of broken fire, an undisciplined mob of men came pouring into the grounds rushing directly at the building, not coming from all sides but almost entirely from the front. The Sikhs under the cool command of their Jemadar – Baldour Singh – held their fire. The Europeans, most good sportsmen, also held their fire. However, Arthur Drummond, the Judge, unsure what he should be doing, did let off a single shot. He then looked round in a sort of embarrassment as he realised that only he had fired.

The lack of any immediate reaction from the bricked up building seemed to give encouragement to the mob as three or four hundred men came running up past all the trees and shrubs in the grounds. It was, however noticeable that the 'redcoats', the sepoy regulars, did not participate in this wild first assault of the siege. The charging mob was composed almost entirely of the released convicts together with a few opportunist characters from the town and the surrounding district. The screaming rabble came running on.

The Jemadar now stood up and in his stentorian voice, which had to reach up to the flat roof as well as down to the lower level shouted out –

"Fire, Fire at will."

Forty-six guns, some muskets but mostly deadly Enfields, spat a murderous fire at what was now close range. Conrad, standing alongside a burly Sikh in one of the lower rooms saw what appeared to him to be about forty to fifty men fall to the ground. It did not seem to him to be real – somehow he was unable to equate any of what he was seeing with pain and death. There was less blood than he would have expected. The reality of course was, as the firing continued, that the bullets had left less of a mark than appeared to Conrad's excited eyes.

Nevertheless at least thirty men fell in that first undisciplined rush. It was not many, but it was enough. As more bullets slammed out from the little fort there was an immediate melting away of the rabble from the open grounds. Further back, the garrison could now see the arrival of the scarlet coats of the sepoy regulars marching forward down the road, too far away at this stage even for the Enfields. Their non-commissioned officers now took control and they moved in and took over the Hamid mansion. John looked on as they entered his house, which was of course empty. He expected excited looting and precious things being thrown out of the windows – but nothing like that happened. Instead, for the first time, a disciplined constant fire from the upper windows of the house, which was about eighty yards away, began.

For the rest of that first day, certainly until about four o'clock in the afternoon, as Saridar Khan conferred in the da Costa house, over one thousand men kept up a constant fire on the zenana house. They fired without much effect from behind trees and shrubs in the grounds. But they fired dangerously from the windows of the Tate house.

This could not last. Eventually the news filtered back to the regimental officers still sitting and talking interminably in the house on the maidan that nothing had yet transpired at the zenana house. The discussions were at last then cut short. The three senior officers moved out and came down to where the continuous firing could be heard.

Arriving at the scene, and still under the impression that this small building contained not many more than fifteen or so desperate men, the sepoy officers took their men in hand. Assembling perhaps as many as three hundred men to one side of the Tate house, and another three hundred on rising ground directly in the front where the road from Darabad forked, and finally yet another two hundred men the other side from the Tate house, they prepared their men for an organized formal assault. It was a formidable sight. These were now British-trained red-coated regulars shaping up for a formal assault by the book for which they were well-trained. The local villains and the convicts had melted away.

The trumpets sounded and they came on as they had been trained, slowly and in disciplined order. Then when each group reached about fifty yards away the charge was sounded and they raced forward shouting and firing. Once again the little fortress had held its fire. However, as the charge sounded, the Jemadar bellowed again and a murderous hail of bullets slammed into the advancing sepoys. Henrietta and Harriet were in the veranda on the upper storey frantically loading muskets and handing them over – while the Europeans continued firing their Enfields until they became too hot to handle. Those in the lower floor were brought replacements by the two boys, who had been told that they were to remain below. The lower floor was of course much safer as it was almost impossible for a bullet to penetrate the narrow loophole at the top of the bricked up half windows.

This charge of 800 men of the 66th and 68th regiments should have succeeded by sheer weight of numbers, but in fact slammed by a rain of fire as they advanced and facing a bricked up building without any obvious means of entry, they fatally hesitated and then fell back to the shelter of the Tate house and the trees. Once this happened it was clear that more planning was going to be needed and that the men could not be persuaded to mount another formal assault that evening. A few of the more courageous sepoys had managed to get right up to the lower walls of the building where crouching down they could not be reached by fire from the levels above. But equally they could not do much damage to the garrison either.

Meanwhile the continuous firing had resulted in two casualties in the little garrison. One of the Sikhs had received a shot in the shoulder. Up on the exposed flat roof, one of the Ghurkas, stationed there as they presented a smaller target than the burly Europeans or the large Sikhs, had received a shot in the stomach. The wounded Sikh made his own way down to Henty's room where he was quickly treated. However, the Ghurka had to be carried down the ladder. His insides were oozing out of the wound and it seemed that he was not going to be able to last. But once in the hospital Henty was determined to try by stitching up the wound as best he could.

Calling out to Marietta he began work at once as the wound gaped open and guts spewed out and onto the floor. He turned and found that the young girl had turned completely white and had fainted as the blood continued to spurt out. Tut-tutting with professional detachment, he shouted out for Conrad, who he knew was somewhere on the lower floor. Conrad heard him and came running in. The sight of all this blood and guts was something he had become used to in the many wanderings round the town with Ali in the early evenings, when they had brought wounded men in to the civil surgeon. Both of them ignoring the poor girl who was groaning to herself on the floor, Henty started work, showing Conrad where he wanted him to hold the soldier's flesh together while he sewed. The young Ghurka said not a word but stared up at the boy and the doctor. Even in this crisis Dr. Henty had managed to yell at Conrad to wash his hands first in the water pitcher at the side.

Sweat pouring down his face, with the continued sound of firing coming from above, Henty worked, cursing and yelling at Conrad whenever his fingers slipped in the blood. It was no use. Even before the end came, Henty knew it was becoming a waste of time. The stitching was completed, but the young man had already died a few moments before from the trauma. Henty, angry with himself at the failure, nodded at Conrad and indicated Marietta who had just started sitting up. Conrad ran out and called Ali, and between them they carried or rather walked the young girl to their bedroom.

That was the first and the last day that Marietta worked in the little hospital. From then on Henty persuaded John and Harriet that Conrad was a natural medical orderly, and that he wanted Conrad to act as his assistant.

No one else in the garrison was injured that first day. The worst that had happened was that the men were covered in a fine red-brick dust as the shots had slammed into the brick walls showering them with fragments of brick and red dust. As night came on and the firing became sporadic and desultory, they stared at each other in a sort of wonder. Not one of the Europeans, neither men nor women, had ever been under fire before and they were awed by the experience and by their own steadiness.

Ali prepared the food in the kitchen below, then he and Conrad ran around with buckets of rice and once again some dhall. After everyone had had something to eat, while still standing at their posts, the Jemadar went round getting his men to stand down except for those scheduled to be on guard. However the Europeans, exhilarated by a mixture of bravado and adrenalin remained for some time at their posts before being persuaded to retire and get some rest according to the schedule already worked out. Neither Ali nor Conrad were required for any guard duty and eventually, loudly declaring to each other that they would never be able to sleep, both collapsed on their shared mattress, dead to the world or to the sleeping Marietta in the other corner.

* * *

That night, as soon as it got dark, the less determined of the sepoys crouching at the foot of the lower level brick walls, melted away and crept back to their comrades surrounding the grounds. But a few, more determined, joined by one or two others who crept forward, began a whispering which went on until midnight. The words were all intended to try and seduce the Sikhs from their loyalty. Neither side could see the other, but the whispering in a poor Punjabi dialect was deadly. The Sikhs were continuously informed that Delhi was in the hands of the rebels, that the Punjab was in flames and that the British Raj was over.

"Man, what have you all to do with these people you are protecting?"

"Come out in the morning tomorrow. Just leave. Give us a sign and we will not shoot. These men mean nothing to you."

"Think, a share of the large loot we have from the treasury is yours."

"Why risk you life for people who despise you and call you – black man?"

It went on and on, but not a man in the garrison replied, though the sibilant whispering was unnerving – particularly to those Europeans on duty, each standing next to the men at whom the whispers were being directed. Everybody was well aware that the Sikhs could have walked out at any time and there was nothing that anyone could do about it.

The next morning, almost immediately after the sun had banished the morning mist which lay over the whole area, the little garrison, already fully awake, washed and even shaved in some instances, standing at their posts ready, heard a great shout from all round the grounds. Sepoys could be seen running towards the road leading from the town. Everyone stood shielding their eyes from the low rising sun and tried to make out what was happening.

Surrounded by a yelling crowd of jailbirds and more rough characters from the district, marching in a disciplined formation was a party of sepoys escorting – what was it? Out came John's field glasses, the only telescope in the fort. Resting the long rather old-fashioned spy-glass on the top of the brick wall John tried to focus it on what was approaching. It was a bronze cannon – the state cannon of the Nawab of Jagpur – being pulled along by the decrepit old retainers of Saridar Khan's bodyguard.

This ancient weapon had not been fired in anger for over ten years. However, rather like an old heirloom it had been kept clean and polished. Following behind was a cart pulled by oxen carrying a considerable sufficiency of cannonballs, all of the right size and all of which had been equally carefully tended, rubbed smooth and even polished. The cannon was technically a 4-pounder – really too small for penetrating well-built walls.

John, of course, was no military expert and he wondered whether his brick walls could stand up to any sustained onslaught by a cannon, however small. He had managed to find and make up some mortar when building them, but most of the lower part of each of his walls were sustained only by the weight of the bricks above them. Would they hold? John watched as the cannon was unlimbered and laid about a hundred and twenty yards away. The Enfields were able to reach that far but not with any great likely effect. However, for the moment no one took any shots. The garrison simply watched fascinated, like a rabbit mesmerised by a snake's eyes.

It took about an hour for the cannon to be fixed in place after some protective barricades and sandbags had been hastily set up around it. It then had to be primed and loaded. The excitement both outside the little fort and within it was intense, though not a shot had as yet been fired by either side. The sepoy officers planned to mount a second assault to coincide with the firing of the cannon. Leaving a clear field of fire down the centre, aimed at the front of the fort, they again prepared two companies of about three hundred men each on either side. Once again this was going to be a set-piece assault – but backed by artillery. The garrison braced itself.

"Fire!"

The cannon spewed out its first cannonball. The elevation was too high and the ball sailed right over the roof of the building. The rather extraordinary silence continued as the cannon was quickly reloaded and the elevation reduced.

"Fire!"

This time the cannon ball went straight at one of the brick walls, raising a lot of brick dust. With a huge shout the two companies on either side charged forward and at the same time a hail of bullets tore into the brick walls and the stone pillars, and from the Hamid Mansion onto the roof. A murderous fire was returned at the advancing sepoys, while cannonball after cannonball now came crashing onto the building.

What the advancing sepoys thought that they could accomplish if the cannon did not open a breach in the walls of some sort was not clear. They had no ladders, and even when they passed through the hail of bullets as they advanced there was little they could do to break in if the cannon did not break down at least one of the walls. As before, some of the sepoys managed to get right up to the walls of the building and crouched down, protected by being too close, waiting for the cannon to do its work. The men inside, standing on the benches in the lower rooms, firing from the narrow openings at the top of the walls bricking up the lower windows, were unable to fire down at the crouching soldiers. But as before there was not much those sepoys could do either. As the first wave assault fell back, all waited to see what would be the effect of the artillery onslaught.

The many years of looking after the cannon had paid off in that it was able to keep up a steady fire almost throughout the whole day. Water was regularly poured onto the barrel to prevent it over-heating. At the same time, not once did the musket fire from the trees around and from the roof and windows of Tate's house cease, keeping everyone's head down, particularly those on the roof.

Paul Kelly, undoubtedly the best shot in the whole garrison, had managed to pick off at least two of the gunners managing the cannon. He himself moved calmly round, being let in at all points whenever he arrived and thought he had a good chance for another precision shot. His expensive sporting rifle was immeasurably more accurate and had a longer range than anything else in the garrison. The most dangerous firing from the sepoys was from the roof and windows of the Hamid Mansion, and in order to counteract this Paul clambered up onto the roof more often than was prudent. It was midday when a bullet finally got him in the left shoulder. The firing just at that moment was particularly fierce, and the Ghurkas on the roof were unable to help as he lay moaning in pain but waving them away to urge them to keep on firing back.

Two of the Sikhs had already been wounded, one in the face and one in the shoulder. They were already in Henty's hospital room being attended by him with Conrad assisting, when Ali ran in reporting that one of the Ghurkas had shouted down to Azimullah in the billiard room below, that Paul Kelly was wounded and that he ought to be brought down. Henty nodded at Conrad and he and Ali ran out up the spiral staircase to the billiard room above. Both boys had been given strict instructions that under no circumstances were they ever to go on the roof.

Their natural instinct of obedience caused them to hesitate at the bottom of the ladder. Meanwhile Paul, who even in his pain knew that he had to get off the roof, had dragged himself as far as the trapdoor from which the ladder emerged. He was hanging down with his head and arms already in the hole. The boys stood helpless for a moment at the bottom of the ladder looking up at Kelly half of his body still on the roof and half hanging down from the ceiling into the billiard room. Then at last the wits of old Azimullah began to work. He was already standing looking up at Paul dangling from the trapdoor in the ceiling. Holding the ladder as steady as he could he motioned to the boys to go up together – it was fortunately a particularly wide ladder. They duly clambered up. Holding their hands up to Kelly's good shoulder and to any other part of his body they could reach, they held him up as best they could as he himself slid down allowing gravity to pull him down onto the boys.

The boys were not quite strong enough to hold up the weight of the man as he slithered down. On the other hand they were able to act as a sort of breakwater, reducing his head-first descent down the incline of the ladder. They all arrived at the bottom in a heap. Kelly, white with pain, passed out as his shattered shoulder fell hard against Conrad's soft body. Helped by Azimullah, who could only ponder philosophically on the ironies which had brought him to this situation, they dragged rather than carried the now unconscious Kelly down the stairs and into Henty's hospital.

Azimullah and Ali left at once – there was simply no room for them. There were already the two wounded Sikhs, one crouching in the corner, the other lying on one of the beds. The unconscious Kelly went onto the surgical table, and Henty began probing at the shattered shoulder to bring out the bullet. Conrad, no longer needing to be told, went first and poured out some fresh water washing his hands carefully with the precious soap. Then coming alongside the busy Henty, he held flesh or widened it where necessary, he threw away things Henty did not require, he handed him things he did require. Mercifully all this time Paul himself remained unconscious. The probing, the plucking, the removal of shattered bone, the cleaning and the stitching went on for almost an hour.

Meanwhile the musket firing and the boom of the little cannon had been going on throughout the day. But in all the excitement and fear, one factor was soon standing out, obvious both to the little garrison and to the sepoy officers outside. The state cannon of Jagpur was almost useless. It made a lot of noise, it was good for morale, but it made little impression on Tate's fort. Those cannonballs, which struck the parts of the building made of stone did absolutely no harm at all. Those, which managed to hit fair and square at John's brick walls, did cause a lot of brick dust to fly about and in many cases dislodged bricks. This occasionally resulted in some slippage of bricks from the top. But these were quickly, though somewhat dangerously, replaced from the inside wherever the wall had sagged at all. If the cannon could have been made to strike the same spot or even the same wall consistently all the time, it might have made a difference, but that element of accuracy with the antiquated weapon was quite impossible.

At about three o'clock in the afternoon, the garrison, by now exhausted and beginning to fear a possible breakthrough, saw the sepoys preparing another built-up redoubt not much more than eighty yards away from the front of the zenana house. Continually concentrating their fire at this they were nevertheless unable to prevent the cannon being trundled forward and relocated at this spot so much closer to the fort. There was little they could do about it.

By 4.00pm the cannon was at last ready to begin firing again. This time there was to be no pointless assault – everyone waited to see whether the cannon, now at almost half the distance away would make a difference. Once again shot after shot slammed into Tate's fort, and once again everyone, garrison, sepoys and onlookers could see that the State Cannon of Jagpur had failed and that it would never be able to decide the issue.

The cannonade and the firing on both sides died away as dusk fell. Desultory shooting continued for some thirty minutes, but then ceased completely, to be replaced once again by the sibilant whispering, which was proving just as ineffective.

* * *

This was now the third night that the garrison had slept in the little fort. They had now stood up to three assaults and the Europeans were exhausted. The Sikhs were in better shape in this respect, but then they were trained soldiers from a naturally military people, as were the Ghurkas.

Not one of the Europeans had ever faced people shooting at them, keen to kill them. They had no military training or experience of any kind. Grant, who had spent almost the entire day next to or near Baldour Singh, was the man most pleased with himself. Not only had he kept much calmer than he thought he would, but also he found that he had created a real bond between himself and the unruffled and dignified Sikh Jemadar. Often exposing himself a little too imprudently in order to get in a better and more accurate shot, he became a bosom friend of all the Sikh soldiers without scarcely ever exchanging more than a word or two. They grinned as he interposed himself between them and stood on tiptoe in order to get a better shot with his longer range and more accurate rifle.

He climbed up the ladder set in the billiard room in order to emerge out of the trapdoor onto the roof. This was the post for the remaining five small Ghurkas, who could crouch behind the low parapet wall and be sheltered by it. But it was too low for GG or any of the other Europeans and he was in some peril while he was on the roof. He had a sort of vague feeling that it would be good for the morale of the Ghurka detachment for him to put in an appearance now and then. Oddly enough, while his bravado – no in fairness his real courage – endeared him to the Sikhs, it had the opposite effect on the Ghurkas. They were in fact irritated by his occasional appearance at their dangerous post, presenting as he did a tempting target to the sharpshooters on the Hamid mansion roof. Needless to say they did not in any way parade their feelings in this respect.

Once darkness fell, the whispering attempt to suborn the

Sikhs started up again. On no night did a single soldier have anything to do with all this whispered attempt at seduction. Their natural trained habit of obedience to their Jemadar, Baldour Singh, whose contempt for all the whispered voices was obvious, was the main foundation for their steadiness. However it would be fair to add that the easy friendship struck up by George Grant with both Baldour and the other men had its effect in keeping the Sikhs firmly on side. Needless to say, no one in the little fortress had any doubt whatsoever that, if the Sikhs had decided to defect, everyone else in the building would have been doomed.

Johnson, the deputy Magistrate, unlike Grant, did not feel that the experience of being under fire was of any benefit to his character at all. He was not afraid. Undoubtedly the effect of John Tate's stout brick walls, together with the thick stone of the original building, made the fighting easier. His tidy bureaucratic mind required him to relive each day's experience by writing it all down somewhere. It was as if the violent events of each day did not have any reality unless and until it was reported. Paper was in very short supply and there were no satisfactory writing implements. Accordingly, armed only with a short stubby pencil, Johnson went into the billiard room on the very night after the first assault and began writing on the long wall opposite the billiard table an account of the main events of the day. The Sikh soldiers who were not on guard duty lay around on the floor leaning back against the walls, smoking and chatting. A few were already sleeping under the billiard table itself. Those awake watched as Johnson stretched up to the highest point on the wall he could reach and started his diary by writing –'Monday 27th July'.

On this first day it was his belief and that of the rest of the garrison that the sepoy regulars would move on in a day or two to Delhi. Even if that did not happen they all believed that the British garrison in Dinapore would very quickly mount a relief expedition. After all, it was the Patna Commissioner himself who had sent the Sikh detachment to them in the first place and accordingly their plight was well known. So, in the circumstances, if it was only going to be for a few days, it was unclear as to why Johnson chose to start expressing himself like this at all. But he did – and it became a feature of the siege that each night right up to the tragic end he laboriously wrote with his stubby pencil all over the wall of the billiard room an account of the main events of the day as he witnessed them.

Dickie Derounian was perhaps the most surprised at his own reactions. He was used to relieving any tensions or fears in his life by a mixture of shouting and coming out with loud, though mild, expletives. He found that in all the noise of the shouting rebels outside and the continuous gunfire on both sides, this simply did not seem to work. He also found that the incentive of mere survival and the automatic instinct of self-preservation was no longer enough. He had always assumed that this was the overriding motive of all people acting under stress, but here it was no longer applicable. He found, for instance, that he was far more worried when the relatively elderly Arthur Drummond unthinkingly stood up too high behind one of the embrasures than he ever was for himself. Several times he called out – "Please crouch, sir, please crouch" as the Judge rather aimlessly passed by. When Ali came scampering round with food, a cold fear would strike him as the boy passed behind where he himself stood which happened to be one of the lowest of the brick walls, whereas on his own he had been completely cool the moment before.

Dickie did not have that easy familiarity with weapons that was second nature for his English colleagues. He was not inter-ested in hunting; going out shooting animals had never struck him as a great sport. Accordingly, the sheer noise and recoil of the guns came as something of a surprise. On the other hand noise he had always been able to deal with and he soon got the hang of the recoil. He found himself banging away with the best of them although he had no idea whether he ever managed to kill anyone.

John, on the other hand, was completely familiar with a rifle. But of all the men in the little fortress it was he who felt the most basic outright fear. Whilst he had as much determination and strength of will to sell his life as dearly as the other six Europeans, he was riddled with an anxiety that they did not have. He was touched with a deep guilt about his children. He knew that in the end Harriet was a thinking adult and had made her own decision and probably would have stayed, like Henrietta, even if there had been no children. So, unlike what all the newspapers in England were yelling about, John did not feel at all badly that Harriet might have to die with him. He felt no guilt – it was her decision not just his complaisance. But he blamed himself for not having insisted until it was too late on Conrad's departure for England.

So the fear which washed over him and which irritated him immensely was for Conrad and the little Chloe. But he did not realise that it was this guilty fear for them that was eating at him and hence he had difficulty combating it. He thought that the fear he was feeling was just plain 'funk' and that of course would have been unforgivable in the circumstances. Of course there was no way at all that he was going to show this inchoate fear to anyone. He well understood the old male hunting requirement that where survival depended on a team effort needing courage, it is vital that you hide any individual fear. It is the collective courage that is important and anything which reduces that, lessens not only the effectiveness of the group but also the chances of survival of the individual within the group.

Harriet of course never recognized for a moment John's fears. Even if she had it would not have made much difference. Unlike so many of her peers she did in fact believe that it helped to overcome stress if you allowed your emotional feelings to emerge. If she had become aware of John's anxieties she might even have been able to analyse the real source of his fears. But of course it could never come to that. If it was atavistically impor- tant for group survival to maintain an outward pose of calm in danger, it was even more vital, culturally, for the male not to show any fear in front of his wife or children. So it was that John never came to terms with the reasons for his uncharacteristic fears.

Arthur Drummond too had never heard or seen a gun being

fired at him in anger. He was the oldest person present with the exception of old Azimullah Hassan, who on that first day had sat quietly in a corner of the billiard room carefully not getting in anyone's way. Arthur had spent so long acting the part of the dignified, impartial, deliberating Judge that he had no other role to play. Unlike Azimullah, Arthur did keep getting in the way. He had no idea why Dickie was always warning him to crouch or why Baldour and even GG were always crossing him whenever he tried to help. He knew that he was not a good shot and so made no attempt to push in and take pot-shots at anything. On the other hand he could find no easy alternative activity. The men could and did shout at Ali and Conrad demanding water or some more ammunition, but even in the middle of all the chaos and strain they simply could not do the same with poor Arthur who was desperate to help but could find nothing to do. Clearly he would have done better to go and sit with Azimullah, but that being culturally impossible he could only mope and get in the way.

Surprisingly this did not apply to Henrietta. She of course had never acted a part in her life. She simply always knew her duty – a duty which she owed as much to the poor deluded Sikh or Hindu as to her fellow-Christian. They were wrong and she was right, but this required her to be even more helpful and charitable. Furthermore, she had a natural feminine understanding of what was required and practical in any awkward situation. 'Awkward situation' was precisely how she would have thought of her present predicament. She carried boxes of ammunition, she made sure the water cans being taken round by the boys were full, she applied bandages to minor wounds caused by the flying brick dust, she encouraged where necessary. A nursery filled with fractious little boys was her natural milieu.

* * *

The failure of the first assault had come as no surprise to the sepoy officers. That first undisciplined charge was the sort of amateur attack of zeal and enthusiasm, which as soldiers of the East India Company army they had been trained to stand up to and defeat without difficulty. They were therefore not in the least concerned when the mob melted away. However the failure of the second prepared assault was more worrying. Then following that failure, while they knew that the stone parts of the building were never under any threat from their small cannon, they were surprised that the makeshift brick walls, which looked so flimsy, had stood up so well to cannonball after cannonball.

So once again that evening there was a meeting in the da Costa house. Saridar Khan presided over the group of three officers together with a couple of havildars from the ranks and the now much subdued Haidar Presaud. The Nawab himself was no longer just indifferent; he was getting distinctly irritated. He missed his crumbling palace with the familiar dusty corners. He missed his wives, particularly to his surprise the undemanding kindly elderly ones. The food cooked by the da Costa servants was uneatable and he felt sure he was getting ridiculously thinner. There was nothing to do, and when that afternoon he had sauntered down to oversee the action, exhausting himself by the unaccustomed long stroll, he could make neither head nor tail of what was going on round the Tate house. He had of course kept well out of sight so it was not surprising that he understood little of such action as he did see; and now the formality of being consulted by these ridiculous Brahminical soldiers. 'God. What a society – where soldiers supposedly belonging to my army, all from poor country families, could be of such high caste.'

He sighed and listened with a distinct lack of interest to the interminable discussions and arguments. Delhi or not? Back to Dinapore to see if they could break into the magazine and capture a cannon before the British garrison could react? Abandon the whole thing and melt away? Open up a proper and disciplined siege? Another copybook assault? At last Saridar bestirred himself and said –

"Jemadar sahib I have nothing to add to all I have heard. As you know I do not have any military experience. So, I feel that it is now necessary for me to return to Jagpur."

"Your excellency, your duty and your future lies here with your army."

"No, this is the field for my generals."

Saridar believed, and he was right, that this was a particularly clever sentence, and he was pleased to note a stiffening in the shoulders of the sepoy officers. He continued –

"I'm sure that as the current Raj wavers and falls there is a lot happening on the political front which requires my attention and that of my advisors. In this way the interests of all of us can be properly looked after."

At this, Haidar Presaud who had also become thoroughly disillusioned by his lack of any political influence in this miserable little town said –

"Jemadar sahib – his excellency the Nawab is quite right. He needs to return to take charge of 'state' business. I will be there to help and advise and I will of course keep your interests always in mind."

"No, no my dear Haidar," said Saridar. "I hereby appoint you as my minister and ambassador with these excellent troops. You must remain here with my gallant soldiers and act as my representative. This will also allow them to have the benefit of your valuable political advice."

The sepoy officers all began agreeing before Haidar could say a word. Nevertheless he managed to shoot a glance of pure hatred at the insufferable Nawab. Saridar, now enjoying himself for almost the first moment since the mutineers had arrived at his palace all those days ago, smiled again and said –

"Well, gentlemen, I will leave you to your military deliberations and go to prepare for my departure early tomorrow morning. My effects have to be prepared and the mahout must be informed so that the state elephant can be made ready for the journey."

He rose, noting with a return of his irritation that none of the others rose in respect, except one of the young havildars who had been included in the meeting. But now this young man, who had not in fact risen out of any deference for the Nawab but because he had something to say, blurted out –

"Yes, of course – the Elephant!"

The Nawab stopped and stared at him. Had the man gone mad, what was he talking about? But the three officers, looking hard at the young soldier then themselves jumped up and said all together and in a jumble –

"Yes, yes, it might work; certainly worth a try; well done young man; what a stroke of genius; sure, yes...."

"What the blazes are you all talking about," said Saridar testily. Everyone fell silent as the senior Jemadar raised his head and looking hard at Saridar said –

"Your Excellency – the state cannon of Jagpur having failed, the state elephant of Jagpur is going to be given its great chance of glory. Tomorrow's third assault will be led by Toto or whatever its name is."

"But you must be mad," spluttered Saridar. "He is an ancient purely ceremonial animal. He has never heard a shot fired in anger, and he is old and slow, What can he do?"

"I'm afraid your excellency that you don't understand. Of course he is not a fighting animal, but he is very large and very heavy; pampered and overweight in my opinion. There is no suggestion of an old-fashioned charge with the beast trumpeting its rage and frightening the wits out of the enemy. No, no, all that the old creature will be required to do is to lumber forward. Once the British see what is happening a murderous fire will of course pour out, but they will not be able to stop the thing. Nothing short of a cannon could stop it once it began moving. No it will continue to stagger forward and then die crashing onto the building. The building will of course stand, but there is no way the brick walls could withstand all those tons of flesh and bone crashing down onto it."

"Yes, yes, I see," shouted out Haidar, receiving in his turn a look of pure hatred from the portly Nawab.

For a full hour Saridar Khan tried every possible argument to pour scorn on the plan in order to save his poor elephant. He was appalled; the animal had carried him from the time when he was only a child riding, with his father by his side, in the howdah swaying on its broad back. But while Haidar Presaud was a lightweight as far as the Nawab was concerned, the sepoy officers were quite a different matter. The more Saridar wailed, the more they hardened their own view of the position.

In fact there could be no meeting of minds: they were all talking at cross-purposes. The officers thought that the Nawab was merely concerned for his loss of dignity in losing his state elephant – how could you be a Nawab or a Rajah in Victorian India if you had no ceremonial elephant. However, for once, Saridar was really not thinking of himself. He felt bad, not only for the faithful old elephant, but also for the loyal and equally old mahout, the animal's keeper, who had also been with him since his father's time. He knew that the old man would be utterly shattered, completely desolated, by the death of his old friend whom he had looked after for over thirty years.

There was only one way the discussions were going to end. Power resided with the men who commanded the soldiers and not with the Nawab. But there was no way, whatever happened, that Saridar would attend and witness the sacrifice of the old animal, and this was accepted. So it was that the next morning the Nawab, with a sigh of relief, left the little town in a commandeered carriage. He could not face seeing either the elephant or the old mahout, both of whom every morning moved from the large back garden of the house to a field in the countryside. Reluctantly he left orders that the old man was to follow the instructions of the Jemadar.

Meanwhile, the garrison in the little fort were in the highest spirits that they ever attained. The way that Tate's little brick walls had stood up to the cannon had given everyone from the Judge down to the youngest new Sikh recruit a huge morale boost. Soon they were all going to be on the verge of exhaustion – all day by day becoming more tired than they realised. The civilians in particular did not have the training or experience that allowed them to achieve a proper rest in catnaps and snatched short periods of sleep. On this, the third morning however, they were all still alert and ready at their posts as the sun rose in the east from the direction of the town. They were aroused to full attention by great shouts of glee and triumph coming from the road leading back to the town. Once again they could not quite make out what was happening, and once again it was John, crouching on the roof behind the parapet with his telescope who called out –

"My God! Oh my God. They're bringing up an elephant. It's a monster. What the hell are they going to do with it?"

Not even the professionals had any idea. The old Sikh Jemadar had served in the Khalsa, the Sikh army, in the forties. He had fought against the British – perhaps even against these very same sepoys. However, even he had never seen an elephant actually being used in any battle. What were they thinking about? For the moment nothing was happening - the beast had lumbered up behind the Hamid Mansion and could no longer be seen. The Jemadar and those Europeans not on duty crowded into the billiard room where there was a hurried consultation.

It was Paul, sitting with his left shoulder now in a very well-prepared sling, who first pointed out that if the sepoys sent the elephant towards the little fort and it was met by killing fire from the garrison it would in its death throes inevitably crash onto their fort, and would open up the way for a direct assault. But if they did not kill it or in some way stop it anything could happen as it arrived at the building. It was, undoubtedly, potentially a dangerous problem – though it was still not quite clear what the sepoys intended.

After further explaining his thoughts on the problem Paul looked round at everyone and said –

"Look, there is really only one solution, but it needs a very good marksman with an Enfield or a good sporting rifle – an excellent top-class shot."

"But Kelly that can only be you."

"Yes, I know. It will be tricky but I think I can do it."

"Hang on a moment Paul. Your left shoulder is shattered and in a sling. I know you use the right shoulder, but can you really hold your position steady enough for your shot to work."

"I will need a helper and of course I will have to go up onto the roof – but yes I think it can be done."

Two of the ghurkas sitting on the billiard table and listening immediately volunteered, almost as if the roof and everything pertaining to it belonged to them and they would not allow anyone else to participate in anything that took place up there, without one of them being present.

There was clearly not much time before the sepoys began to do whatever they were planning with the elephant, and so with an enormous amount of pushing and pulling Paul, using only one hand, managed to clamber up the ladder and onto the roof. Here he took up position behind a low sandbag redoubt that had been erected by the ghurkas to protect the exit from the trapdoor opening to the room below. Here, with his rifle ready resting on the shoulder of one grinning kneeling ghurka, and with the other soldier holding him steady, Paul, still puffing on his pipe, waited.

Meanwhile, in the other camp, shielded by Tate's house, the elephant was being prepared. There was no question of any howdah – no one was prepared to sit up there on any seat on that great swaying back. The old mahout had already been swung up by the elephant in the same way that it had done daily for thirty years, and was now sitting on the beast's neck between its ears. Poor man, he really had no idea what he was meant to do, but he sensed the impending doom of the old animal that he had looked after ever since he was a young man in the service of the former old Nawab. All he had been told was that he was to ignore all the shouting or any rifle shots and simply steer the great pachyderm towards the building over there in the grounds.

The sepoy officers intended that fire should commence as soon as the elephant appeared from the back of the Hamid mansion. It was to be regular and highly disciplined. Only those to the sides and in the Tate house were to fire, and of course they had strict instructions to avoid the elephant completely. Behind the elephant and to each side three assault groups of about two hundred men in each group were ready to charge in the event that the plan worked and the beast died as required.

It took a fairly long time to prepare everything to the officer's satisfaction and it was nearly 10.00 am when the order to commence firing was given. The fire was not returned as the garrison waited to see what was going to happen. At last the great elephant lumbered out from behind the Tate house and began walking somewhat hesitantly in the direction of the zenana house guided by whispering and leg movements of the experienced old mahout sitting between its ears. The animal was already nervous and in some distress from all the firing coming from all sides. It was however a majestic sight and a good deal more frightening than any number of the charging yelling crowd that had tried to rush the building on that first day.

Up on the roof Paul steadied his rifle as the great animal came into view. The shooting coming from the sides and from the Tate house was being aimed at the foot of the building and at the first floor embrasures, not at the roof, and that made it a bit easier. It was a small and swaying target at which Paul was aiming. Difficult, but undoubtedly the best way to stop the elephant in its tracks. Everyone had agreed with Paul's analysis that to shoot at the elephant and to kill it, would not stop its forward momentum wherever you managed to hit it. But, if you killed the mahout, that would be likely to be decisive immediately. Paul had reckoned that he could get in at least four shots before the moment came when the elephant would be too close and killing the mahout would be too late.

Paul's left shoulder was beginning to throb with pain. The ghurka holding him steady was holding too tightly, while at the same time the ghurka kneeling in front of him upon whose shoulder the rifle was resting was so tensely still that that too was affecting Paul's aim. The elephant came lumbering on. Paul steadied himself and two shots rang out in quick succession. Everyone in the building, knowing what was coming, had held their fire, and at just that moment firing from the other side had also stopped. In the short silence, everyone on both sides saw the old mahout, with a great look of surprise on his face, slowly keel over to the side and then topple off the elephant's back.

Despite all the shouting and yelling behind him and the increased firing that then broke out, the old elephant stopped at once and turned to look down at and nuzzle with his trunk the fallen and dead mahout, whom it had known and trusted for over thirty years. The sepoy officers were beside themselves with excitement. The elephant was after all now only about thirty yards away from the little fortress. Could it not still be persuaded to die for the greater glory of the state of Jagpur? There was only one thing for it. The order to fire at the great beast was given, and a rain of musket balls, most of which missed their target, fell on the elephant. The poor animal, standing now between the two combatants had no idea what to do or where to go.. But in order to nuzzle the dying mahout who had of course fallen behind it the elephant had already turned back. The effect of all the shots now slamming into its leathery sides angered and alarmed it. The beast gave what it believed was a great bellow of rage – poor old thing it came out more like a squeal – and began lumbering as fast as it could go to get away, forwards. Forwards, however, was no longer towards the Tate fort, but away to the boundaries of the park and to the countryside beyond.

The little garrison gave a cheer as the elephant picked up speed and ran off. The forces, waiting at the sides for the antici-pated breach in the walls which would allow another charge, never moved. Thus the fourth attempt at a direct assault petered out.

But those two shots that had killed the old mahout had not of course gone unnoticed from the vantage points of the Tate house. The sharpshooters in the house, aiming from the roof and from the upper windows, opened up a murderous fire onto the exposed roof of the zenana house. All three, the two ghurkas and Paul, were hit before they could scramble back and down through the trapdoor, falling rather than climbing down the ladder.

Conrad and Ali, both of whom had been staring at the elephant from a space in one of the lower floor windows, raced up and helped the three men down and into Henty's hospital room. The elephant danger had been seen off, but Paul would now be completely out of action as his right arm had now been hit in the elbow. After a hasty inspection and yet another sling Henty confirmed that it would not recover for weeks. One of the ghurkas had a minor wound and waited patiently while Dr. Henty now began working hard on the second ghurka who had been shot in the stomach. Sweat pouring from his brow, determined not to lose another man, he probed through the gaping wound; he fiddled and picked out the musket ball; he delicately straightened twisted bone and removed bone splinters; he pulled and pinched and eventually sewed while Conrad stood by his side the whole time, holding instruments, passing bandages and replenishing clean water. Ali left the room as did Paul and the second ghurka, whose wound was fairly superficial and who bandaged it himself with Conrad's help.

The surgical work was brilliant. The young man regained consciousness in the early afternoon and was able to welcome the other four ghurkas who came to see him, hold his hand and touch his forehead before leaving. Henty knew he had done a job of which any great London surgeon, even with all the help that they would have had, would have been proud.

However at about six o'clock in the evening, shortly after drinking a small cup of water, the young man died, with Henty still sitting by his side.

PART III

The Siege

Four direct assaults against the fort had now been attempted – two on the first day and one on each subsequent day. Each one had failed. The Nawab had left and surely there was now nothing to prevent the remnants of the two regiments from packing up and marching off to Delhi. But Haidar Presaud, although increasingly disillusioned by what he saw as the feeble weakness of his chosen leader was still present advising against such a move. It was not so surprising. Delhi was after all the home of a once foreign and Muslim power. Here around Darabad in the district of Shantapur lay the homes of most of the men. Surely they would command more influence staying put rather than moving seven hundred miles away to an alien atmosphere. Without knowing it he was repeating exactly the same arguments that had persuaded the Nana Sahib at Cawnpore to turn back and to crush poor General Wheeler and all the people, European and Eurasian, for whom he had been responsible.

So it was that the two regiments, still officially acting in the name of the Nawab of Jagpur, stayed on. By now they amounted to only about fifteen hundred men in total as they had been losing men on a daily basis. Those with families nearby simply drifted away. One thing was clear to the three senior officers; those men that they still led did not have the motivation to mount yet another assault on the determined men skulking in their ridiculous little fort. So, as another assault could no longer be considered, it would have to be a set-piece siege.

These officers had learnt their trade well. They knew how sieges were supposed to be conducted, and they began well. The headquarters and nerve centre of the siege was of course to be Tate's house - the Hamid mansion. Here those sepoys on duty received their food and their daily orders. It was here in the main sitting room that the priorities of the besieging force were mapped out. Not all the men were needed to be on duty every day, only enough to keep the whole enemy garrison alert all the time in order to wear them down. The classic way to resolve a siege where direct assault had failed was to construct a tunnel. The tunnel was started not much more than forty yards away from the front of the little fort, after a well-protected redoubt of earth and sandbags was first built up to protect the tunnel entrance and the soldiers involved in digging and working there.

The mutineers were not short of assets. About seventy thousand silver rupees had been found still left in the Darabad treasury, and even after Saridar Khan had got his hands on some of the money there was more than enough left to keep the two regiments maintained and the local farmers happy.

However there was a gap in the siege dispositions. The building was not completely surrounded day and night. There seemed to be no reason to post men in the jungle behind the fort on any regular basis. Relief could only come from Dinapore and through the town. If, on the other hand, by any chance the garrison broke out and escaped to the back and melted away into the jungle and the wilderness beyond, this would be all to the good. They would be much more easily hunted down and at the same time it would remove this whole little thorn in their side.

The garrison in Tate's fort soon realised that at night there were no guards posted behind the zenana house. In fact the sepoys were on the whole amazingly slack in keeping proper military watches. However, gunfire would continue throughout the day. Although not much damage could be achieved, such regular fire forced the defenders to remain alert and keep their heads down, and it served to mask the activity of the tunnelers whose comings and goings could be seen from the roof. On the third day after the failure of the elephant assault there was in fact one more casualty. One of the Sikh policemen was shot in the face and died instantaneously. This raised to three the total number of dead – the two ghurkas and now one of the Sikhs.

Something had to be done about the three dead bodies. The garrison was aware that there was no strict watch being kept during the night. But now, with all the arches and the lower windows all bricked up, it was as difficult getting out of the building as it was getting in. Whatever they did would have to be from the lower rooms and from the back of the house facing the jungle. On this side there was the Tate's room in one corner, and Marietta and the boys in the other. The Well was in the bigger middle room, which also contained the charpoy used by the elderly deputy collector Azimullah Hassan. No assault had ever been mounted on this side. From the sepoys' point of view this was the least likely place for any successful attack, as the walls were stone above the lower windows right up to the roof. The wide verandah that went round the front and sides of the building did not join round the back.

In order to take advantage of this and come out of the building some bricks would have to be removed from those walls built to cover up the half windows in the lower storey. The Well room was the one chosen for the exit. After the death of the third defender, working as quietly as possible during the night, several layers of these bricks were quietly removed, bringing the wall down lower towards the level of the earth outside. These layers of brick were then replaced by several stout wooden beams, previously stacked in a corner, which had been left over from the railway materials brought in by John when he had been constructing his little fort all those weeks ago. These beams wedged in and as secure as the bricks to any assault, could be removed instantly and quietly when necessary. Azimullah moved his charpoy out of the way and it was carried up to the billiard room where in any case he had spent most of his time.

The next night a burial party consisting of four Sikhs, two Ghurkas and GG himself, took down the three wooden beams, slithered over the remaining brick wall and were handed the bodies. They moved off towards the jungle twenty yards away carrying the three corpses. It was two o'clock in the morning, there was no one stirring as they melted into the jungle behind.

There were no words or ritual of any kind. A shallow grave was dug for each body and the bodies simply placed in and covered. Throughout the whole of the two hours that all this took there was not a murmur or any interruption from the besiegers.

This satisfactory mission was the start of several expeditions that George Grant made, usually with one of the Ghurkas, to scout the area at the back of the fort. It was fairly unnecessary really, but it was exciting and good for his restless and active spirit. For by now, the length of the siege was beginning to have its consequences. The dirt, the smells and the total lack of any privacy was effecting the morale of almost everyone except the Jemadar Baldour Singh who remained a tower of indifferent strength. The well continued to work, but nevertheless the water had to be rationed carefully and everyone was feeling unwashed. The smells from the little ablution rooms were becoming overpowering despite all Henty's attempts with various medicaments to counter them.

As it happened Henty had brought in a fairly copious supply of bleaches and soaps, but much to the surprise of the rest of the garrison he did not use them to lessen in any way the aroma from those essential little rooms. He explained to Conrad one afternoon the importance of the biological breakdown of waste – a biological effect that would be hindered by the use of chemical bleaches of the sort that he had and which he needed to keep his little hospital as clean as possible. Conrad did not in fact understand much of what he was being told, but for him Henty was becoming a great hero figure and he never let on that this was really all above his head.

Apart from the problem of the disposal of waste, there was also the fact that the fresh drinking water in the great pottery jars was fast disappearing. The water from the well was drinkable, but it was muddy, tasted bad and eventually would either run out or at least need to be deepened. However these were long-term anxieties. The immediate current major problem was the tunnel openly being worked on thirty or forty yards away. The water table here in Darabad was very high and this had been helpful to the garrison when constructing the well. It was undoubtedly also causing difficulty to the sepoy tunnellers, who had to keep shoring up the walls of the tunnel as they advanced. Sooner or later, however, the tunnel would arrive below the fort, after which it would only be a matter of time before it would be filled with gunpowder and exploded with devastating effect.

The classic reply to tunnelling by besiegers was to build a counter-tunnel and blow up the approaching tunnel before it arrived under the walls. Baldour Singh discussed this regularly with his two havildars and also with Grant. The consensus was that the garrison was now too small for this to be possible. With Paul now unable even to hold a gun, and a Sikh and two Ghurkas dead the strain on those left would have been too much.

Grant suggested that they make a sortie late one night, starting out from the back of the fort over the wooden beams in the Well room. A meeting to discuss the problem was held in the billiard room in the middle of a whole bunch of sleeping men. Baldour Singh presided and both the two havildars were present together with Grant, Tate and the Judge.

"I agree with Grant sahib," said the Jemadar, "the work on the tunnel is the single biggest danger that we are now facing. Once it reaches here and is properly blown under us, even those that survive the blast will have no more chance."

"But is it likely to be properly blown?"

"Yes I am afraid so. I have never met those senior officers of the 66th and the 68th, but so far as I can see they know their job. The direct assaults having failed, this tunnelling is their obvious and militarily correct next step."

"Well, what exactly is Grant sahib's suggestion?" said one of the Sikh havildars.

"I suggest," said GG "that one night we make up a small assault party which gathers at the back of the building. You all saw how fairly easy it was to arrange the burial party. I have succeeded in going out on a couple of occasions since then without any problem. Once gathered and ready we come round and either immediately rush the redoubt and the tunnel head, or creep up to it as close as we can first and then take it. I leave that to you professionals."

"Yes, yes, that is feasible. The element of surprise would be decisive. But while we could certainly take it in the first rush, there is no way we could hold it for more than about fifteen minutes once the alarm is raised."

"Of course – but we only need those few minutes in order to lay our own charges of gunpowder, already primed and ready, which we bring with us on our initial charge. We blow great stretches from the entrance of the tunnel, as far back as we can and then we scamper back."

"But George, this could only ever be a one-off," said John. "They will start again won't they, and our capacity to come out at the back will be known and we will not be able to use that exit ever again."

"That may be so, but we will have gained another two weeks at least. What do you think Jemadar sahib?"

There was a short silence while everyone looked at the bushy beard and grand moustaches of the bulky Sikh. His eyes not being visible as he looked down at the billiard table.

"We will have to go over the details very carefully. Every man chosen must know exactly what he is to do. But yes, once and only once it might work. The later we do it the better of course. My havildar here, who was at the siege of Kuraon, has calculated that they are still less than halfway, perhaps even less due to the difficulty caused by the high water-table. We will wait another week and plan this very meticulously."

The decision having been made the meeting broke up.

The garrison went back to the long boring days of dirt and smells, of intermittent firing, and of tasteless and repetitious meals without any fresh vegetables or meat. There was too little water with which to wash and too little water to drink and too much hard alcohol to make up for it. Paul Kelly became more and more gloomy each day with both his shoulders now out of action and causing continual pain. Dickie drank and shouted a bit, though he never got aggressive. Grant, with his excellent relations with the Sikhs remained in a state of febrile excitement, though he had to curtail his nightly excursions in case he gave away the existence of the hidden exit. The married men, John and Arthur were the most sober but John remained racked with fear and guilt as he contemplated his daughter Chloe. She, however, was now recovering fast and had begun running about all over the building. She was protected by her small size from even the occasional stray bullet. The whole garrison observed her uncaring innocence with enormous pleasure and satisfaction. She was even vying with GG for the affection of the Sikhs.

Meanwhile, another week passed as the tunnel grew ever closer to the little fort.

* * *

As day after day passed with no possibility of knowing what was happening in the rest of India away from their own predicament, the strain began to affect the Europeans in ways completely different to what they had expected. Arthur Drummond, despite the stern resolve and calm example provided by Henrietta, began to wilt. He had always been clean-shaven contrary to the current fashion for burly beards in all shapes and sizes, but he now stopped shaving. It suddenly seemed pointless. But this made him look older and shabbier as the resulting beard took a long time to grow out of being mere stubble. He continued to insist on taking his turn in the night watches, but never having fired a gun in anger it was clear that he would not be much use. There was no room for him at the walls during the day either and he just did not know what to do with himself as tedious day passed after tedious day.

Azimullah, the deputy collector, was in much better shape even though he was a good deal older and frailer than Arthur. He could sit cross-legged on the floor of the billiard room for hours on end just contemplating his own incredible folly in having come to this spot in the first place. He rocked back and forth, he played with his beard and he smiled rather vaguely at everyone. He too did nothing all day, but it did not worry him. He had no desire or pressing need as did Arthur to be up and about organising something or someone.

Henrietta, in contrast to her husband seemed to get stronger every day as Arthur deteriorated. Domestic details which she had ignored and left to her servants for years, suddenly sprang up to confront her. She found herself dealing with them sharply and decisively. She made no direct attempt to help Ali or to interfere with his preparation of all the food for the garrison – but she did take over the careful management and rationing of all the stored food. She made Ali's task much easier by leaving out for him on a daily basis just the right amount of ingredients for the day's cooking. The ending of the three days' attempts at direct assaults meant that the garrison was now facing the drudgery of a possibly long-drawn out siege. The stored food and drink was no longer required just for the few days before the sepoys marched away to Delhi. Whatever was keeping the sepoys here, it had become clear that they were intending to remain until either they had overrun the little fort or starved them all out. The provisions therefore had to be carefully husbanded in order to last as long as possible. It was Henrietta who first grasped this point and took in hand the necessary curtailment of Ali's rather lavish and wasteful methods of cooking.

As the days passed, even though cleanliness became almost impossible, never once did Henrietta fail to wear her tight-laced corset and her heavy long skirts. How she managed to remain so controlled and an object almost of awe to the Sikhs in the cramped building was a complete mystery to Harriet. She of course had the added burden of a little girl of three years old to care for. As the little Chloe's health improved that became more of a trouble. She was of course long past the use of the nappies of the time. But keeping her clean and amused was nevertheless a laborious task. Rather like Henrietta she too had, until now, relied on servants and the faithful ayah to deal with all this.

In the course of the one or two times that she and John had managed to be intimate together she had wormed out of him some of his fears for her and the children which had been eating at him. Accusing him of male arrogance, she made it as clear as she could that she considered herself to be the main, indeed the only, architect of their present predicament. Furthermore she refused to feel guilty in any way for the fact that the two children were going to suffer the same way as their parents and were likely to die with them. Chloe had survived the cholera when so many others, statistically the majority, would have succumbed. That was a cause for joy not for the gloom under which he was labouring. She did not actually use the words – 'snap out of it' – but she felt it and made it clear to him.

John himself did not entirely get rid of his feelings that he had let his family down. His anxieties about the two children and Harriet remained. But that state of fear that had been with him during the days of the four assaults passed away. As the siege progressed, as Chloe got visibly better, as Conrad stayed as cheerful and active as before, he himself overcame his fears.

This was not however quite so true of most of the other European men. The excitement and the adrenaline rush of the days of the assaults gave way to the deadly strain of a siege. Lack of any good sleep; having to remain continuously on the alert when nothing was happening; the poor and monotonous food; above all the dirt and the smells; all contrived to make them morose and snappy with each other. Dickie became less bouncy. Johnson just sat and smoked his damned pipe, often not noticing when the tobacco burnt out and the pipe went out. Paul moped, being particularly irritated by his inability to hold a rifle anymore. He buried himself in his Gibbon. Having passed the final end of Rome he was into the many pages of the follies of Byzantium and the interminable arguments over the nature of Christ that went on and on for ever. But Constantinople had survived siege after siege for a thousand years. It had protected Western Christian civilisation for all that length of time. It was an inspiring metaphor for the present situation in Darabad. But of course it did finally fall.

Only George Grant was in his element. On two more occasions, with the agreement of the Jemadar, he slipped out quietly by himself from the Well room and reconnoitred exactly step by step how the raiding party would advance to take what was now referred to generally as the 'Tunnel Redoubt'. His night vision was excellent and he only needed to stand at the corner of the building to see every tree and all the variety of the ground between the fort and the redoubt. His enthusiasm was like that of a boy. It was this that gave him his extraordinary rapport with the Sikhs, together with an easy familiarity with Conrad and Ali whom he treated almost as adult equals, a relationship which was going to get him into trouble later. Sleeping in the room next door, they always awoke on the days that he slipped out at the back. He was never out for more than half an hour and they always remained awake until his return.

But for these two real boys, the days of the siege had given rise to a new complication – the close presence day-in and day-out of the young Marietta. Marietta herself was in a confused state. She was well aware that it was almost certain that she was now a widow. However, just as the marriage had been a whirl-wind romance which had burned brightly very quickly, so the grieving had been violent but had also burned out almost at once. She was only sixteen after all. Like everyone else in the garrison she had difficulty keeping clean. Her clothes were dirty, water even from the well was far too precious to spend on washing clothes. Far less capable of maintaining any sort of dignity in these circumstances than Henrietta or Harriet, her hair was all over the place. All this, together with the increasing failure to maintain much privacy had made the boys, whose dirt and odour were somehow more natural, look at her increasingly as a girl only a little older than themselves - a friend rather than a lady.

Both the boys were right in the middle of approaching puberty and both now suffered – if that is the right word – embarrassing erections. But both were totally innocent, even for those times, of any 'impure' thoughts about the young woman whose room they were sharing. Yet despite all the excitement and drama of the siege, when they went to bed at night they could not help but glimpse in the candlelight the occasional soft skin and rounded curves. They could not help but be disturbed by the shining eyes and warm red lips of a girl who, despite having consummated her marriage, was innocent of the effect that she was having on the two twelve-year-olds sharing her room.

For the two boys the effects of the siege, which for them was not the slightest bit boring, left them in a state of exhilaration. This adventure as they conceived it, together with the different excitements of the night, listening to GG's exploits on the one hand and experiencing the disturbingly sensuous presence of the young Marietta on the other, was leading to a state of heightened stimulation. which matched GG's overactive mind. It was all going to have its dangerous dramatic effect a week or two later.

But meanwhile the siege dragged on and the tunnel crept closer every day.

* * *

The group that were going to make the surprise assault on the tunnel was carefully chosen but only after a lot of argument among the men involved. Everyone agreed that it was going to be a difficult and dangerous exercise. The Jemadar felt that he had to go with the assault force for at least two reasons. Firstly that he should be leading from the front in such a perilous action. But more than that he felt that in the event of any really major problem only he had the requisite military training to extricate the little expeditionary force. However, Grant also wanted to go in the party. He felt that as it was his own idea, he should be the one risking his life. Furthermore he had reconnoitred the whole landscape and knew every foot of the way. Above all – and really his argument here was overwhelming – if in the last resort one or two of the men might not make it back, the one person the loss of whom would put the survival of everyone in the little fort at the greatest risk was the Sikh commander.

Baldour Singh saw the strength of that point fairly quickly and conceded that he himself could not go. However he insisted that one of his Havildars should be in command in the event that any decision had to be made.

"Look Grant sahib" he said at the final meeting called to discuss and plan the night attack, "I have no doubt in your capacity to lead a spirited offensive of the type envisaged. What

I am concerned about is the requirement of a retreat in the very real possibility of impending failure. Where military training comes into play is the capacity to see that a plan has failed, or is at the inevitable point of failing. At that point it needs training to have the capacity to take the decision to pull back and save lives. The enthusiastic amateur, and I mean no disrespect, will never see until it is too late that the moment has come to retire."

"Very well, very well, I accept that. Could I however add that it is not enough just to capture the sandbagged redoubt. We have to hold it for at least five to ten minutes to enable us to set the charges and blow the whole thing up."

"Yes, yes – we've gone over all that already. Once the redoubt is taken, everyone left here in the fort will open up in all directions. We will particularly aim at where most of the sepoys are sleeping with everything we've got. We won't need any accuracy; it will be in the middle of the night; just a murderous fire for the ten minutes needed to deter the inevitable counter-attack. So, Grant sahib, who will you be proposing for the detonating party."

"Well I would have taken Paul – he is certainly the most expert in explosives – but that is obviously now out of the question in his present condition. It will have to be another of the railway men, and as between John and Dickie I think it will have to be Dickie. John might have had a little more experience with explosives, but not so much more as to override the fact that John is a family man with wife and children."

"Yes, I agree. Very well, Mr. Derounian it will be, But he will need an assistant to help in the sheer chore of laying the fuses and dealing with the detonators. I don't think that that should be you – you would be better placed helping with the inevitable counter-attack, taking over command in case of the incapacity of my havildar and liasing between the fighting party and the detonating couple."

"Then I suggest Johnson, my assistant. He has the one great virtue that he will carry out to the letter and without question whatever Derounian will ask him to do while they are both down in the tunnel laying the charges."

"Right – so Grant sahib we have the plan complete. You will

be in charge of the two Europeans and will liase with my havildar. I think we will not need for the assault much more than eight men. More than that would be cumbersome and unnecessary, for the assault will depend largely on surprise for success. The less you take with you the less chance of casualties."

"Fine, but that already makes a total of twelve – almost a third of the whole garrison - the havildar in charge, eight men, me and the two in the detonation party. All twelve will be part of the preliminary assault – but then that will leave only ten to hold back any counter-attack while Derounian and Johnson get to work."

The two men grinned at each other – the one too professional to show any concern, the other too amateur fully to appreciate the dangers.

Every detail of the attack was thrashed out for days, using the top of the billiard table until every man knew exactly what he had to do, how long he had to do it and every possible aspect of the plan. The boys, eyes popping with excitement, watched and listened in a corner of the room, totally unaware that blood was going to flow and that excruciating pain was likely to be an associated part of the whole proceedings. The status of both boys had subtly changed. There was not a single man in the room who thought for a moment of getting them to leave for the reason that, as children, their presence was in any way improper. Childhood seemed to have vanished and that too had its effect on the events that were to occur two weeks later.

On the evening of the night on which the attempt was going to be made, John spent the last remaining hours of light on the roof with the ghurkas, watching with his spyglass focussed on the redoubt. He carefully kept track of how many came in and out and how many left once it began to get dark. Once the daylight totally faded he continued to keep watch as best he could on the candles and the shadowy figures seated eating their evening meal round the cooking fires.

At about eleven o'clock he scrambled down the ladder and into the storeroom/kitchen on the lower floor which had become the assembly point for the little force. The group were of course due to clamber out of the Well room at the back , now with its removable wooden beams. John took in the rather bizarre scene - nine Sikhs with black cloth pinned over their turbans and three Europeans with GG still in the process of blackening his face with burnt cork. He reported that in his opinion there were currently about six soldiers in the redoubt. When he had left his post there appeared to be only two sentries, but they were still sitting round the fire and it was unlikely that they could see much until they put the fire out.

The rifles and the ammunition were inspected by Baldour Singh. Dickie fussed with his gunpowder and broke the slightly hushed atmosphere by vociferously arguing the whole time

with Paul, who was continually trying to interfere and give last-minute instructions on the handling of the detonators. Johnson just sat and puffed on his evil-smelling pipe, making no objection when GG began smearing his face with yet another burnt cork. Grant then turned to Dickie to do the same.

"Oh for God's sake GG, what the hell do we need that for?"

"Because, old man, your lily-white face is going to shine out like a great beacon whenever the moon or any other light catches it", replied Grant already smearing the spluttering Dickie with the foul stuff.

"But GG haven't we deliberately chosen a night with little moon?"

"Oh, shut up Dickie – just sit still. You wait and see, once the sepoys are alerted and the shooting starts there is going to be lots of light."

By midnight the expeditionary force was ready. At the last moment George took the decision, agreed to by the Jemadar, that there was no need for Dickie or Johnson to carry a gun as well as the gunpowder and charges already prepared. One or two more or less in the first assault would make little difference, whereas what was the most important element in the whole plan was the speed at which Dickie could place the gunpowder and set the charges.

The whole garrison were up and waiting at their posts along the veranda. Both the boys were detailed to remain in the Well room to be there to lend a hand to anyone tumbling in from outside and to be ready to help in replacing the wooden struts after the last of the assaulting party had returned.

Complicated night attacks are notorious in military lore for producing enormous disasters. However on this occasion there was no fiasco in the attack. – no blundering into each other – no mistaking which was the enemy and which the friend. It helped that every one of the twelve men had been staring for days at the terrain they were to cross. After climbing out of the room quietly the party crept up to the corner of the zenana house and peered round. No one stirred as they shuffled forward in a crouched walk. The night was quiet save for the usual nocturnal animal cries. Dickie, weighed down with all the gunpowder, imagined as he shuffled forward that he was making enough noise to awaken the dead – but still no one moved or cried out.

Then at last, when they were only about ten yards away, there was a piercing cry from the sole sentry leaning against the sandbags. The twelve men themselves now gave a shout, stretched up and began racing forward. The six soldiers in the redoubt – John's estimate was exactly correct – never had a chance. The sentry got off a couple of wild shots which hurt no one; one of the sepoys managed to dive over the sandbags and got away; but the sentry and the other four died from the bayonets of the Sikhs with scarcely a murmur.

The two planners, Baldour Singh and George Grant, had totally overestimated the speed at which the sepoys would react. Candles and lanterns were indeed immediately lit throughout the Hamid Mansion. Fires and more dim lights quickly appeared in the woods and behind trees all round. But nothing actually happened. No one appeared or started firing for what seemed to be an age – certainly for far longer than GG or the Jemadar had anticipated.

However this was fortunate, because they had both badly underestimated the time it would take for Dickie and Johnson to prepare and lay the gunpowder and charges where they would do the most harm. Their first task was to scramble down into the tunnel and go along it as far as possible to lay their furthest charge. But the tunnel had been badly made. It was fairly deep and had been constructed for smaller men than the bulky Derounian and the tall Johnson. Dickie took one look and then immediately called out for some wood or cloth or anything. It was clear that neither the gunpowder to be piled up at the end, nor the long fuses that would be necessary leading back to the entrance, could be laid on the wet floor of the tunnel – there was water everywhere.

There was nothing available – it had to be the coats and tunics of the dead sepoys. Newly dead and with no rigor mortis it did not take long to strip them and hand them down to Johnson, while Dickie himself crawled forward through the pools of water in the suffocatingly small tunnel. The time gained by the incredibly slow reaction of the sepoys now began to expire as shooting broke out both from the Hamid Mansion and from the surrounding trees as the soldiers finally found their muskets and their senses.

The moment that the first sepoys appeared out of the mansion, a huge and noisy fire opened up on them from the fort. No one appeared to get hurt on either side, but the sight and sound of all those musket bullets plunging into the walls and ground around them, as they stepped out, caused the sepoys to stop and shelter until they could be formed into a proper assaulting party by their officers. Meanwhile the Sikhs and GG in the redoubt kept a careful watch on the waking sepoys in the trees around but held their fire until they too began appearing also waiting for orders.

Grant could now see the mansion clearly and both he and the havildar saw the arrival of one of the officers, who began taking the men in hand and preparing for the inevitable counter-attack. It looked to him as if there were already several hundred men gathering, even without counting the men now taking pot-shots from the woods. The havildar thought that there were less, but whether they were one hundred or three made little difference there were now more than enough to overwhelm the little party holding the top of the tunnel. Grant scrambled back and shouted down the tunnel –

"For God's sake Dickie, wherever you are however much you've done, we've got to go – now – now!"

Johnson, who had been holding a candle all this time behind Dickie as he worked, backed slowly out and GG now heard him shouting at Derounian who was still far ahead. The shooting seemed to redouble in sound and fury. The Havildar now shouted back to GG –

"Grant sahib, we are about to be charged. In all this dark there is no way they can be stopped. I am now lighting the flare which will tell the fort that we are about to retreat. For God's sake get Mr. Derounian out of there now. Now!"

Grant turned back in despair and saw to his relief Dickie being dragged out by his feet by Johnson, who miraculously still had his pipe in his mouth, and above all had not lost his grip on his lighted candle, dangerously close to Dickie's trousers.

It was clear that every second counted as Derounian struggled out. He had lost his own candle, but he grabbed Johnson's, then turned and shouted, and at last the stentorian voice came into its own, -

"Out everyone, out – the thing is going to blow in less than thirty seconds," muttering under his breath as he turned back to the tunnel with the candle, "that is if my calculations are right." The Havildar had already lit the signal flare and this had resulted in a burst of really heavy firing from the fort directed at the mansion.

Carefully shielding the candle, Dickie lay down again and stretched the candle down into the hole of the tunnel and lit the more than adequate trail of powder leading back down the tunnel to the far end. He then leapt up and threw himself over the sandbags. He was immediately followed by Johnson, who had loyally waited for him in case, even at this late stage, he needed any help. Everyone else, the Sikhs and GG, were already out racing for the shelter of the fort.

There was a cry of triumph from the sepoys already prepared for a copybook charge, who began pouring forward after the fleeing twelve. The garrison in the fort had stopped firing a few seconds after the flare had been lit and the sepoys raced forward at top speed as fast as the expeditionary force was retreating. The retreat had been rehearsed as thoroughly as the original assault. It had been anticipated that Johnson and Derounian might well be behind the others and in more danger. So as the main party reached the back corner of the zenana house, three of the Sikhs knelt to fire back at the foremost sepoys racing up, while the men in the fort opened up again. Derounian and Johnson came racing past. The others had all thrown themselves over the first wooden beam, already in place, and into the Well room and onto the mattresses placed on the floor. They jumped up, grabbed the other two beams from the boys pushing them aside and stood waiting with these other wooden beams at the ready. Johnson, having raced past the kneeling Sikhs at the corner as arranged, stood by the entrance and once all were in he gave a yell to the three kneeling Sikhs who abandoned their weapons and sprinted back. Johnson pushed each of them through. But the last one, wounded in the leg, was slow. The sepoys had already turned the corner as Johnson pushed him through the open edge. They stopped and opened fire just as Johnson himself made his own leap. The bullet caught him in the back as he tumbled into the room, and as the sepoys came rushing forward.

Then, at last, not much more than Dickie's estimate of thirty seconds, there was an enormous explosion which shook the ground and lit up everything for a short moment. The sepoys outside stopped, but in the Well room the Sikhs, with their adrenalin pumping, fitted the last two wooden beams into place, lifting them as if they were matchsticks, Grant, having stood at the side, continued firing at the stunned sepoys through the opening at the top once Johnson had tumbled in until the moment it finally disappeared.

No one that night could see what damage had been done to the tunnel, but not a man had failed to make it back and the celebrations went on most of the night. But down in the hospital room Dr. Henty worked all night, with an exhausted Conrad by his side, to remove the bullet from Johnson's spine. At the same time he worked to try and save the leg of the wounded Sikh. He refused to accept that Johnson might not survive the trauma of the long operation to remove the bullet and clear up the wound. Furthermore, he found that he could not do much about the leg of the wounded Sikh lying on the other table. His excellent hasty first aid work meant that the Sikh would certainly live – but could he save the leg or would he have to amputate. Henty made sure that no one else was aware of the critical situation for both men. The garrison needed – it was a medical opinion he gave himself – to celebrate this night. The bad news could be absorbed tomorrow.

* * *

"Sir, we cannot just sit here doing nothing. Already we should have reacted as soon as we heard that the bastards had rebelled."

Several other voices were saying much the same thing as old General Lloyd looked round at the Council of War he had himself called. He had been tired and confused ever since the news of that first outbreak in Meerut had reached him two months ago. He did not lack courage, but he did now lack that certainty of command, that capacity to take a decision good or bad and act upon it and to hell with the consequences. He must surely have had it as a young man, he thought to himself, as he looked round at the young men around him. He certainly did not possess that capacity anymore; but this lot all shouting out their opinions had been mere babies when he had undertaken his first charge at the head of sepoys with fixed bayonets. My God, what fine chaps they all were forty years ago – ready to follow him to hell and back. What had happened?

"How long ago was it since they mutinied and left?"

"It has been several days ago now, sir. Heaven knows where the 7th, 8th and 40th have now reached. However, I happen to know that the 68th marched off to Revelkhind and joined up with the 66th."

"I knew that our sepoys would not harm their officers."

"Well, perhaps sir, but that is only because we all knew that a mutiny was looming, and so we acted in a way so as not to be caught off-guard when it happened."

The old general shook his head sadly and mused as the others in the group began arguing with each other as to the best course of action. How could it have come to this? He thought of the battles he had fought with these self-same sepoys right behind him – or wait a moment now he came to think about it, more probably their fathers or uncles. Service with the army of John Company was sought after in the villages of Bengal and Bihar. There was a pride in the regiment, and often when the soldier went on leave during his last period of service he would return with a sixteen-year-old son or nephew whom he would recommend to the commanding officer. The General, musing on, thought of how often the boy would be accepted without question in view of the status of the introducer.

The old General's hearing was not good and he did not hear the comments passing between those junior officers at the other end of the big table –

"the old boy's passed it, the man's in his second childhood,"

"he's done nothing at all, he...."

"we could have stopped the bastards and disarmed the lot before they could take a step off the parade ground – but there were no orders, absolutely nothing was...."

The truth was that General Lloyd had indeed done nothing. This was partly because he was out of his depth and had not known what to do. But there was another reason for his inaction. He thought rather like the thought processes of an Admiral who would not risk his ships unnecessarily on the basis that so long as there was a fleet in being somewhere it would continue to have an effect on an enemy, however strong that enemy was. The moment the fleet ceased to exist, sunk and at the bottom of the sea, it would cease to have any effect at all, however many of the enemy it took down with it.

General Lloyd was conscious, perhaps too much so, that his was the only effective force left between Calcutta and Delhi. So long as he did not fritter away his force of six hundred men in minor romantic actions, the way remained open for the reinforcements coming to Calcutta from Singapore and other imperial possessions to pass through on their way to the disaffected areas.

"Gentlemen, gentlemen, to order. Let me see. We have discussed and agreed all the necessary further defensive measures needed for Dinapore here, and to keep the city of Patna under control. I would like to hear again the proposal put forward by Lieutenant – er – Captain Reith-Davies."

"Thank you sir. As you know, the 68th and the 66th from Revelkhind have joined forces and are besieging a small party of Europeans together with a Sikh police detachment that had been sent to help, holed up in some sort of a bungalow or house in the town of Darabad. I believe, sir, that your first reaction was to refuse to weaken our position here by sending men to relieve them, and...."

"Certainly I remember. Look what happened to Captain Dunbar in his attempt to relieve that other place when I was persuaded to send him with a small relief force."

"Well, yes, but it did get off to a bad start and the ambush into which it blundered could have been avoided. On the way back the steamer bringing them got badly stuck on a mudbank in the river and can't get off. Now, sir, we have another steamer that has just got in with about 150 passengers on board on their way down to Calcutta. Sir, if we commandeered the boat and went off straight away, we could get the first steamer off the mudflats, so that one of the steamers could come back to take on the passengers. Then I, knowing the way well, could guide the rest of us including those on the marooned boat down to the Sayed Ghat, where we could disembark, relieve the besieged in Darabad only five miles or so away and return with them on the steamer. We would have saved one steamer and done much for morale in relieving a garrison in danger. I believe a hundred men would be sufficient."

"But look all of you, this is precisely what I have been trying to avoid all this time – frittering away our strength with one hundred men here and one hundred there."

"Sir," said another voice "this is a party of Europeans that now include, I understand, some women and children, and thirty or forty of our own Sikhs. It is not just a question of honour that is at stake – but morale, sir, morale. That is...."

"There is no need to shout Lieutenant" said Lloyd. "I understand the situation perfectly well, but there are many factors to consider. After all the greatest concentration of non-combatants – women, children and civilians of all types are right here in Dinapore and Patna."

"Sir, are you suggesting that we abandon the stuck steamer, requiring the men left on it to march home, and at the same time show the residents of the district of Shantapur that we are indifferent to the distress of fifty supporters of the Raj besieged in their midst."

There was a long silence. Everything the old General had believed in for the last fifty or so years, all the old loyalties, the old easy-going relationships, all had gone. His will was wavering. He no longer had the courage of his convictions and he was facing the complete certainty of all his officers.

"Very well, Captain, you must take command. Commandeer the steamer that has just arrived, the civilians can be housed in the church hall till the other marooned steamer arrives back. No cannon. I will not risk the loss of any more cannon. This Council is closed."

The General then washed his hands of the matter. He could not see where there was any possible military advantage in sending out a force of 200 or so regular troops to face in the open two to three thousand trained sepoys, only to relieve a group of civilians, who at their own choice happened to be holed up nearby. Of course he was only thinking in terms of a purely narrow military advantage or disadvantage. He was not seeing how the effect of leaving this small group to its inevitable fate at the hands of rebels could turn the whole province of Bihar completely against the Raj. In fairness, however, the young Captains and Lieutenants present at the Council also had no such realisation either. In their minds all they could think of was the forming of a heroic relief force. For them it was indeed exactly the sort of quixotic romantic tilting at the dragon, which the old general deplored and had sought to avoid.

The old general was wrong but for all the right reasons. His young officers were right, but for all the wrong reasons.

The upshot was that after a morning of utter confusion when over a hundred civilians in the steamer tied up in Dinapore were forced off the boat, and one hundred men – a detachment of about 70 British regulars and about 30 Sikhs - clambered aboard. It took almost the rest of the day before this steamer arrived at the spot where the first steamer still lay marooned on the mudflats of the Ganges. It took a further two hours to take all the men off the stuck steamer, and tie up the second steamer to the first. Then with the power of both steamers pulling in reverse, the boats eventually sucked away from the bank. Stores, arms, men and ammunition were now transferred to the commandeered steamer. The old marooned steamer with the wounded on board went back to Dinapore, while the new steamer went carefully on and into the river leading to the Syed Ghat and the abandoned and ruined railway bridge.

Once moored up to the ghat the men came ashore unopposed in the evening. The whole force now numbered over 300 men, 200 British regulars and more than 100 Sikhs. There were no cannon, but it was known that the rebel 66th and 68th regiments also had none.

The force settled down for the rest of the night. It was very quiet and very dark, without much of a moon. They were only at the most six miles away from the zenana house on the other side of Darabad. In the middle of the night the sentries heard the muffled boom of what must have been a large explosion and they saw the flash of a bright light in the sky to the west. But no one else woke and it was ignored until the morning. It was the 8th August - the night of the blowing up of the sepoy tunnel. The siege had now lasted two weeks.

The next morning the relief force moved slowly and carefully forward. The troops on the marooned first steamer had suffered a major ambush in the action they had undertook further north almost a week ago. This had been due to a precipitous advance without all the usual necessary reconnaissance. The young Captain Reith-Davies was determined not to be caught out in the same way, particularly after all the doubts of his senior commander - General Lloyd. Accordingly he advanced by the book, sending out scouts at all points, and carefully guarding his flanks. As they inched forward it was clear that the sepoys were now fully aware of the arrival of this relieving force. Every mango grove, every stream and every small hill, was now being stoutly defended by well-placed and well-drilled soldiers. Without any artillery the relief force could only advance in the slow classic manner: move to the next obstacle: be met by a spirited sheltered defence: exchange fire while looking around for some flanking or sheltering advantage yourself: more firing: then the full bayonet charge yelling at the top of your voice. The enemy often then melted away to the next line of defenses, not much more than a couple of hundred yards further back.

It was obvious that the sepoys were being well led – but then so were the British. Nevertheless, as the force moved slowly forward they were always losing a handful of men each time they advanced. Furthermore, as the hours and days passed and as the little force advanced further down the road towards the town, more men had to be kept in the rearguard so as not to lose contact with the detachment at the Syed Ghat guarding the steamer waiting to take everyone off.

Of course this was not regular warfare. There were no rigid lines through which it was difficult to cross. The captain did send out Sikh observers in an attempt to find out what was going on in the town and try to contact the besieged garrison. But ever since the explosion of the 8th August, the sepoy officers had increased and tightened up their night guard round the little fort and there was no way that any spy could get close enough to speak to anyone in the building. On the other hand they were able to report that the siege was continuing and that the garrison appeared to be holding out.

The same problem of not knowing what was going on was being faced by the defenders in the fort. They too could hear the firing slowly approaching day by day and which soon appeared to be only half a mile away from the town. But with that rear exit now being carefully watched every night, there was no way that they on their part could find out what was happening on the other side of the town.

* * *

No one in the zenana house had slept during that night of the 8th August. All the men who were not on guard duty had celebrated in the crowded billiard room with copious quantities of Dr. Henty's 'medicinal' liquor. No one knew for certain whether the explosion had done the trick, but it had certainly made a lot of noise. Meanwhile, as the celebrations continued on the upper storey, Dr. Henty, with an exhausted Conrad along-side, laboured all night on Johnson's back and the young Sikh's leg. As if in further contrast to the celebrations above, in the opposite corner from the hospital room, the little three-year-old Chloe had had a relapse and had developed a sudden high fever. Harriet, dirty and dishevelled, desperate for her child, had suddenly lost all her will-power and could only sit staring at the little girl for whom she had already sacrificed so much.

Henrietta bustled in and took charge in her bossy but invalu-able way. She brought in drinking water from the fast dimin-ishing pottery jars and a cloth with which she gently mopped Chloe's feverish brow. She talked to the little girl and tried to keep her amused, while Harriet just sat and stared. Finally Henrietta lost patience – probably the best thing she could have done in the circumstances –

"For God's sake Harriet – snap out of it. You are doing no good to anyone sitting there staring. If anything you are making matters worse. The little mite can feel your anxiety. Look, I'll sit here with her. I'll call you immediately if there is any change. For heaven's sake just go away and sit with the others for a bit – and take a glass of brandy. Go on – go on – you're depressing me, never mind what you're doing to your daughter."

Henrietta in full cry was fairly irresistible, and Harriet duly went out, though she did not go upstairs but walked about in the kitchen and soon returned somewhat more ready to face her problems.

The next morning was a Sunday as it happened – perhaps the first Sunday in all her previous adult life that Henrietta ever missed celebrating and worshipping her God. The two sides took stock of the situation as the first light began to arrive from the east. The lovely grounds, already churned up from the assaults, were now in a complete mess. The sandbag redoubt had disappeared and was now a large muddy crater. The whole line of the tunnel, almost up to the zenana house, had collapsed in, in a great mass of earth, wooden supports and above all mud, as the explosion had disturbed the whole water table beneath. It was fairly clear that there could now be little question of any new tunnel.

But the euphoria of the night before drained away very quickly. Somehow the devastation in the ground around them left them all depressed even though it was a consequence and proof of their own success. The news then filtered through that Johnson – the quiet, pipe-smoking, courteous Johnson, - was very ill. His life appeared to have been saved, but Henty reported that he might remain paralysed from the waist down for the rest of his life. Then there was the matter of the shattered leg of the young Sikh. He was in good spirits lying in the hospital and had been visited by many of his friends. But Henty had to inform Baldour Singh privately that he ought to amputate. The doctor doubted that the leg would heal. This would bring about gangrene which in the cramped and unhygienic conditions in which they all lived would almost certainly bring about the lad's death. The Jemadar replied that the decision must be put to the young man himself – but not today – let him rest first. Henty agreed.

On top of all that, the garrison now heard of the returned illness of Chloe. The little girl, padding round the veranda whenever Harriet had allowed it, well protected from any stray bullets by her small size, had become a sort of mascot for the men. The news that the cholera might have struck again, leaving her ill and with a high fever had a further depressing effect.

That Sunday, by no means the most dangerous day spent in the little fort, was nevertheless one of the gloomiest. Yet like a yo-

yo, the very next day the mood changed once again. In the afternoon, the men, standing wearily at their posts exchanging desultory fire with the besiegers, heard for the first time the sound of firing from about three miles away to the east. An excited murmur arose. The roof was the best place from where to judge exactly what may have been happening. But the roof was also the most dangerous spot in the fort. It had become the accepted preserve of the Ghurkas. They were never too pleased to be visited by the large and conspicuous Europeans or Sikhs who, on arrival on the roof, would almost always call down a storm of fire from the Hamid Mansion. Nevertheless, braving their scowls even more than the enemy bullets, GG and Baldour Singh clambered up. Taking shelter where they were advised, they listened carefully. There really was no doubt. The sound of regular and sustained shooting coming from two or three miles away was quite clear. A relief column of some sort was surely on its way.

The news flashed its way round the garrison and chased away all the gloom that had settled on everyone the day after the blowing-up of the tunnel. The atmosphere swung straight back. Relief was on its way – they had not been forgotten. Though their actual physical circumstances had not yet changed, everything was turning more and more on the matter of morale and the new optimism was enormously important. The sounds of approaching relief must mean that the Raj had not as yet fallen. Perhaps it had all been worthwhile. Meanwhile, in addition to the spark of hope, there was also a significant lessening of the daily grind of bullets. Obviously there were at the moment far less numbers crowded around them.

At no time had both mutinous regiments been fully operational against the little fort. Many of the sepoys had melted back into their villages; then there were always some enjoying the comforts of the town or living it up in the surrounding district. The officers never really knew for certain upon how many men they could rely on any particular day. But now, as the danger from the relieving troops of Captain Reith-Davies became generally known, many of the missing men surprisingly returned and rejoined the regiments. The sepoy's opposition to the relief force moving up on the road from the Syed Ghat got tighter and tighter. It was an extraordinary phenomenon. The same two sepoy regiments that had so far failed so dismally to storm the little fort containing less than forty amateur combatants, were putting up a brilliant and effective defence against a professional army of over three hundred men.

As day after day passed the sounds of the firing seemed to get closer, though never decisively so. Then came a day when the firing seemed to be coming from the same spot as the day before, not more than a couple of miles away. The nerves of the little garrison swung alarmingly back to despondency. It was as if each mood swing got wilder and wilder like a pendulum increasing its swing on each turn. Finally came the next day when there was an ominous silence from the direction of the town – all firing seemed to have ceased or was too far away to be heard. It seemed to be absolutely vital that they found out exactly what was happening.

On that very morning when, straining their ears as much as they could, they could no longer hear anything, Johnson died. Henty was beside himself with a sort of professional rage. Then right on cue, as if the fates were determined to pile on the agony for him, gangrene set in above the knee of the shattered leg of the young Sikh. There had never been much quinine in Henty's stock and if the leg was to be amputated it would have to be without any anaesthetics. He hated having to do it and of course the poor lad hated it even more and appealed to his comrades. But everyone could see that death was the only other option. Screaming and cursing the boy was physically held down as Henty sawed and hacked at the groin. He had decided that Conrad was not to be present on this occasion, but after the butchery was done he dismissed the four burly men who had held the boy down and called for Conrad to come and help him with the sewing and bandaging. The young man had thankfully lost consciousness as his leg came off and the dreadful screams had stopped. Crutches were fashioned for him for when he came round and recovered. The garrison was fast coming down below forty effectives.

It began to seem imperative for the wavering morale of the garrison to know exactly what was happening on the road leading from the Sayed Ghat to the town. The euphoria that had arisen with the thought of relief had given way to an equally extreme despair. Had a relief of the siege really been attempted, or was it all a fantasy? If there had indeed been some attempt at relief, was it still under way? On the day after the death of Johnson, the whispering at night with offers to the Sikhs to deliver up the fort started up again and GG began to feel that a crisis was approaching and that it was up to him to deal with it.

The problem was that the exit from the back of the building, out and over the timbered section of the half window of the Well room was now no longer available. Since the sortie on the night of the capture of the redoubt and the blowing-up of the tunnel, it was clear that some sort of watch was now being kept every night on that potential exit. It was of course a question of how efficient such a watch would be, and GG considered that despite the risk there might be a possibility of one of the Ghurkas slipping out over the top at the dead of night and making an attempt to find out what was happening. Grant realised that it was really not feasible. Even if he managed to get out unobserved, he would not be able to converse with anyone or be seen in the town or get any information, and in any case could never get back again to report his findings..

It was while GG was in this frame of mind that a series of events now unfolded in a way that caused him to take a step which would give him more mental anguish than during the worst moments of the siege to date.

* * *

It all started with Henty having a quick ad hoc chat with GG as he made his rounds, suggesting that he might have a word with Conrad and give him some official-sounding praise for the really hard and tiring work that he had been carrying out in the hospital. GG readily agreed and had gone round almost immediately to the boy's room in the other corner. As chance would have it, Marietta was away with Henrietta. They were ministering to Chloe, the distraught Harriet again being persuaded to leave the bedside for a short break. Conrad and Ali were in the room together resting on their shared bed. Occasional shots were being exchanged outside as always, but everyone had got used to this and only silence would have caused any worry. The boys stood up when Grant came into the room.

"Ah – Conrad – I've come to tell you what a good job you've been doing helping the doctor. Everybody is really proud of you – a true brave English soldier doing his duty."

GG could really be most dreadfully pompous. But Conrad blushed with pleasure and shuffled his feet. Grant, complete extrovert though he was, was no fool and he immediately added –

"Ali, too, you've been invaluable. Both of you deserve to get some sort of medal after all this. That is if we get through it all."

"Did all that shooting on the other side of the town mean that there was a relief column coming, sir?" said Conrad.

"I just don't know – I just don't know. It's very frustrating. I'd give anything to know what is happening. But there is no way for anyone to be able to slip out and find out about that relief force or whatever it was."

"Sahib, if there was such a way, do you believe it would be really important to get the information."

"Why yes, Ali, certainly."

By this point Grant had already lost sight of the fact that he was talking to two twelve-year-old boys. Having been aware of Ali running round for three weeks ignoring the bullets and the noise, feeding the men and acting just like one of the rest of the garrison, he had reached the stage where he saw Ali as no different than one of the Ghurkas. He continued to muse out loud, talking to the 'two men' about morale and the importance of knowing what was happening beyond these four walls.

Ali and Conrad, already thrilled by the praise heaped on them by the man they thought of as the overall commander, looked at each other. Conrad nodded and Ali said the words that begun the chain of events which George Grant was to come to regret so much.

"But Sahib – there is a way that one of us could slip out and report back to you."

"What are you talking about lad?"

"See sir," said Conrad eagerly. He went over to the corner and pulled the mattress away, disclosing the broken bricks of the drain that they had discovered all those weeks ago.

"Good God – what is it?"

"Sir, it is a drain of some sort. We have explored it thoroughly before and removed all the debris blocking it. It goes off for about twenty yards and comes out right over the stream over there in the jungle. That exit was not uncovered when father cut back the jungle growth. It is quite safe – we have been down it several times and when you get to the other end it is easy to peep out and make sure there is no one around."

Anything at all, any little thing, might have given that vital pause that was needed. If Marietta had returned; or if Conrad had used the word 'dad' rather than the word 'father'; or if he had not at that moment turned away and crouched down to put on his shoes. Instead it was Ali who took over and said –

"Sahib, if it would be really useful, I could slip out right now. I'll make sure that no one is around when I move away the brushwood at the entrance to the drain at the stream. I could creep round to the town – I know the way well. I can find out exactly what is happening and I could get back easily before it gets light tomorrow morning."

"But...."

"There is no fear that I could give away the existence of the drain. It is much too small and narrow for any adult even to get in. Even I have difficulty wriggling through."

A combination of factors now led inexorably to GG's fatal decision which led to the desperate events that followed. First there was his own character, which contained within it a sort of adolescent irresponsibility. This led him, on the positive side, to be a natural and decisive commander ready to take quick decisions and stick to them. However, it also led him into a romantic, thoughtless, gung-ho recklessness as well. Then, there was the fact that Grant had already perceived the boys as if they were one of the adult soldiers in the fort. He completely forgot that he was actually still talking only to a boy. Finally and fatally there was also an element of class and racial arrogance. He was a product of his times and he saw Ali as only a servant – a cook-boy – who, while clearly Eurasian, was nevertheless only a native – a servant to be ordered to carry out tasks. Conrad, sitting in the corner tying up his shoes, was no longer even in his vision. He became excited.

"Could you really do it Ali?"

"Certainly, sahib, but what exactly do you want me to do?"

"Listen – be very careful. Don't whatever you do wriggle out at the other end until you are absolutely sure no one is around. Work your way round in order to approach the town from the south. It is still fairly early so there should be a lot of people still around. Be very careful and find out what you can about what is happening on the Syed Ghat road. If you get the chance see also if you can pick up any gossip about what is happening in the district."

"Yes sahib. I will avoid people who might know me."

"Be careful – don't stay out once people start going to bed and the streets begin to empty. Creep back here whether you've got any information or not. My God this is a great chance."

"Sahib, you will have to arrange for someone else to deal with the meal tonight."

"You're right – you're right. I'll go and get Marietta to take over. Let me see – can you still get down there – it looks dreadfully small."

Ali opened the hole and then wriggled down headfirst into the sloping drain. The last that Grant saw of the boy was his wiry brown legs swaying and kicking in the air as his body inched forward. It was possible even then that if Grant had stayed for just half a minute he would have heard Ali call out from under the ground –

"Light the candle Conrad"

If he had heard, it might even at this last moment have

brought his mind to the realisation of what he was setting up.
But he did not hear. Instead he in fact made his final move which
set the seal for the drama that was going to break the unity of the
garrison, which had so far been its greatest strength. Without
another word, muttering about seeing Marietta about the
evening meal, he turned on his heel as he saw Ali's bare feet
wriggling down the drain, and strode out of the room.

What followed had an inevitability about it which, in any
other circumstances, a reasonable adult would have realised at
once. Conrad, who had now managed to do up his shoes, stood
up and without giving it a second thought got hold of one of the
candles they had been using before and which they had left
hidden under the bricks. He had heard Ali calling out to him to
'light the candle', and he knew surely that GG had heard as well
and had said nothing but had walked out. The Lucifer matches
kept carefully for just this purpose fired immediately. The
passage through and down the narrow drain was quite straight,
but it was frankly scary without the feeble light of the flickering
candle coming up from behind. The boys had wriggled through
many times during their explorations in the previous months
and were aware of the importance of the comfort of having the
man behind with the candle – always well back, but always able
to come forward and grab hold of a kicking leg if there should be
any trouble.

Conrad was not being the slightest bit mischievous or disobe-
dient or thoughtless. No one had said that he was not to go with
his friend – and his friend had called out in the presence of an
adult for him to bring the candle. They had done this many
times before. It simply never crossed Conrad's mind that the
adult who had urged his friend on to the venture would have
been horrified if he had realised what it might lead to.

So he called out down the drain, holding the lit candle before
him –

"Here it is Ali – I'm right behind you. Wait for me when you
get to the end."

With that, he too went down headfirst into the drain, holding
the candle carefully in front of him as they had done so often in

the past. He wriggled forward, still, despite his thinning body, with a good deal more difficulty than the naturally wiry Ali. The room behind them lay quiet and empty.

* * *

Like most English men in British India in the eighteen-fifties Captain Reith-Davies was young. He had impossible romantic dreams about dashing and courageous young men riding to the rescue of women in distress. But he had not achieved the rank of Captain over and above all the other eager young Lieutenants in his peer group for nothing.

As each day had passed since the night of the explosion the odds against his little detachment breaking through to Darabad got longer and longer. He was not blind to the military realities and he began to consider for the first time the likelihood that the drive to relieve the garrison at Darabad might not after all be possible. An attack on the small detachment of about thirty men that he had stationed at the Syed Ghat to protect the steamer still moored there had already taken place. It had been beaten off fairly easily, but meanwhile his already small force was losing men at each attempt to break through the stubborn defense of the sepoys. This was what these regular soldiers of the East India Company army were trained for and good at – open defensive warfare in prepared positions against other soldiers.

Furthermore, as he considered his options, there was another thought at the back of the young man's mind. What if he did break through into the town? He could not simply remain there, he would have to withdraw, bringing with him with what was left of the garrison. His imagination pictured the spectre of having to escort defenceless women and pathetic children - how wrong he was - all trying to make their way back to the dubious safety of the steamer at the Syed Ghat.

He saw that he had to husband his already dwindling human resources and this meant that he could not risk squandering the lives of the men under his command to the point that he would have difficulty retreating. Inevitably, this meant that his attacks on the defending sepoys became more carefully planned, more dependent on complicated and time-consuming flanking movements. Against the rebel sepoys, this was in the long run less effective than the usual ear-splitting charge with cold steel that had won so many battles in nineteenth century India before. He also had to be more wary of his line of retreat and the security of the men guarding the Syed Ghat.

But to abandon the enterprise entirely was too much for him. How could he possibly abandon 'those poor fellows over there' in order to cut his losses and turn back? It was just not the action of a gentleman and an officer.

However, as more and more men of the two regiments filtered back from their villages to rejoin their regiment, the decision was being taken out of his hands. With only a mere two hundred or so men now maintaining the siege over Tate's fort, the officers of the two regiments, now commanding over 1,000 fully armed men, decided that the time had come to mount their own offensive. They did it carefully following to the letter all the manuals. They made the most of their overwhelming numbers by also sending a force away from the road and towards the Syed Ghat. The intention was for them to get between the men of the main British force, now only half a mile away from Darabad, and their comrades at the River.

The attack, when it came, was a conventional daytime assault. The two regiments started off, unwisely, with a prepared advance. The British and the Sikhs stood firm, now firing from their own defensive lines. There was the usual slaughter where 'rifled guns' with ranges of up to a thousand yards met advancing infantry and the sepoys fell back. But the infiltration on the flanks was growing. Young Reith-Davies, still beardless but with a thin moustache, could see back down the road for quite a long way. There were sepoys behind him reaching the road and he could now hear shots coming from the Syed Ghat. His position was becoming hopeless and a military disaster was in the making if he remained. He gave the order for a retreat.

For once it went according to the textbooks. First the British troops knelt and stood holding the line as the Sikhs with the supply wagons in their midst went through. Then they in their turn stopped and knelt holding the new line as the British regulars went through. And so it went on with no counterattack from the flanks until they reached the top of the Rajiv hill from where they could look down on the River and the Syed Ghat, where the steamer still stood calmly at anchor and intact.

This position was held for some time as Reith-Davies and his two young lieutenants took stock. They had now retreated over three miles back from the outskirts of the town without many losses – but there had been some. The two lieutenants were all for making a stand where they were. It was a good defensive position and they could pose a threat, though somewhat remote now with such a small force, to the mutineers in Darabad. At the same time they would be in a position to defend the Syed Ghat, and the steamer, their ultimate escape route. From their point of view it was always the same argument –

"How can you think, sir, of abandoning all those chaps fighting for their lives?"

But military command was as much about knowing when to abandon a failed plan as making the plan in the first place. Simply sitting on the top of the hill, neither being able to move forward nor choosing to move back, made no military sense and Reith-Davies knew it. At least back in Dinapore, cannon could be added to the force, more supplies obtained and a new attempt might be made. He ordered a retreat to the River. Efficiently and with a minimum of fuss the men carefully retreated again without losing cohesion or a single wagonload of supplies. The mutineers followed shooting at everything as the men embarked, but the two hundred yards range muskets were simply unable to cope with the Lee Enfields, which again took many lives.

The sepoys were quite unable to prevent the steamer, already belching out thick black smoke from its single funnel, from slipping away. It turned and swung down the River to go back to the Ganges and Dinapore. But the attempt at a relief was over. An ominous silence now arose over the whole area –the silence which had so worried GG and the rest of the garrison on that same day.

The numbers involved in this attempt to relieve the belea-
guered garrison in Darabad were never completely clear.
Certainly the relief force had set out the week before with a
minimum of three hundred men, two hundred British and one
hundred Sikhs. But there were sure to have been extras and
volunteers, particularly among the Sikhs who had friends and
even relatives holed up in the zenana house. About two hundred
men returned to disembark from the boat when it reached
Dinapore. More than one hundred men, therefore, must have
died on this escapade.

General Lloyd was right – a small-scale attack of this kind
without cannon would not work and would simply fritter away
resources. But he was also quite wrong. The whole district of
Shantapur was fully aware of the failure of the mutineers to
dispose of the little garrison in Darabad. If the British had done
nothing at all, the adverse effect on imperial prestige, already
wavering, would have been considerable.

But, meanwhile, the siege was set to continue. The garrison
knew nothing of what had happened, and it was this that had led
to the dangerous departure of the two boys.

* * *

An unusual, unrecognised, aspect of having over forty souls
living together day and night in a confined space like that of the
zenana house was that people tended to lose sight of each other.
Where every room, every corridor, every space was filled with
people – standing or sitting or lying on the floor - a sort of filter
descended which allowed you to wander around, sifting out the
terrible crush otherwise pressing on your senses.

It was this perhaps which accounted for the fact that the
absence of the two boys from the little building was not noticed
for about three hours. Marietta duly produced the evening rice
and dhal mixed with some chutney. She had taken it round
herself. Without any one helping it had taken her much longer
than Ali and Conrad usually managed and Dickie who was on
sentry duty for the first three hours of the evening was one of the

last to be served.

"Where's Ali then this evening," he said as he took one of the eight plates which had to make do for all and began eating.

"I don't know, Mr. Derounian. I haven't seen him around. Mr Grant told me to prepare the meal this evening."

"Oh well, I suppose he's not well or something."

But Dickie, after finishing and giving his plate back to Marietta as she returned, began considering that after all he had not seen the boy for some hours. By now even the most defiantly civilian of the Europeans felt themselves to be good soldiers and Dickie was no exception. He was not going to abandon his post until he was properly relieved by the next guard on the rota, and this was due at 10.00pm in only a few minutes. But once his relief turned up, he immediately hurried down to the boy's room in the corner – to find it empty.

Dickie was not the most imaginative of men, but he was observant and he immediately saw what appeared to be the uncovered opening to a large drain in the far corner which he had never seen before. He stood staring at it wondering what it could possibly mean. He had left the door open and as he stood he was aware of Marietta in the kitchen outside.

"Mrs. Postern," he called out in a voice now a little hoarse with anxiety. "Could you please go and ask Mr. Grant to come down here as quickly as possible."

Grant, meanwhile, had been fairly active ever since he had left the boy's room. But the little task that he had set for Ali had not slipped his mind and he had already decided that once his chores were completed he would return and spend the rest of the evening with Conrad waiting for Ali's return. When he got Marietta's message he immediately hurried down thinking that Ali must have already returned.

"Grant – can you tell me where Ali has got to," said Dickie the moment GG appeared.

"Ah! Derounian, I've been meaning to tell you but you were on duty and I missed the chance. He volunteered to slip away and find out for us what may have happened to the relief force. I reckon he will be back soon."

Dickie stared at him totally lost for words perhaps for the first time in his adult life. His mouth opened and shut like a fish. GG, noticing nothing at all, went into a long explanation about the drain, Ali's experience and understanding of the position and finally the importance to everyone in the garrison of knowing exactly what was happening to the relief force.

"You blithering great stupid idiot," shouted Dickie, suddenly getting his voice back. "What were you thinking about? The boy is only twelve years old. You've sent him out into that hornet's nest....at his age...."

Dickie was beside himself with rage. His fists were clenched and his face, usually pale and sallow, had gone completely red. He began shouting again, cursing – and of course his voice was as always too loud. Only Marietta was in the kitchen and there was no way that she was going to intervene in what was shaping up to be a major quarrel as GG tried to explain while Dickie got more and more incoherent. But along the corridor was the little room of the Tates in the other corner. Here John and Harriet were lying in the dark, hoping that Chloe would not wake up from her first unbroken sleep for some days. John quietly rose, tiptoed out of the room and came walking down to where the shouting was coming from.

"For God's sake fellows," he said. "Can't you keep it down."

"John, John," spluttered Dickie, only with difficulty managing to speak coherently. "This bloody idiot has allowed – no probably encouraged - Ali to wriggle down that thing there....that drain or whatever it is....in order to go and get some information about what is happening out there to the relief force. It seems that the boys had been using it as a game before all this trouble began. The fool....the lad is only twelve. He'll be caught – my God he 'll be tortured. What right do you have man, what right?"

"Look, he volunteered. He showed me the route and it is clear that only a boy can use it. This is vital information that we need....life and death circumstances....he is in it like all the rest of us. He's one of the garrison – a soldier."

"You pompous idiot – he's twelve – only twelve."

"He's his own man. He has no father whom I could approach.

He was ready to...."

At this something snapped in Dickie's mind and it showed in his face. The anger, the sheer hatred that shone out of his face made GG take a step back, and caused John to catch his breath and hold himself ready to intervene to restrain the man in case he resorted to violence.

"You bloody fool! I'm his father. I'm his useless pathetic father. He should have relied on me – my protection – but you...you...you tricked him like a..."

Derounian put his head in his hands. Unquestionably, a moment before, he was about to go for GG to punch him in the face. What prevented the whole matter descending into fisticuffs was that a wave of the sharpest guilt washed over him. Dickie had always assumed that everyone had long since come to realise that Ali, clearly a Eurasian, was the illegitimate fruit of his own loins with an Indian mistress. He suddenly became conscious that it was his own failure, his selfish negligence in not openly acknowledging the relationship that may have contributed to GG's failure to consult anyone. Dickie sank to the floor and squatted on his heels muttering –

"He's only twelve....he's only twelve."

John, whose first reaction had been simply to stand close to Dickie to restrain him in case he lashed out, staring at GG with a dawning horror, said

"For God's sake, George, where is Conrad?"

"What. Oh no – I left him here to wait for Ali's return."

John turned and ran out. There was a silence in the little room. It was however really already clear. It did not need Tate's frantic rush all round the fort. Conrad too must have gone out with Ali down the drain. Until that moment GG had really not felt that he had acted in any way unreasonably. Native boys matured fast. There were plenty of twelve-year-old drummer boys in the British Indian army. How was he to have known that Dickie was the boy's father ... and so on... and so on. But the unpleasant fact was that as soon as it became clear that Conrad had also gone with Ali he came face up to the fact that while not directly ordering anyone, he had connived at sending two twelve-year-old boys out into terrible danger. Furthermore there was nothing, absolutely nothing, that he or anyone else in the garrison could do about it.

John returned, white as a sheet, and in a state of despair said, without shouting –

"George – even if it was never your intention that Conrad should go out, how could you have left him alone in this room supposedly to wait for the return of his best friend. It's no use talking about the requirements of Empire, or that everyone must play their part, or all that 'stiff upper lip' nonsense. These two were only twelve, neither of them even in their teens. For God's sake Grant, his white face is going to stand out like a great shining beacon."

"Tate…. I never thought for a moment that the boy would follow Ali. I never intended….Oh, heavens, Derounian, believe me I had no idea that Ali was your…."

At this point John too sank to the floor, leaning back against the wall and stretching out his legs, ready to wait all night in the hope that the boys would shortly return. Dickie took his head out of his hands. He looked up at Grant and using his first name, probably for the very first time, he said quietly, almost a whisper for him –

"George, please go – leave us. We'll wait here for the boys to return. Just go – there's a good chap."

Grant looked at the two men for a moment and then turned and walked briskly out.

For some time the two fathers sat side by side with their legs stretched before them saying nothing – but it was not a comfortable silence. The fear for the safety of their sons preyed hard on their minds and in the end they had to talk about the boy's chances – like picking at a sore until it bled. They went through every possible scenario, inevitably getting more and more despondent. But this could not go on for ever, and it then opened up other thoughts -

"But Dickie, old man, why Ali? I think we all knew that Ali must have had a European father – but why the name Ali? It made it very confusing – particularly seeing him in church with you as well."

"It's difficult to explain, John. It was the name his mother wanted – but I accept completely that in the end the decision was entirely mine. On the positive side I really did and still do feel that all the Portuguese or English Christian names given to these mixed race kids don't help them in the snobbish and segregated society in which we live. The Europeans snigger with snide remarks about ' a touch of the tarbrush don't ya know'. The Indians draw away from any human warmth or contact due to stupid fears about loss of their precious caste if they even talk to him."

"But what about religion? What religion were you...."

"Oh God, John, religion is the worst of all. Everything in this bloody country comes down to that doesn't it. The whole country reeks of cloying spirituality. On the one hand there is an enormous amount of horror and violence and sheer misery spewed out in the name of one or another of the three intolerant Semitic religions. Then on the other hand there is the same misery that stems from the other side's bloody stupid caste rules and regulations. I despise them, I despise them all."

"Oh Dickie – it's not quite that bad surely, don't take your frustration out on the priests, mullahs, rabbis or gurus or whatever. In any case that still doesn't entirely explain the decision you made of the name - Ali."

"I know, I know. I can't deny that there is a negative side to my decision of which I am now deeply ashamed. If I gave him an Armenian Christian name like Paul or Petros, I would be trumpeting my parenthood. The Calcutta Armenian community is even worse than the British in rejecting anyone marrying out. I was weak – I didn't want the trouble, so I didn't marry and I never openly acknowledged the little boy. And so the boy has gone to his death without the protection on which he should have been able to rely that of his father – his own father...."

It was all too much. Dickie's head slumped even further. John struggled hard against a lifetime of emotional restraint. To his eternal credit he overcame it and stretched his arm round the man's back and held him tight. And so they sat and waited.

* * *

The successful defence of the road from the Syed Ghat to Darabad, together with the return of many of the original mutineers from the countryside, boosted the morale of the two besieging regiments. The sepoy officers felt a return of confidence. They were well aware that they had not been facing the whole of the Dinapore garrison, but nevertheless it was a victory of sorts and they trumpeted it around the district accordingly.

Saridar Khan, meanwhile, had been finding that his return to a life of ease and pleasure in his old palace did not seem to satisfy him anymore. The one hunt that he managed to organise lacked any excitement or flavour. In the backwater of Jagpur he had no means of finding out what was happening in the rest of India, and somehow the days of eating good food, the occasional hunt and cavorting with his younger wives no longer seemed to give him as much satisfaction as before.

As the days passed, he tried but found it impossible to analyse his own reactions. He knew that he was certainly not having any stirring of any thoughts about the independence of some new independent state that he might form. He had never been taken in by the talk from Haidar Presaud of the rise of a new state of Jagpur. Nor was there any question of him hankering after the military exploits of his past warlike ancestors. He knew well that that was not in his nature. So what was it that led him to take the step of leaving his life of ease and comfort, saying farewell to his adoring wives, and returning to Darabad to rejoin the sepoy regiments he actually despised.

He never quite worked it out for himself. There was an element of wanting to be where there was some positive action going on. He had felt isolated and alone back in his crumbling palace in Jagpur, and to tell the truth he had also felt a little afraid. Though he considered that he had in reality done little to call down the wrath of the British if they ever returned, nevertheless he began worrying how his actions could be misrepresented if he was not around to explain. He was in a complete dilemma and he could not decide whether to make his way to Patna and throw himself on the mercy of the Commissioner – Mr. Taylor, or stay shivering in his palace until something turned up. But there was a third alternative - to go back and rejoin the mutineers where he would be physically protected, would know what was going on, and would at least earn the admiring approbation of all his wives.

Whatever the true motivation in his mind, the day after he received the news of the defeat and retreat of the relieving force of Captain Reith-Davies, he set off immediately in the state carriage with Sunitra, his youngest wife, in tow. He was followed by a small train of oxcarts, which contained some gifts for the sepoy officers, some comfortable furniture for the da Costa house, and above all carrying his cook with his spices and chutneys

He was met at the outskirts of the town by all six officers of the two regiments. With them riding alongside, he made an impressive entry into the town. The officers, still anxious to retain some semblance of political legality for their actions, organised to have the maidan flanked by two lines of ceremonially dressed soldiers standing at attention and fully armed. But their efforts to get the local populace to stand behind them, hopefully to wave and shout, was a complete fiasco. Apart from a few ragged bands of boys who were always on the streets in any case, the population of Darabad gave an enormous yawn to the whole affair. The Nawab himself was not aware of this. He had not expected any sort of formal welcome anyway. He was pleased by the military reception and was in a surprisingly good mood as he emerged from his carriage. He was even more elated, when he looked up at the da Costa house and saw down the side the unmistakeable lines of the state elephant of Jagpur wandering contentedly in the large back garden.

"Jemadar – is that my elephant?"

"Certainly, your Excellency."

"Well, well – what happened? How come it is here?"

"Your Excellency, I believe you received our report about the unfortunate death of the Mahout and the failure of our attempted assault on that third day. The death of his old friend and trainer affected the beast badly and he ran off into the woods. He was pursued by the many bullets fired at him by the heartless enemy, but these failed to kill him or even to harm him much. Eventually he was found and brought back to the town. We placed him here in the back garden of your residence. He is being looked after by the junior mahout."

Saridar made no comment on the Jemadar's statement that the bullets which caused the beast to panic and run off had been fired by the enemy from the fort. His own private information from others who were present suggested that it was the sepoy officers who had ordered the hail of bullets in an attempt to fulfil the plan of having the old animal die directly onto the building. However, he said nothing but strode into the house, where all Alphonsine's staff were at the door bowing and scraping.

The Nawab was not so happy then to find that Haidar Presaud had also settled into the da Costa house himself while he had been away. Haidar hurried up as Saridar Khan arrived and gave a grand salaam with a deep bow –

"Your Excellency it is pure pleasure for me to feast my eyes again on the person of the Nawab of Jagpur and to welcome him to the bosom of his devoted army, ready at a command to do his bidding."

It was not clear which of the people listening to this little speech was the closest to being sick. The Nawab together with the Jemadar were a close equal second, but undoubtedly the one most likely to vomit with disgust was Haidar himself. Everything had turned to wormwood in his hands. First the Nawab had not turned out to be the dynamic leader thirsting to set up a new independent power in Bihar. Then the sepoys of the two regiments had themselves turned out to have their own agenda and were in no way under his control or even influence. Finally he was beginning to receive disturbing news from his spies and commercial contacts that the British Raj might not after all be on the point of collapse. It appeared that they were completely secure in both the Madras and Bombay presidencies and were even beginning to make a come-back here in North India. Having urged these men to revolt he was now beginning to think of ways to distance himself from the whole affair.

A formal council was now clearly necessary and the Nawab decided that it should take place immediately. The senior Subadar gave a report in which he referred to the four assaults that had already been made against the zenana house. He referred to these as - the rabble assault – the first formal assault – the cannon assault – the elephant assault. He explained the difficulties and above all the fact that they had no cannon. He crowed over the ability of the two regiments to hold back the relief expedition, not dwelling in any way of course on the disparity of the numbers involved.. He failed to be able to explain why the two regiments had succeeded in driving back the Relief force while being unable to dislodge a handful of men from a mere fortified house.

Once again the issue of a march to Delhi was raised. But by now it was clear that as most of the men had families nearby they would be increasingly loathe to move away. The sepoy officers did not have the information that the wily Haidar was receiving. There were so many contradictory rumours as to what was happening in the rest of Hindustan that every bit of news was discounted unless it could be verified personally. Above all there was a provincial and local attitude that applied to everyone at the council except Haidar, who was the only one present who was aware of the bigger picture. Even the fairly well-educated Saridar tended to see things very much from a purely provincial viewpoint. It was Jagpur first, Shantapur district next, Bihar far behind, with no thought of India as a whole at all.

And so it was that sheer inertia triumphed. The sepoy officers agreed that the siege would continue on the basis that it was unlikely that the little garrison would be able to hold out much longer. Haidar Presaud suggested that, now the Nawab was personally present again, the cause would be better served if he himself returned to Patna. He raised the possibility of the clandestine procurement of some cannon capable of smashing the flimsy brick walls of the fort. This was enough to get the sepoy officers interested. At the same time Saridar Khan jumped at the chance of getting rid of a man whom he had come to dislike.

Accordingly it was agreed that Haidar was to leave that very afternoon and make an attempt to obtain the cannon he believed existed and which was available for direct purchase. If he succeeded it would mean the end of the garrison once and for all.

* * *

Ali reached the end of the drain well before Conrad could arrive. The flickering candle behind him had been the usual comfort as he wriggled forward. Conrad took much longer to arrive breathless behind him. He was now relatively thinner but was nevertheless stouter than Ali and had more difficulty pushing his way through the drain. He also had to hold the candle ahead of him as he struggled through. However, eventually there they were together. The candle was extinguished, and it and the sulphur matches were set below a stone. Ali grinning back at Conrad slowly and carefully pushed aside the shrubs and stones hiding the entrance. They waited while they got used to the darkness of the outside. Only Ali, of course, could see out – there was no room at all for Conrad who remained behind his friend as Ali peered out, wriggling himself forward so that he could look carefully all round. The stream below him was low and flowing only sluggishly.

"It's all clear Conrad – but be very quiet," he whispered back and slid forward only just managing to stop himself before slipping into the muddy stream. This did him no good, however, as Conrad anxious to get out of the drain slid straight out after him and right onto him as he was struggling to rise. This had the effect of braking Conrad temporarily, but pushed the hapless Ali right into the mud and water of the little stream. Ali, dripping with mud and water scrambled up onto his feet and this then had the effect of causing Conrad who was still lying chuckling on the bank to slip down further himself and end up in the muddy water of the stream.

Both boys in their efforts to stop giggling out loud hiccoughed and spluttered. Neither boy had the slightest realisation of the danger they were in. Conrad, throughout the whole of his twelve years of childhood had always felt completely safe in the Indian environment in which he had been brought up, indeed far safer than any boy of his age would have felt in the streets of Victorian London. Ali was more fearful, but only with the excitement of the coming 'adventure'. Both boys were in the habit of trusting adults – and this was after all clearly an adult-supported expedition. They were not stupid or completely thoughtless. They knew it was important not to be caught. What they did not know or even contemplate was the terrible possibility of torture and death that being caught might mean.

Their first task was to stretch up the bank and replace the shrubs and stones hiding the opening of the drain. They then splashed across the little stream and melted into the jungle beyond. Keeping the Hamid Mansion in their sights to the left they wound their way round and eventually into the back of the town coming in from the south road. As GG had worked out there were plenty of people about in the maze of little alleys to the south of the maidan. It was at this stage as they wandered into the town that the boys had their first misgivings. Hunkering down in a little doorway, they began considering their options.

"Oh dear Conrad, it's a good thing that you fell into that muddy stream. The town is big enough so that not everybody knows everybody, but nevertheless you do stand out a bit. Why do people say 'white' when actually your face is red?"

"That's only because we've been pushing our way through woods. You know well enough that I get red when....oh shut up. You are right though. There are still likely to be some of the boys about who would know us from our fights in the past. Do you think they would tell on us?"

"What do you mean 'tell on us' – we're not in some English boarding school."

"Oh come on Ali you know what I mean – would they raise some sort of alarm and go and tell the soldiers?"

"Of course they would. Look – let's wait a bit until the kids go home for their evening meal or whatever. Then we can approach some adult or other who doesn't know us and ask him about the relief force and find out what has happened to it."

Conrad grinned at Ali's use of the word 'kids' to refer to the other boys, almost all of whom would have been bigger and older than Ali. In any event that is what they did – keeping themselves as inconspicuous as possible, they wandered round for about an hour squatting here and there and moving on when they felt they might be attracting attention. Eventually they felt it to be safe to start approaching the occasional single man walking in the street. Most simply ignored Ali completely and strode on. Nevertheless, by being very careful who they chose to approach and moving off quickly if they ever started receiving awkward questions themselves, they managed to piece together exactly what had happened on the road to the Syed Ghat and that the British had now been forced to withdraw.

Ali had done all the talking while Conrad had shuffled about in the background keeping his face turned away. The dirt and mud of the stream had helped to keep him inconspicuous. His knowledge of the local dialect was as good as Ali's and between them they could work out exactly what the men were saying.

It was getting late. The streets were emptying and the boys decided that they had found out enough. Everything seemed to be turning out as GG had anticipated. They sidled their way down the south road and turned off to the right and back into the jungle to the west. They could see that there was a good deal more activity as they passed the Hamid Mansion than when they had left in the heat of the late afternoon but they pressed on. It was a good thing that they had done the trip several times before, as returning to find the entrance to the drain was a good deal more difficult than leaving and going to the town. Twice they had to stop for a whispered consultation as to which way to go. But eventually they reached the stream and recognised trees and objects. They relaxed and pressed on a little faster following the stream to the point where they could cross and wriggle back into the drain.

They had almost reached that point and were about to plunge into the stream when they saw a small party of sepoys sitting sprawled about on the other side of the mud – away from the hidden drain but within sight and earshot. Had they not relaxed just that shade too much as they recognised the end of their adventure, all might still have been well – but they were making more noise than before. Two of the men who were lying down and smoking sat up and stared towards them and then shouted out getting up onto their feet.

The boys were not to know that ever since the sortie from the back of the zenana resulting in the exploding of the sepoy's tunnel a guard of about six men was posted each night to stay on watch, keeping the back of the little fort in view from about 11.00pm until the dawn of the next day. At the shout the boys panicked and turned to run, not now caring about noise. The shouts continued pursuing them, and they both had visions of a horde of sabre-bearing soldiers chasing them. But as it happens the two sepoys had seen even in the dark that they were only boys – children, and assumed them to be kids from the town creeping through the woods simply out of mischievous curiosity. Nevertheless they yelled curses at what they thought of as two scamps from the town, but did not chase them. Laughing at the cheek shown by these urchins, they settled down again for the night's vigil.

In some ways the boy's panic and noisy dash away through the undergrowth was probably the best thing they could have done. They had been seen and if they had tried to creep away quietly they would have aroused suspicion and the soldiers might have come over to investigate. As it was they ran off in a blind reaction which the sepoys thus ignored, which was of course all to the good. However, in their panic and in the even deeper dark of the jungle they immediately lost each other. During the whole time that the shouting of the sepoys could be heard behind them they both continued fleeing but in totally different directions.

Ali was the first to realise that he was not being followed. He had heard one or two of the curses and shouts of the soldiers and realised that these were the words of men irritated by the mischief of children rather than worrying about anything sinister. Puffing with all the exertion he finally came to a stop and found that he was alone.

But Conrad was already far away and still running on. He was now deeply afraid for the first time that night. He eventually stopped due to sheer exhaustion and stood bent over gasping for breath. For the first time he realised that he was totally alone. Both boys now spent a further fruitless hour wandering about getting further and further away from each other until they both saw how pointless an exercise it was.

They both sank to the ground deciding to wait till the morning to deal with their predicament. Ali, always more anxious about life than Conrad, was no more fearful than his usual state and soon fell fast asleep. But for Conrad the fear he felt was new. It was not just the fear of men who wanted to hurt him, but also, for the first time in years, childish imaginations of serpents, werewolves and eastern djinns all gathered round in the dark of the jungle around him waiting to pounce. But eventually, exhausted in mind and body he too finally fell asleep.

PART IV

The Imminent End of the Fort

The siege had now lasted almost three weeks. During that time there had been moments of fear, moments of despair and moments of euphoric triumph. Nevertheless, regardless of all the vicissitudes of mood, the resolution of the garrison as a collective whole had never faltered. The Europeans remained determined throughout to sell their lives dearly. The Sikhs and the Ghurkas never questioned their decision not to surrender to the blandishments of the sepoys whispering to them from outside. Quite apart from the extraordinary quality of their leader Jemadar Baldour Singh, they felt sure that it was unlikely that they would be spared by the excited mutineers if they did decide to surrender. Even if this may not have been true in the first few days, it was certainly true once the fighting had gone on for a week.

But by now the sheer dirt and squalor of the continuing siege had begun to affect everyone. The fresh drinking water from the great pottery jars was running out. The stored wood for the cooking was almost finished. The well was still operating, but the water was increasingly muddier and only just drinkable. Furthermore it was filling up much more sluggishly. The well water had already had to be rationed as strictly as the water in the jars. It was clear that if the siege continued much longer any sort of washing would have to cease.

The makeshift arrangement of the two little rooms which had been turned into a latrine and an area for the disposal of excrement was already breaking down. Henty's store of bleaches was running out and the smells were becoming insupportable.

Already the odours of over forty men, three women and two boys cooped up in the confined space of the little house were beginning to become unbearable. It was becoming stiflingly hot during the day and the whole building, bricked up as it was, lacked any air. The fresh air, such as it was, coming through the embrasures and loopholes for the firing was simply not enough even with the trapdoor in the roof always left wide open.

Any sort of privacy had of course been impossible right from the start, but now after three weeks the effect of being unable to get away from the pressure of other people with their insufferable smells milling about was beginning to wear everybody down, leaving all the men intolerant and irritable. But in the end, as three weeks went by, everyone suffered fairly willingly and with a basic hope, each with their several and different levels of fortitude and resolution; until, that is, the morning after the disappearance of the two boys.

John and Dickie had spent all the night wide awake in the corner room. Marietta had not dared to disturb them and had spent the night in the kitchen area dozing on the floor under the table. Her attempts at producing a hot meal which Ali and Conrad had been dealing with so competently had been dismal. No one complained, but the dhal was uneatable and the rice had been overcooked and had ended up like porridge.

As the sun rose the next morning it became clear to both men that their sons were not going to turn up. All passion was spent. The two men looked at each other as the defused light began to come through the opening at the top of the bricked-up window. They rose stiffly and without another word to each other left the little room.

When John went into the Tate's room at the other corner of the building, he walked into the same scene he had left in the night. Harriet was lying stretched out on the one charpoy with Chloe sweating and still in a fever on the other. Henrietta was still there sitting on the floor by the side of Harriet holding her hand. Both women knew of the boy's departure on the task put to them by GG. Both immediately realised from John's weary and haggard appearance that neither boy had returned.

John in a turmoil of guilt and anger was now desperate at the added thought that Harriet, already shattered by the return of Chloe's illness, would crack up completely. He failed to be able to say a word to either woman. Henrietta shuffled to her knees, then leaning forward on the bed with her hands clasped together she began to pray. It could well have been this conventional act of religious piety which was the catalytic moment which turned it all around. Harriet, who had also spent a sleepless night dwelling on the possible death of both her children looked at Henrietta kneeling beside her muttering her senseless prayers, then up at her husband whose ravaged face showed a strain so extreme that it looked as if he would collapse at any moment. She sat up, swung her feet onto the tiny bit of floor left to her next to the kneeling Henrietta and stood up. She bent down and kissed the top of Henrietta's bowed head and said firmly without any embarrassment or apology –

"Henrietta, my dear, you have been an absolute brick. Thank you, thank you so much for staying with me all this terrible night. It was a great comfort. But please now cease your prayers. We don't need to try and persuade any deity to intervene. We will have to face this, as we have to face everything in life, with our own human will and efforts."

"Harriet," said Henrietta as she struggled to her feet in the cramped space, "you will act as you believe you must of course – but prayer works and is always good for your own soul even if it doesn't appear to make a difference. Either way I will leave you both, but understand that whatever your own feelings in these matters I will be praying for the safety of your children."

The moment she turned and left John shut the door and held Harriet tight. They stood like that in the tiny area left by the side of the bed – bodies tightly clasped together – lips on lips – and this continued until one of them broke into harsh sobs. It was not Harriet, it was John who was weeping. Harriet was not the slightest bit upset by the sight of what John thought was his unacceptable weakness. She sat him down next to her on the bed and held him tight. Then at last it all poured out; his fears for the children; his guilt at not having organised Conrad's departure earlier; his supposed failure as the paterfamilias. Harriet wisely said nothing and let it all pour out. Who knows how long it might have gone on, but at last the little Chloe made her presence felt, She moaned out the word 'Mama' guaranteed by centuries of evolution to bring to an end any other thoughts in the minds of parents. Harriet began busying herself to look after and comfort the little girl – but, as Chloe remained quiet, before doing anything further, she said as John rose to go out –

"John, you must know perfectly well that I am as much to blame for the situation in which we have placed Conrad as you. You have always maintained that you look on our marriage as one of equals, and that means equal in the poor decisions as well as the good ones. I don't ever need you to play the heavy-handed decisive male for me to love you. I don't want any unthinking muscular hero – I want a good man and that's what I've got."

John hesitated at the door and turning back, flashed her a devastating smile of real warmth, and then said as he turned to go out –

"Well lets pray all will still be well."

By then Harriet had picked up the little girl and rocking her gently said with a smile back at him –

"Neither of us need to sink to our knees to pray for the intervention of some deity or another – we will face what is to come as two thinking and loving human beings."

However, the disappearance of the two boys did not just affect the Tates and Dickie Derounian – it affected the whole garrison, Europeans and Asiatics alike. For the Sikhs and the Ghurkas the absence of the two boys and the thought of what could happen to them was an added depressing factor in an already deteriorating situation. Without thinking much about it, all these men had come to look on the happy and rather carefree manner in which Conrad and Ali had run about the building with boyish enthusiasm doing all their many little chores without a word of complaint, as a positive part of the otherwise confined and squalid life in the zenana house.

Meanwhile for the Europeans the effect of their absence was even worse for they divided into two bickering camps over the question of GG's personal responsibility for what had occurred. The Drummonds and Paul Kelly, whilst obviously sympathetic to the fear of the two fathers did not believe that the Senior Magistrate had acted in any way improperly in requesting Ali to do a 'reconnaissance' on behalf of the whole garrison. The boys had freely shown him the drain and Ali had openly volunteered to go and find out the information that the garrison needed. It was not GG's fault that Conrad had gone too. Henty could not agree and he also had more sympathy for Dickie than the others, probably because he had always suspected that Derounian was the natural father of the boy.

No one came to any blows or even bitter discussions about any of this. Nevertheless the tension and the anxiety of the parents pervaded the whole garrison. The heroic epic quality of what they had been facing over the past three weeks disappeared. The squalor and the worsening situation began to take over all other considerations. The collective will, the collective resolution began to waver. It was still not fear, it did not even make any difference to the determination to resist to the end – but the joy in shared adversity, the grinning bonding of collective courage and action had gone forever. All that seemed to be left was to wait for the inevitable end as the water and the provisions ran out.

* * *

It was possible to buy almost anything in the British India of the mid-Victorian era if you had sufficient money. Haidar Presaud was not simply being devious to get himself away from Darabad when he referred to the possibility of paying a sufficient bribe in order to purchase a cannon. He knew of a small cache of some cannon originally made for the Khalsa – the Sikh army – ten years before. How these four cannons together with a sufficient quantity of cannon-balls came to be in the storehouse of a Bihari merchant who dealt in the import and export of grain was a mystery Haidar never even attempted to solve.

He still believed that the British Raj was on the point of collapse. Delhi had still not been recaptured despite a considerable British force now besieging the town. In addition there were signs that one or two more districts were on the point of joining the rebellion. However, Haidar also saw that none of the major independent Rajahs appeared to be throwing in their lot with the rebellious sepoys. In the circumstances, added to the continued complete calm of the Bombay and Madras presidencies, Haidar was no longer quite so sure.

He was already quietly covering his tracks as best he could. Meanwhile, however, he intended to keep on good terms with the officers of the two regiments currently controlling the district of Shantapur. Once settled back in Patna he sent a message to Darabad confirming that he could certainly get his hands on one or two cannon, but that they were about 150 miles away. They were held secretly in a warehouse in a small town on the road to Cawnpore. The regiment would have to send a detachment to escort whatever they required back to Darabad together with 5,000 silver rupees for one gun.

On the very next day after the messenger arrived in Darabad, the jemadar of the 68th together with two men arrived in Patna. Although there was no British garrison, the nearest troops being the 600 British regulars commanded by General Lloyd at Dinapore, the town was still nominally under the control of the British Commissioner – William Taylor – , and the three were accordingly dressed in civilian clothes when they presented themselves to Haidar.

"Your Honour, we have come to make the necessary arrangements for the delivery to us of the cannon you promised," said the young Jemadar.

"Ah, Jemadar sahib this has nothing to do with me you understand. The four cannon are the property of a grain merchant currently in Jaunpur, who purchased all four from loot recovered from the battlefield after the battle of Gujrat ten years ago. You have to go to Jaunpur – it is about 140 miles away on the road to Cawnpore. This is the list of the four guns available.

The Jemadar looked carefully at the list.

"It would appear that there are two 6-pounders, a 12-pounder and a great 24-pounder siege cannon."

"Ah, Jemadar, surely you could never be sure that the 6-pounders would be effective. What you need in order to be sure is the big siege cannon...er...that will cost..."

"No, that won't be necessary. It would need about 100 oxen to drag it along – and think of the fodder needed to keep them going – and the cost. No, no. I do agree that the 6-pounders would be a risk in view of the way the walls stood up to the Nawab's cannon. We will need the 12-pounder. Only a few discharges from that would be enough to finish the job once and for all. But even that will require at least 30 bullocks for the gun and the powder and shot."

"Well Jemadar you know your job. I will send my man to the merchant to warn of your arrival....when?....very well in 3 days at the most. I will make sure that he will have the necessary bullocks and carts and everything ready for when you arrive. You must be sure to have your rupees with you."

The sepoys rode off to collect a proper detachment from Darabad. Haidar watched them leave, relieved that their arrival had not caused any unhealthy curiosity. He was of course earning a large commission from the merchant in Jaunpur who had been holding the cannon for some years. The grain merchant had despaired of ever being able to get rid of them at a profit as of course he could never have off-loaded them onto the Company.

Haidar himself went the next day to sign the visitor's book at the home of the Commissioner. He also sent round a large donation with a note explaining that he had sent this with a view to helping the British war effort in the area. He received and carefully filed an effusive letter of appreciation and thanks signed by the Commissioner himself.

Once the Jemadar got back to Darabad all was immediately put in hand. The siege continued but a detachment of 100 men, armed with the necessary silver rupees obtained from the looting of the treasury, rode off to pick up the cannon and begin the slow laborious task of trudging back with it to Darabad. The transaction itself went smoothly. The 12-pounder was loaded up and the whole caravan began its slow laborious trek through the still lawless countryside on its way to Darabad.

Meanwhile, about 200 miles away, on the road from Raniganj, the current terminus of the Calcutta – Delhi railway line, a major relief force was heading for Oudh and the centres of the rebellion on the Ganges plain. This comprised the final part of the 90th Highlanders that had been hurriedly despatched from South Africa and sent forward piecemeal as they arrived. They were due to be accompanied by the Fifth Fusileers who had already arrived from Mauritius a few days previously and were further up the road. Their objective was Cawnpore and the Central Provinces, with the possibility also of using the combined force to break the current stalemate at Delhi.

The principal danger in India for most British regular soldiers was the terrible heat and the diseases that they could not combat. Unquestionably far more men were wiped out by sunstroke and cholera than by any enemy action. Throughout the whole of the Mutiny less than 3,000 men of all ranks were killed by enemy action. Compared with the horrific slaughter in the American Civil War which began only a couple of years after the end of the Mutiny, this was less than the loss of men in only one day of any one of the major battles in that war. As against this however nearly 10,000 British soldiers died of sunstroke and other diseases.

So it was that troops such as those comprised in this large relief force first travelled by train to Raniganj. Rather than being required to march through the heat, they were then transferred to convoys of bullock carts which lumbered up the dusty roads with the oxen being changed at regular intervals,. These huge convoys, paid for from the Company's coffers, or provided by friendly princes or zamindars en route, plodded along covering about 30 miles each day. The cannons, together with the shot and gunpowder, followed along behind, usually arriving at the camp two or three hours later. Whenever the system broke down as it inevitably often did, the men would have to march, rising well before dawn to avoid the searing heat of the middle of the day. This would then reduce the daily average to only 20 miles a day.

Back in Dinapore, General Lloyd still commanded a substantial force despite having lost men in a series of minor engagements – all against his better judgement. These had been mostly minor engagements, where he had been persuaded to send off detachments to help other outposts where Europeans had been caught out and attacked by the rebels.. But news of the force approaching from Raniganj gave him some comfort and believing, mistakenly, that the whole force was headed in his direction he was persuaded again to send a small force to join up with the relief force while it passed through the area. Accordingly, a small force of about 100 British soldiers with some 50 or so Sikh volunteers, again under the command of Captain Reith-Davies, was sent to rendezvous with the coming relief force and until their arrival to hold the Syed Ghat crossing.

So it was that as the siege continued the officers of the two mutineering regiments waited in the certain knowledge that the fort would collapse the moment their newly acquired cannon arrived. At the same time Captain Reith-Davies with his 150 men approached the Syed Ghat aboard a steamer. He duly landed there for the second time and garrisoned both sides of the river, waiting for the arrival of the force supposedly coming up from Raniganj. Desultory attempts to dislodge him by the sepoys were not pressed to any conclusion in any way once it was clear that he was not proposing to move out.

Neither group moving slowly towards Darabad were aware of the other. If the Khalsa 12-pounder cannon arrived first that would be the certain end for the Europeans in the zenana house. Yet no one, neither the garrison in the little fort, nor the sepoy officers conducting the siege from the Hamid Mansion, nor Captain Reith-Davies, nor the officers of the relieving 90th Highlanders had any idea that there was any sort of a race. The bullocks on both sides plodded slowly on.

* * *

When Ali awoke the next morning it was already becoming light. He was deep in the rather sparse jungle that lay south of the zenana house. The sun easily penetrated here and he woke to a world of dappled sunlight and of the sounds of many birds and insects. For a moment he lay back enjoying the fresh air, the varied scents, the buzzing of all the insects and the sound of the birds all around him. But then as memory came flooding back he sat up and began thinking fast. He had to find Conrad – that was undoubtedly the first priority.

He knew that there was no point in just wandering blindly about in the jungle undergrowth. He tried to think what his friend would do and cursed that they had not had the foresight to make some arrangement together beforehand as to where to meet if they ever got separated.

One thing seemed clear. It was very likely that Conrad too would reject the idea of wandering around in the jungle looking for him. So the only alternative was to go back to the town. The only way they could get back to the fort was once the evening set in and the shadows lengthened and they could creep back through the jungle unseen to the hidden entrance to the drain. But they would have to pick just the right moment. Too light and they might be seen from the Hamid Mansion, but too dark and the nightly guard would be back watching.

Ali carefully worked his way through the trees back to the outskirts of the town. He had not run that far the night before and he soon came out onto the road going into Darabad from the south. It was early morning and there was the usual throng of farmers and workers plodding into the town using both sides of the dust road, down the centre of which moved bullock carts belonging to the wealthier peasants. These were filled with products destined for the morning market on the Maidan. Interspersed with the bullocks were donkeys patiently trotting along, weaving round the slow-moving carts, either laden with farm produce or carrying a fat Brahmin whose legs almost touched the floor as he was borne along.

Ali did not feel the slightest bit afraid. All the excitement coupled with the tinge of fear that he had experienced the evening before seemed to have disappeared. Light-skinned Eurasian though he was, he knew that he did not stand out in any way. The only danger was if he came across someone who recognised him. He felt self-confident as he walked out from the trees and joined the slowly moving crowds walking into the town. But when he got into the jumble of town streets on the southern side of the Maidan, he began to realise how hard it was going to be to find Conrad. It was unquestionably going to be much more difficult for Conrad to wander about in the streets without attracting attention. The light whitish-brown skin of Ali may have marked him out as half-European, half-Indian, but few would give him a second glance. On the other hand the chubby red face and blue eyes of the tall and well-built Conrad would stand out like a beacon.

Ali wandered round all morning visiting every spot and secret hideaway in which they had played together and spied on the adults during the last two years – but all to no avail. As the morning went on the heat began to increase and the time would soon come when the streets would empty again as people sought the shade of their homes, their bullock carts, or the awnings in the market on the Maidan. Already Ali was being careful to keep his head down and to turn away whenever he glimpsed any of those bigger boys who had tried to bully him but been prevented by the formidable sight of the red-faced anger of Conrad standing by his side with his fists up.

He was just about to give up, thinking that in order to avoid the risk of returning to the town for the day Conrad might after all have decided to remain in the jungle to try and find the hidden entrance of the drain on his own. But then for the first time he thought of Dr. Bannerjee. Yes – that was the answer. It was after all the only house in the town that they both knew and which they could both find easily. The buildings in the Judge's compound were already burned to the ground and this was the one neutral house they both knew. That was it – that was it! It was now nearly midday and Ali hurried off to find Dr. Bannerjee's house. The closer he got the more certain he felt that Conrad would probably already be there waiting for him. He did not consider any alternative possibilities or that the timid Brahmin teacher might be too afraid to let Conrad into his house. Ali simply hurried on and eventually arrived at the door and knocked.

Meanwhile, Conrad had awoken even earlier than Ali while it was still dark. There was just a hint of pink in the sky over the trees as he sat up cold and hungry. He was not used to doing without breakfast even in the straitened circumstances of the siege. His tummy was already rumbling and demanding food and water. He was dirty and dishevelled and his clothes were torn and filthy. He had followed Ali out of the fort the evening before without a thought, dressed in completely unsuitable clothes. His white shirt had fortunately already been stained and dirty and had not been conspicuous, but the grey shorts, grey socks and leather shoes of a European schoolboy marked him out. The dark and the presence of Ali as they sought the information GG had required had constituted just sufficient protection, but it was not going to quite so easy on his own in the bright light of the morning.

Conrad, unaware that he was not being chased, had run on much further than Ali. He had not understood the mild good-natured curses of the sepoys or heard their laughter over what they had thought were village boys bent on mischief. He had been, perhaps for the first time that day truly terrified and had run on and on until exhausted. But he too, once he came fully awake, realised that it was hopeless just wandering about in the scrub of the jungle in the hope of finding his way back to the hidden drain or of meeting Ali. He would have to go back to the town where he would surely find Ali and then they could both make their way through the part of the jungle they knew well from the town to the back of the fort. He found it was easy heading eastwards towards the rising sun, and eventually after dirtying and tearing his clothes even more on the thorns and branches in his way he too came to the end of the jungle and looked out onto the road leading up to Darabad from the south.

As he peeped out he saw the same line of villagers and farmers, donkeys and bullock carts, lumbering their way up the road to the town. The evening before it had been Ali who had been nervous and afraid – today it was Conrad. He could immediately see how conspicuous he was compared to the line of plodding peasants. Quite apart from the red face and the grey pants, socks and shoes, he seemed to be the only boy of his age. There were plenty of babes in arms or little kids running along beside their mothers. There were also boys of fourteen or more helping their fathers with all the produce, but somehow his particular age group - 11 to 13 – was absent. Conrad shrank back nervous and fearful into the shade and safety of the trees.

What got him moving again was the pressure of his hunger and thirst. The people slowly passing in front of him all seemed to be munching away; a mango here, a banana there; a dry well-cooked chapatti, a fresh naan wrapped round some dhall; breakfast on the move. Conrad couldn't take his eyes off it all. He had to do something and at last he began to think. He was still frightened, but he brought to mind his father's words about overcoming fear – 'Conrad, when you are afraid and in a panic, if you can, just stop – stop doing anything – just sit, take a deep breath or two and consider what is the worst that could happen immediately. Then decide how best to avoid it and act, a step or two at a time.'

So he sat and stopped staring at all the food being consumed in front of his eyes. Also simply thinking of his dad helped. What was the worst now? Well right now the worst was that he had no food or water. So for now what he had to do was go out and ask for some or steal it. Then if he did that, what was then the worst that could happen, Easy – to be recognised as an English boy or even as a European from the fort. Right – so he had to prevent that. Conrad pondered.

The shoes and the socks were the biggest giveaway. Conrad peeled them off and threw them further away into the trees – he was now barefoot. The grey shorts were still a danger, but he couldn't walk about in his underpants so they had to stay. However a bit more mud on them and on his face would do no harm and he set about that, including extending many of the tears and holes. Then at last, looking as scruffy as he had ever been in his life, with his heart pounding and butterflies in his already rumbling stomach, Conrad stepped out from the trees. He walked with his head down right up to the road, joined the line and began walking alongside a bullock cart piled high with melons.

This particular cart was being managed by a surly looking old man, who peered down at Conrad walking alongside. Conrad looked back up at him. He didn't trust himself to speak but pointed at his mouth and mimed his request for something to eat, indicating one of the melons. The old man grabbed a stout stick and flashed it menacingly at the boy, muttering some curses at the same time.

Conrad glared at the old man but trotted forward and then found himself alongside a family group walking together at the side of the road.. This party consisted of a man walking in front carrying over his back an enormous jute bag of some root vegetable which looked like carrots. Walking immediately behind him was a woman also with a load of some vegetable, smaller and lighter than the man's, and with a baby against her breasts rocking in a shawl tied round her neck. Next to her, trotting alongside and holding onto her sari was a little boy of about five years old carrying yet another bag of what looked like bunches of fresh herbs. This bag though not very heavy was large and cumbersome and was giving him some trouble. Conrad, whose hunger was making him cunning and brave, smiled at the little boy and took his bag and slung it over his own shoulder. Smiling at the mother he then took the boys hand, trustingly given, and marched along.

The man ahead, obviously the father, looked round but said nothing. Conrad, growing increasingly confident now offered to carry the woman's bag as well. This turned out to be heavier than he had first thought but he was strong and it was manageable. He was patient as they all plodded on, but his tummy was making really alarming sounds of distress and eventually he mimed to the woman that he was thirsty. The family stopped, moved off the edge of the road and moved to the trees where they sat while the woman gave water to the three males and at last, welcome sight, produced some chapattis freshly made that morning.

Conrad grinned with pleasure as he wolfed it down. The father nodded and stood up to go off again. He could not afford to arrive at the market after all the other carrot and herb growers had already started selling. The family prepared to move off again – the little boy took Conrad's hand again as if he had been doing it all his life.

Conrad himself was still not thinking too hard about what was to happen next. His idea was to get into the town with his new family, settle with them in the market on the maidan, perhaps give the father a helping hand in setting up his produce, and then drift off to look for Ali, if he had not seen him by then. So it was that Conrad Tate – a 12-year-old English boy and erstwhile defender of Tate's Fort – found himself helping an unknown Indian small farmer from the Shantapur district set up a little makeshift awning on the edge of the great vegetable market on the Maidan of the town of Darabad. He helped the man setting out his vegetables and herbs, he sprinkled water provided by the woman on them, and he even held the baby for a mercifully short moment.

But the sun was well up and it was approaching eleven o'clock when Conrad finally gave his salaams and took another couple of chapattis and a few carrots. He gulped a last cupful of water and wandered away. He had no idea who the family had thought he was. It was fortunate in any case that they must have been of a fairly low caste, as if they had been of the Brahmin caste they would never have taken the risk of giving him any of their water.

He had to find Ali. He was sure that he too would have come into the town. But where to start, where could he go, where was the best place that they could meet. He again followed his father's advice, found a shady spot, hunkered down and started to think. Dr. Henty's house and surgery? No, being a feringhi property it would certainly have been attacked and ransacked by the rebels. The judges compound? No, surely they had all seen the flames coming from there on the very first day.

Ah! Got it! Got it! Dr. Banerjee's house. Yes, yes Ali would go there – it would not have been attacked by the sepoys – one way or another it was certainly the place they could meet, or at least leave messages for each other. Conrad, excited by his own impeccable logic, unaware that as noon approached the streets were getting dangerously empty, rose and began hurrying to the old teacher's house.

* * *

The 12-pounder cannon mounted on a large cart, drawn by a team of eight oxen, set off from Jaunpur early on the morning of the 14th August. This cart was followed by a reserve of eight bullocks with a further eight pulling along the carts filled with the fodder needed. The whole caravan was escorted by the Jemadar major of the 68th together with a detachment of about 100 men. They were about 150 miles away from Darabad. Bullock drawn carts, if well-fed and on fairly good roads could make about 30 miles each day. Accordingly they were expected to arrive on the 18th or the 19th August.

Meanwhile the small British force comprising the last section of the 90th Highlanders was moving up from Raniganj. They were scheduled to join the Fifth fusiliers who had moved up earlier and were waiting at Dumroon a little further down the road. The senior commander of this force had been told that, once merged, his force was to march on to Cawnpore and the troubled Central Provinces. However, he was authorised, if he considered it safe and prudent, to peel off a detachment of the Fifth fusiliers – not more than 100 men - to meet with a small force being sent from Dinapore in order to make a second attempt to relieve the besieged fort at Darabad, which had now been under siege for over three weeks. The meeting was to be at the Syed Ghat.

The Fifth fusiliers had an assistant surgeon attached to the regiment, Doctor MacAlistair. He kept a careful journal of all his travels and experiences with the regiment including all the details of this march to Darabad. When the detachment finally peeled away from the main force at Dumroon, there were about 150 men including Doctor MacAlistair who marched off to the rendezvous with Reith-Davies at the Syed Ghat. MacAlistair was new to India, having only just arrived from Mauritius and his narrative was accordingly fresh and without any prejudices. The entries in his journal which formed the basis of the report which was eventually deposited with the local Commissioner read –

"Our route from Raniganj at first lay through about 50 miles of fairly straight and level road which had once been the main road from Bengal to Delhi. However this had been superseded by the Grand Trunk road which was further inland, but which we were specifically instructed not to use on this expedition. Our route passed between woods and mango groves. It passed over many rivers all well bridged.. For this first stretch we had no delays or any difficulties. The old camping grounds still lay at the usual intervals where there was sufficient room by the side of the road to set up a camp, the ground having been kept clear of cultivation.

We marched with as little impedimenta as possible – but we had six cannon with us and this inevitably meant that we had to camp fairly early in order to enable the gun carriages to catch up. Also as well as the bullock carts there were two elephants carrying the tents and the great-coats. The weather was rainy though the full force of the monsoon had passed. The heat was excessive but due to the occasional downpour the nights were sometimes cool. The first nights march away from Raniganj was of the usual trying nature for beginners like me. But after that uncomfortable first day, uncomfortable whether I walked or sat in a cart, I began to enjoy the march. The beauty of the countryside and the friend-liness of those natives that we met in those first few days left me excited and unaware that there might be any latent danger.

We arrived at Dumroon about 60 miles away from Darabad on the 16th August. The cannon and the rearguard were particularly late in catching up that evening. We were now in Bihar and the attitude of the people appeared to have changed markedly. The next day the last section of the 90th Highlanders arrived having caught up with us after leaving

Raniganj. Here in Dumroon there was an influential and wealthy Rajah. Responding to our commander's call for assistance he sent servants to our camp promising to provide food, shelter and baggage guards. But at the same time he gave excuses for not making any sort of appearance himself, or of inviting any of the officers to his residence. It was already clear that we were now in country infested with mutineers and that they were aware of our numbers, our equipment and our movements. It seemed likely that the information was being passed on by this same Rajah of Dumroon.

In fact the very next day after we left the town one of these mounted spies fell into our hands. Dressed in white and riding alongside the column he was at first mistaken for one of our own men, but on being challenged he rode off and was chased. He was at last taken, but not before he received a pistol shot in the arm. I was sent for and found his left arm broken. He would not give any account of himself though it was clear that he had come from Dumroon. I splinted and bandaged him up, and as none of us had as yet experienced any of the horrors of this war we let him go after he finally confirmed that he had indeed been sent by the Rajah to report on our intentions and movements.

I should explain that the force had separated at Dumroon. I was now with the small detachment of about 150 men with four of the field cannons on our way to join a certain Captain Reith-Davies who was waiting for us at a ghat on the River, with a view to the combined force making a second attempted relief of the garrison at Darabad.

That first day that we split off from the main force we marched on well beyond darkness as it was a cool and pleasant evening. It was the rainy season and we were all anxious that we might be overwhelmed with tropical rains causing flooding which would delay our march. We had the four guns, the ammunition wagons and four or five more carts and so we were tied to the road. Furthermore, unlike our earlier route before Dumroon, this road looked as if it could turn to a sea of mud at any time.

It was now the 18th August and for the first time the enemy began to make his presence felt. We were only about ten miles from the Syed Ghat where we were supposed to meet the detachment which should have been sent by steamer from Dinapore when we first had to fight. We had one more minor river to cross. We heard from our own spies that the sepoys were ahead of us trying to break up the bridge. We moved forward at the double leaving the supplies behind. We arrived to see the sepoys milling about on the bridge. A few shots from our rifles soon scattered them. Not much damage had been done and it only took us an hour to repair it enough to allow the carts to pass later. The two villages on either side were burnt down. I doubt if any of the villagers were the slightest bit involved – we had after all only seen soldiers on the bridge – but, well, we were all getting jumpy.

That evening we finally arrived at the Syed Ghat on the River, having had to go into line to return defensive fire on two further occasions before we finally made it. The Ghat was well held on both sides by the troops from Dinapore who numbered a little more than 100 men all of whom knew the area well having taken part in the first failed attempted relief. It was the night of the 18th August. We were only about five miles from Darabad. We knew that the enemy were all around us, but the night remained calm and quiet."

Meanwhile coming from the West the detachment of the 68th Regiment escorting the 12-pounder cannon from Jaunpur together with all its attendant carts, fodder and ammunition, had made good time as far as Buxar, but here only about 20 miles from Darabad their easy rate of travel ended. They had to cross the River Soane, bridgeless at this point, which while not in full flood was nevertheless wide and flowing fast.

It took time to collect together large boats and rafts. Meanwhile men began preparing to cross on the two small boats immediately available. The great unwieldy cannon was slowly manoeuvred down to the point on the bank chosen for the crossing where there was a small village on each side of the river. But to the consternation of all, patrolling up and down the Soane was the same steamer which had previously got stuck on the mudflats. Still commanded by a European pilot captain, it happened to turn up round the corner up-river just as a second boatload of the 68th arrived at the far bank. Amidst a great deal of shouting and yelling the Captain came up fast moving down-river and tried ramming the boat from which the sepoys were hurriedly disembarking. However an ominous scraping below drove him off into the deeper middle of the river before he could do any real damage.

But it was clear that while the steamer remained on station, even without any guns on board, the sepoys could not risk loading the cannon and the animals on the large but flimsy rafts. The steamer was manned by a nondescript crew of low-caste natives who were largely indifferent towards the high-caste sepoy mutineers. There were also a few European civilians on board together with the determined British Captain. Having moved on past the villages the steamer now stopped and turned back. It pushed its way upstream, moving a good deal more slowly, past the crossing point receiving musket shots as it struggled back up the river. It then turned again and stationed itself upstream ready to charge down with the current and ram anything trying to get across. The Jemadar soon discovered that it was no use chasing up the river after it with men armed only with the old muskets – the steamer simply backed away but remained with steam up ready to come racing down as soon as the captain became aware of any cross-river activity. It was the 18th August. The Jemadar was not aware of any great urgency, but he had promised delivery on the 18th or the 19th at the latest. Hours went by. It was surprising how long the delay was before the obvious solution at last struck him. After all for once he had artillery. It took time to get the cannon set up under some camouflage. He then had to tempt the steamer forward. Ostentatiously he loaded a raft with eight soldiers, carefully chosen as being good swimmers, together with two bullocks.

With a great deal of excitement and shouting they were launched. The steamer immediately hooted and drove forward with the current, full steam ahead.. Too late the captain became aware of the cannon as the branches hiding it were pulled away –

"Fire!"

It worked. There was no fiasco, no exploding barrel, it turned out to be a 'pukka' gun which was going to be able to do the business in Darabad easily. The very first shot struck the oncoming steamer on the front bow causing the ship to swerve off course. It raced on and just missed the raft with the soldiers aboard who all started shooting as the ship swung by. Meanwhile the cannon had been dragged round and a second shot hit the fast-moving ship in the stern causing yet more damage, this time to the rudder. The Jemadar watched as the steamer went on and away down-river, the captain unable and unwilling to try a second round.

The escorting detachment of the 68th spent the rest of the afternoon crossing the Soane. Once across they were only about twelve miles away from Darabad and over the last obstacle. But they had been delayed by almost a day. It was now the 18th August. The Jemadar sent a messenger forward to warn the besiegers that he would arrive by the afternoon of the 19th and that he was able to report that the cannon had stood the test of a firing and would undoubtedly crack the defence of the fort in less than an hour.

* * *

When Ali knocked at the door of Dr. Bannerjee's house the sun was already high overhead and the heavy heat of midday was already beating down forcing everyone back to their houses, or at least to seek some shade. The house was only a mere 20 yards away from the maidan. The pedantic old man was finishing his late morning prayers in front of the little shrine in the corner of his sitting room and was not pleased at being disturbed by a servant who padded in.

"Master – there is a young boy at the door, Ali the servant of Derounian sahib, craving to have a word with you."

"I really have no idea what you are talking about – a young boy – a young boy – at this hour. Who did you say sent him? Derounian. No, no, that's impossible – send him off – send him off, some scamp trying to...."

"No sir, no sir, it's the boy who used to take lessons from you before all the troubles began."

"Oh yes, yes, why didn't you say so before. What does he want? Didn't he go with his master into that ridiculous fort which is giving those dratted mutineers such trouble? Well don't just stand there – what does he want?"

"I don't know, master. He wants to talk to you."

"Oh well – let him in and bring him here. But, wait a moment, Abdu, make sure that there is no one else about in the street when you let him in."

During all this Ali had been left outside the door, which had been closed on him. Even he was now feeling the midday heat. There were less and less people about in the streets and out of the corner of his eye he saw some of the street boys who would certainly have recognised him from the days when he and Conrad brawled with them. They were sauntering up towards him and he was contemplating running off and returning later, when the door at last reopened and the servant beckoned him inside. Ali, relieved, went into the welcome shade of the hallway of Dr. Bannerjee's house and on into the sitting room.

"Well, boy – what is it? Do you have some message for me?"

"Good morning sir" said Ali nervously, wondering where to start now that it was immediately clear to him that Conrad was not here."

"Did you say – good morning? My dear young man I can well recall teaching you the difference between 'good morning' and 'good afternoon'. Midday has passed and in the English language you say 'good morning' only before midday. You also don't go visiting people after midday unless it is very urgent. What do you want?"

Ali felt a sort of relief that in this wildly changing world Dr. Bannerjee remained much the same. He began to tell his old tutor why he was there and who he had come to find. The fussy old man listened fairly tolerantly, until Ali got to the point of confirming that Conrad too was out there somewhere in the town. Ali explained that he believed that Conrad too would eventually get round to coming here as being the only place left which they both knew.

However, the fact that this British child, a son of one of the men holed up in the little fort in the grounds of the Hamid Mansion, might suddenly turn up at his house demanding some sort of sanctuary, left the old man in a state bordering on panic.

"He can't stay here – not for a moment. No, no! I can't

possibly be seen to be sheltering a feringhi boy. No, no – and you too…you must leave at once. Go away go." Dr Bannerjee was beginning to jump up and down in his agitation.

Ali saw that further argument was pointless – but all he needed to do, he realised, was to get out of the old man's way before he called out for one of the servants. The good Doctor was not about to change his habits of a lifetime. He would devote some time to finishing his midday puja, and would then sink onto his charpoy, already set up in the corner, and sleep. So all he said was-

"Yes sir, yes, of course. I will leave now from the back through the kitchen, where I can no doubt stay for a moment and have some water."

"Good – good. Hmmm! Give my regards to Mr. Derounian," replied Banneerjee relieved that Ali had not insisted, and waved him away.

Ali carefully closed the door behind him saying to Abdu who had been waiting in the dark hall –

"Your master doesn't want to be disturbed as he his ready for his siesta. I am to wait for a time in the kitchen and have something to eat and some water to drink. I am expecting a friend – you remember the other boy who came with me to lessons. If he comes, no need to disturb the master, just tell me and we will be off together."

This seemed to satisfy the servant who came with Ali to the kitchen at the back. The house stood quiet.

Meanwhile in the slowly emptying lanes and alleys of the old quarter south of the maidan, Conrad was making his way to Dr. Bannerjee's house. He had usually come to the house from the direction of the maidan. Trying to find it from the warren of little lanes and streets from the south needed a bit more care and attention.

Concentrating on making sure that he went in the right direction, confident now that he would find Ali waiting for him, he was unaware of the emptying streets. At the same time the increasing heat was getting at him particularly as he had no head covering of any kind. He turned the last corner and recognised that the house he was looking for was up at the end of this lane. He strolled forward impatient to get out of the sun and then stopped dead. There in front of him were four boys whom he recognised even with their backs to him. They were also heading north toward the maidan on their own way home. Even then all might have passed off without incident. Conrad was behind them. He became immediately aware that the street was empty. He realised at once that they were the bullying gang whom he and Ali had stood up to in the streets all those weeks before. He froze and then quietly stepped sideways into the shade of the houses along the side of the lane. But fate intervened. He had stepped sideways without looking with the idea of pressing up against the wall until the boys passed on. But in so doing he stepped right onto the tail of a cat which had been dozing in the sparse shade provided. This scraggy animal gave a piercing shriek and leapt away. The four boys ahead turned and stared at Conrad as he stared back at them.

This was the moment for Conrad to turn and bolt back into the warren of streets behind him. But instead he waited for those fatal seconds of indecision. It was not in his nature anyway to run away, but above all the whole atmosphere of British India where he had been brought up made it difficult for him immediately to take this sensible course. Within not more than ten seconds three of the boys, all bigger than him, were onto him. The fourth boy ran off. Bringing him down to the ground with a crash two of them rolled about all over him in the dust of the beaten earth lane. They were intent on getting their revenge for the many times Conrad had stood up to them preventing them from bullying Ali. Even fate was not neutral – lying to one side was a stout broken leg of a chair, a sturdy weapon which the third boy grabbed.

Conrad was bleeding – what clothes were still on him were tattered and in shreds. Blows rained down on him as he fought back desperately never letting them pin him down completely. But eventually numbers told and exhausted, frightened by the ferocity of the assault and alone he stopped fighting back and curled up in a foetal position with his hands up to protect his head. At this, the two who had been rolling about with him on the road trading blows stood up with a view to giving the boy who had the stick a free chance to strike. He set to with a vengeance, beating Conrad on the back and legs as he lay curled up on the road.

But the removal of the two who had been rolling about on top of him and preventing him from escaping gave Conrad that one moment of chance. The two had stood back to watch with satisfaction their comrade delivering the punishment they so craved to inflict on the arrogant feringhi boy who had stood up to them so often before. Conrad took several viciously delivered strokes on his back and legs. Then, forgetting all that rubbish about standing and fighting, with a great rush of adrenalin, he uncurled himself, jumped up and without looking back ran back down the lane from where he had come.

There was nothing political, or racial, or class about this attack. They all acted as they did because they were 12-year-old and 13-year-old boys. Nothing more. Nevertheless, it was something that could not have occurred at any other time than during those days of the mutiny. Conrad, aching, bleeding and in real pain scampered away. The three boys did not follow. They had soundly defeated their enemy of the streets and they turned back to continue on their way home with a triumphant yell. It would have ended there but for the actions of the fourth boy. As the three boys began walking on towards the maidan, they saw him coming back down the street with four armed sepoys – three soldiers and a havildar who came quickly up to them –

"Well – where is this feringhi boy? Are you sure that he was one of the British children? It surely can't be possible – they all left weeks ago."

"Yes sir, certainly." In the presence of adults impinging on their way of life, the boys became more subdued and a good deal more nervous. They sincerely wished that these out of town soldiers, whom their parents had been grumbling about for weeks, had not been called. But there it was – they had been and they now had to face a barrage of questions. It was hot – it was the middle of the day and their story was muddled and excitable. Nevertheless one thing came out clearly – a young lad, one of the children of the British families who had lived in the town, was wandering the streets. Where he came from; where he had been hiding and what he was doing was a mystery – but one way or another he was going to be found.

It was hot, everyone was irritable and the sepoy soldiers were not about to go chasing around in the streets. They returned and passed on the information to their officers. The four boys thankful to get away from them went on, crossed the maidan and went home to their lunch of rice and dhall and a siesta. The rebel officers, without quite knowing what they would do with him once he was found, agreed that in the afternoon they would mount a full-scale search for the missing boy. Meanwhile the midday heat bore down and everyone slumbered, except for one bedraggled frightened and bleeding European boy seeking bits of shade here and there in the streets, and one anxious Eurasian boy trying to remain inconspicuous in the kitchen of a house just south of the maidan.

* * *

After jumping up and fleeing from his tormentors Conrad had run back southwards. Once he realised that he had not been followed he stumbled into a corner where there was a little shade. The alley was deserted and relieving himself against a wall he managed to shed some of the angry tension. His face was dirty and scarred. His nose was bleeding and his hands were scratched and blood-spattered where he had struck out at his enemies. To make matters worse he was not used to walking about barefoot and so his feet too were in pain and as dirty and injured as the rest of his body. The beating itself had not been so bad – it had hurt his dignity more than his body; after all the wielder of the stick was himself only a boy and it had not done any real damage.

As he sat hunched up against a wall his fury and agitation began to fade and fear began to creep back in. He was of course unaware that his presence was now known to the mutineers, or that a search was about to be organised to smoke him out. While the two boys had been together they had bolstered each others morale; they gave each other courage simply by being together. But now, alone, uncomprehending, unable to think clearly any more, Conrad was reverting to childhood. He desperately wanted someone to comfort him and tell him what to do. For the very first time in the whole of his life in India he felt himself to be an alien, unwanted by anyone and with every man's hand against him.

He had no idea what to do or where to go. Somehow, going back to the street where he had been waylaid and beaten was out of the question for him. On top of all his other injuries he now felt a sticky mess on the top of his head, He realised that he must have hit his head on the road during the fight and it was now bleeding. The loss of blood and the heat of the mid-afternoon was beginning to give him a headache, and his vision was getting hazy.

He could not stay long in any one position – the occasional person who passed stared at him curiously. He started walking on aimlessly and eventually he came out onto the maidan. The market was still there but all the carts were covered with ragged awnings under which most of the vendors were fast asleep. Conrad slipped across the road – why – he did not know or care. He wanted to get away from the scene of his defeat and by now what with the loss of blood and the unbearable heat and with his head throbbing he scarcely knew what he was doing. He drifted into a lane on the other side and stumbled down it alongside a low wall. Then, looking up at the wall, his tired eyes filming over with a heat-induced exhaustion he saw something which at first he thought was a hallucination. It was an elephant!

It was as if he was in the middle of a dream. Standing in the garden behind the wall stood a large elephant. Conrad was too tired, too emotionally exhausted to work out that this must be the same elephant that he had glimpsed from between the broad shoulders of the Sikhs firing out from the fort. It just seemed to be magic. Without thinking, acting instinctively, Conrad managed to find footholds in the crumbling wall and pulled himself up to the top of the wall and fell over into the garden on the other side.

Conrad had arrived in the grounds of the da Costa house. He lay for some moments on the scrubby grass and stared up muzzily into the sky. Then he felt the trunk of the elephant nuzzling him and sniffing. This frightened him a little and he got up, or rather shuffled up and moved rather gingerly away. He saw a shed up against the wall with an open door. He crept into this – blessed shade – and saw that it was filled with hay and cut grass and with great pails of water. He had no idea where the water came from or whether it was good to drink – he simply went on his knees and slurped it up like a puppy. He then lay down on a bale of hay and prepared himself to start thinking again, but almost immediately fell into a deep sleep before he could do so.

Ali crouched all afternoon in Dr. Bannerjee's kitchen, becoming ever more despairing about what might be happening to Conrad. As the sun slowly began to sink and the heat to abate, he knew that he would have to leave. He waited until Abdu told him that he would shortly be taking his master his afternoon cup of tea. Ali thanked him for the rice and water he had been given and was let out at the front door.

He started wandering the streets again, keeping a look-out for Conrad as the small shopkeepers started opening their doors and shutters and people began coming into the streets again. He listened out for all the gossip going the rounds and heard nothing other than more confirmation of the departure of the relief force. Above all there was no mention of the capture of any English boy. Trying to spot Conrad was hopeless and Ali knew it, but somehow he could not bring himself to start making his way back to the hidden drain without him. In the end he had to go – after all he considered Conrad might now be there waiting for him. He knew, as Conrad too would have known, that they only had a short window of opportunity between the onset of dusk and the full night. They could not get safely through the woods until dusk fell – but the guard posted to watch the rear of the zenana house would be set as soon as the evening meal was finished.

Ali crept round through the trees, now moving with much more care and attention than on that first night, only twenty four hours ago, when it had all seemed such an adventure. This time he did not falter or miss his way even for a second. He approached the entrance to the drain, still camouflaged and undiscovered. Conrad was not there. He wriggled his way in feet first, carefully pulling the twigs, boughs and moss back into the opening as they had done together so often before. A candle had been left burning at the end of the drain below the opening and he wriggled his way backwards towards the light.

The two fathers had been taking turns all day to wait in the room, but at this moment both were present. They called out as they heard the noise – "Ali" – "Conrad".

"I'm coming" called out Ali.

When he got near he saw the light of the candle disappearing as it was lifted away, and then as his feet appeared out of the opening willing hands drew him up by the feet until he was standing. He was grabbed by Dickie who held him in a tight almost painful embrace. Even in this dramatic moment Ali felt that Dickie's embrace was somehow different from the bear hugs with which he normally greeted people and with which he had greeted Ali in the past. There was a passion, an emotion, flowing out of the man he had always thought of as a sort of kindly uncle. He felt it, but could not understand it.

Ali was mature for his age and was already thinking hard about what he was going to say to Mr. and Mrs. Tate. For the moment there was silence and then the floodgates opened. Ali told both men everything that had happened – the first evening in the town – the panic when they were challenged on returning to the drain – the failure after that to meet the next day. He had to admit that he had no idea where Conrad might now be, but he helped to keep some hope alive by his last comment.

"One thing I can say Mr. Tate, sir. If Conrad had been recognised and captured the news would have been all round the town, and I would have heard about it when I came out of Dr.

Bannerjee's house. I have no doubt that if he had been found and arrested the bazaars and the streets would have been buzzing with the story within minutes."

It was not much, but it left a glimmer of hope and John and Harriet clung on to that. In addition Arthur also pointed out that if he had been captured the mutineers would almost certainly have paraded him in some way before the defenders of the fort.

That same night Ali was made to recount everything that had happened in a meeting held in the billiard room. He reported, as faithfully as he could, all that he had gleaned during those hours the night before while they were wandering the town. It was now clear to all of them that a relief had indeed been attempted but that it had failed and the relieving force had retired. But by listening carefully to all the bits of conversation that Ali reported, everyone realised that whatever had been the fate of the relieving force here on the road to the Syed Ghat, the Raj itself in the rest of India had not collapsed. It was also clear that the people of Darabad had not fallen in with the mutinous regiments and were remaining aloof and waiting to see what would happen. This must mean that a counter-attack was proceeding and that the Raj was fighting back.

The dirt and the squalor, the dwindling supply of fresh water and all the other problems were all still present, but the garrison now again swung back, somewhat inexplicably, into a more positive mood. The Europeans remained heavily divided between those who did not blame Grant for the disappearance of Conrad and those who did. But everyone remained determined to resist to the end, an end which was clearly soon going to be upon them if no relief came. No one however was aware that a 12-pounder cannon, capable of bringing down with only a few shots all the brick walls, was on its way and would by the 18th August be only twelve miles away.

* * *

Saridar Khan could never quite understand why he had left the comforts of his palace at Jagpur and returned to Darabad.

But whatever the underlying reason he did feel safer here than alone in his old crumbling palace. In Darabad he was receiving more information about what was happening in the rest of India. Although Delhi was still in the hands of the rebels he was already receiving reports that a recapture could not long be delayed. None of the great independent Rajahs had joined the revolt and Saridar saw that the possibility of an eventual victory for the British Raj was becoming more and more likely. Already he was making sure that those of his servants who were present when Haidar Presaud and the officers of the two mutineering regiments arrived at his palace were clear about their recollections. He did not put words into their mouth – he knew that it would be better if their recollection were entirely their own.

"Yes, certainly Your Excellency – I remember well the occasion. The Subadar pulled out a gun, er... yes some sort of pistol and his deputy...yes, yes I remember, drew his sword."

But why then had he rejoined the two regiments voluntarily? Saridar pondered this question over many hours. It was a mystery in a way to him, and he knew that it would be an equal mystery to whichever British official would eventually be ordered to prepare a report as to what had happened here in the district of Shantapur; that is of course if the British Raj did survive and return to this area.

It was the afternoon of the 14th August. There were still three or four days before the cannon purchased by Haidar Presaud was due to arrive. The attempted relief of the fort by the troops sent from Dinapore had failed two or three days ago. Those troops had re-embarked on their steamer and returned back up the River. It was a particularly hot day and Saridar missed his cool palace and the cold sherbets he would have been drinking. He was pondering all these matters as he sat in the da Costa sitting room, which he now thought of as his audience chamber. But somehow, in a way he could not analyse, he was glad he was here in the midst of all the action. His warlike ancestors would have been proud, even though he himself had not yet raised a finger in the unfolding events. His reverie was interrupted by the junior mahout, who since the death of the senior mahout now looked after the state elephant on his own

"Your Excellency"

"Yes, yes my good man – I'm awake. What news of your charge – well I hope?"

"Your Excellency is kind – the state elephant is well. But Your Excellency we have a slight problem. We have come across a boy – er a youth – asleep in the shed holding the fodder."

"Come, come, junior mahout...er, what is your name? – Oh never mind. Just deal with him my good man. Give him a couple of strokes with your cane – then give him some chapatties and throw him out."

"Yes certainly sir, that would indeed have been my intention and I would not have worried you. However, sir, when I and the two sweepers who found him woke him and held him fast ready for me to give him a little gentle correction before throwing him out, I discovered – er – I found...."

"Well what did you find – out with it man."

"I found, sir, that he was a feringhi. In fact sir, despite the ragged clothes, the blood and a large bump on his head, he is undoubtedly a European."

"A Eurasian then – you know what I mean."

"No sir, a European. I said nothing to the two sweepers but left them holding the boy and hurried up here to see you."

Saridar, who had been lounging back on his divan, sat up. He knew the man to be intelligent, comparatively well educated, and unlikely to be mistaken. He told him to bring the boy – but on his own without the two sweepers who should be told nothing.

It was already late in the afternoon when Conrad, with his hands tied behind his back, was brought in to the Nawab by the mahout. Conrad was in a defiant mood. His aches and pains were still troubling him. But when he had been woken, he had wrestled with the two sweepers who had been holding him and he had shouted out – in English – as the mahout had come forward with the obvious intention of giving him a few strokes with his cane or whip or whatever it was he was holding. The mahout had stared at him after he had shouted and had then turned and disappeared for some minutes while the two sweepers held him fast. When he returned he had brought some rope and tied Conrad's hands together behind his back, but had not done so viciously or with any intention to hurt. He had dismissed the two sweepers and had then hurried the boy up into the house to come face to face with the Nawab.

The Nawab looked at the filthy ragamuffin with grey shorts so torn that it looked as if all he was wearing was his cotton underpants. Hardly any of the shirt was left and his feet were dirty and bleeding. But the mahout was right, he was undoubtedly a European, probably English. Saridar Khan motioned to the mahout to untie the boy's hands and to go and sit by the door. Then he turned to the boy and said in good English –

"Please sit down over there. Would you like some tea?"

"Oh yes please, sir" came Conrad's polite automatic reply.

Conrad was at an age where he teetered between boy-child one moment and a youth the next. He had coped with the fight in the street as a boy, he defied the two sweepers and the really rather gentle mahout as a young lad, and now he reacted to the well-bred drawing room drawl of the Nawab, as he had been brought up to be – polite and civilised.

Tea was brought in, together with some cakes. Conrad who was ravenously hungry nevertheless ate daintily and politely as he had been taught. He told Saridar exactly who he was and who his parents were. He skated over the issue of where he had been during the last three weeks and left Saridar with the impression that he had been left outside the fort when the two regiments had first arrived.

They were almost at the end of this polite teatime conversation when a servant knocked and entered after the Nawab had nodded at the mahout to let him in.

"Your Excellency, the Subadar-major has requested an audience with you urgently."

"Oh – where is he at the moment?"

"Waiting in the hall at the bottom of the stairs. I have arranged for coffee to be served to him and his assistant."

"Tell him I am coming down right away. Junior mahout – please note that you are now the official senior mahout of the state elephant. Please stay here and see that the feringhi boy does not escape. Keep this door locked and do not let anyone in until I return."

Then reverting to English he said to Conrad –

"I'm sorry old man, I have to see to something for a moment. Please finish the cakes, I'll be back shortly."

Saridar hurried out and heard the mahout locking the door behind him. He walked downstairs to where the Subadar and Jemadar of the 68th were waiting for him.

"Ah – Your Excellency – it is good of you to see us so promptly and you do us honour to come down in person. We are making a search of the houses in this area. An English boy – the son we now believe of the previous senior officer of the East India Railway Company, appears to have slipped out of the fortified house in the Hamid Mansion grounds and is roaming the streets. He was last seen somewhere in this area."

"Well, well Subadar sahib, I am grateful for the information though I'm not sure why you have gone out of your way to keep me informed. I'm sure you will find him if he hasn't already fled into the countryside."

Saridar waved airily in a gesture of dismissal – but the officers were not going to be put off so easily..

"Your Excellency – to be sure of apprehending the boy the whole area must be thoroughly searched including, sir, this building and the gardens."

For a moment the Nawab thought of pulling rank and going for a haughty superior tone. But then decided not to raise the stakes in that way. Thinking far quicker than he was wont to do and with a satisfying quickening of his senses he said –

"Why of course. This house is full of servants and it is most unlikely that he could be hiding here, nevertheless he could certainly have got over the wall and be in the garden. There are sheds and outbuildings all over the place. Get your men to search the grounds now, while I arrange for my household here to be ready for you to search in here if you don't find him."

"But I would prefer...."

"No, not another word. Come Subadar you will want to see

the ladies quarters too won't you? Well those of the zenana must be given a minimum moment to get veiled and ready for you to enter."

"Of course, of course, I understand – I will make sure that only officers will enter the zenana."

The sepoy officers salaamed and strode out and Saridar heard them giving instructions to the small group of soldiers at the front door. They all went round into the back gardens. Saridar waddled up the stairs and called to the mahout to open the door. He hurried into the room and stood thinking hard. Staring at Conrad he was in a quandary as to how to deal with the situation. Up to this moment he had acted instinctively. He was not a brave man but he was determined that he was not just going to hand the boy over to the rebels. Once again it was impossible to analyse his motives. It was a combination of a refusal to be bullied anymore – a quixotic desire not to see a child harmed – a cynical thought that the protection of the boy might be helpful in the face of any future vengeful retribution by a recovering Raj. He came to a decision as Conrad, aware of a new tension, stared back at him.

The Nawab said to him in a heavy man-to-man English, the only kind he knew,

"Look my dear fellow, those soldiers outside are looking for you, and you are going to have to hide. Do you understand?"

"Yes sir, I do. I am sorry to cause you trouble – I could run away if you prefer."

"No. Just follow me. How old are you?"

"Twelve, sir"

"Oh dear – a bit old. Well it can't be helped." Saridar thought to himself as he contemplated what he was about to do that after all it was known that the feringhi did not mature as quickly as Indian boys.

Motioning the newly promoted mahout to follow him, he led Conrad out of the room and down a corridor right up to a door at the far end where he knocked and waited. The door was immediately opened by an elderly lady, who at once drew her shawl over her mouth and nose and bowed to the Nawab. The mahout standing behind carefully looked away. Saridar spoke to him quickly and he sat down cross-legged in front of the door facing back down the corridor. The Nawab pulled Conrad in behind him and went through into a suite of rooms. The door closed.

Conrad knew that he was in the ladies quarters – the zenana of a high-class Indian family – where normally the only male allowed in was the husband. There were strange scents and a cloying sweetness in the air – rosewater - and he felt awkward, dirty and dishevelled. Saridar knew that the officers would demand seeing over the whole house and the zenana was the only place he could think of for hiding the boy. But now that he was here he had no idea how to set about it. He found his young wife - Sunitra – and explained the situation to her hurriedly. Conrad standing behind him shuffled his bare feet and reddened at the sight of the young woman in front of him who he assumed was the Nawab's daughter. He waited understanding only snatches of the Nawab's words.

Saridar, relieved that someone else was now going to look after the problem of hiding a small and dirty boy, looked hard at Sunitra. She looked back at him and nodded, indicating that she would deal with it. Saridar turned, shook hands with the now thoroughly bemused Conrad and said –

"Stay here with Sunitra, old chap, and do what she says. She'll see that the soldiers don't catch you. Good luck."

He then wandered off to an accompaniment of some bowing and scraping, calling back-

"Sunitra hanum, you only have about twenty minutes at the most before they will be here at the door."

The zenana quarters of the Nawab's establishment, which would have been full of many females of different ages in his palace at Jagpur, here in Darabad consisted only of the old lady who managed the house, Sunitra herself and one attendant who, like herself, was only sixteen. The three ladies having seen off the Nawab now turned their full attention and their huge kohl-enhanced brown eyes onto Conrad.

Conrad, in confusion, tried a shy smile. He was not afraid but felt somehow that he would have preferred fighting off the toughs who had beaten him up in the street than his present situation. However pure instinct had come to his aid and the shy smile did the trick. The two girls and the woman broke into giggles, came up and began touching him and chatting at speed together as to what could be done. Of course they had no English and Conrad could only understand one or two of their words. But although Conrad remained shy as he was poked and prodded he understood that they had come to a decision and were trying to help him, so he stayed still.

In the next fifteen minutes he was hustled into a bedroom and the old lady came in. Conrad had to strip off all his clothes while the old lady bustled in and out carrying bowls of water and a towel. Conrad did not feel at all embarrassed as he washed and towelled himself, but he was uncomfortably aware that the door was open and that two pairs of eyes were watching.

Once cleaned up, at first Conrad was unclear what the old lady was handing to him to wear after he had put his underpants back on. The shalwar kameez looked to him as if they were flimsy long trousers – but as more clothes were thrust at him he realised that he was being dressed as a girl. In almost any other circum- stances Conrad would have objected, but by now noises coming from the rest of the house were making the women nervous. Sunitra and her companion came in and they were no longer giggling. Conrad felt the new tension – a fear instead of a latent sexuality – and he stood still as a shawl was thrust over his hair and then pinned up to cover his mouth and nose.

There was a knock at the door. Sunitra looked at the old lady and was about to nod when she looked down at Conrad's bare feet. No longer dirty or bleeding they were nevertheless big feet and undoubtedly masculine.

"Oh God – look at those feet. Too late to change to a long sari! The slippers – the slippers – the frilly ones,. Never mind, never mind, let them crack at the back, just push them on."

Tears came unbidden to Conrad's eyes as his feet were brutally forced into a pair of pink slippers far too small for his feet. But he too could see the incongruity between his bare feet and the flimsy delicate attire in which he was dressed.

More loud knocking.

The old lady hurried out as Sunitra draped herself over a sofa and motioned Conrad to kneel by her side holding a bowl of some sort of aromatic oil with a rather disturbing musky smell. The companion stood behind him in a sort of tableau as they waited for the arrival of the soldiers.

PART V

The Battle of Darabad

It was the morning of the 19th August. Dr. MacAlistair awoke early. During the night he had remained with the cannons, the bullock carts and the two elephants on the east side of the River. The rest of the 5th Fusileers had crossed over during the previous evening to join the Dinapore detachment, commanded by Captain Reith-Davies, holding the Syed Ghat on the other side of the river. The crossings were easy as the small steamer that had brought the troops from Dinapore was still moored at the Ghat.

As it happened, fortunately, Reith-Davies outranked the young Captain who was in command of the small detachment which had peeled off from the main force at Dumroon. There was therefore no problem about the experienced Reith-Davies taking overall command of the combined force. He was supremely confident. He now knew every twist and turn of the road from the Ghat to Darabad, every possible ambush site or defensive position. On top of that his eyes gleamed with professional confidence as he saw the four cannon which had been brought up from Dumroon slowly and carefully being off-loaded from the steamer which had been steadily crossing and re-crossing the river all morning. There seemed to be no hurry. Spies had already gone ahead and returned reporting that the little fort was still standing firm, though there was continual shooting going on.

Reith-Davies explained the terrain and the general situation to the even younger Captain Garner of the 5th Fusileers. The first obstacle the Relief force had to surmount was the Rajiv Hill which could be seen just over a mile away. This was now well-defended by the sepoys who were always at their best when defending and holding firm in prepared positions. But of course this time there were cannon to redress the balance.

"Look Garner, I believe for this first obstacle we can have no more hesitation, no more cumbersome and time-consuming flanking movements. We go at them with the guns, and the moment they are softened up and any ramparts broken down, we assault with cold steel."

Garner agreed and both officers began the necessary preparations. By this time MacAlistair had crossed over with all his stores and medicines carefully carried by two native bearers whom the doctor had been grooming to help him with all his medical requirements.. He listened eagerly to the short discussion of the two officers. He looked up at the low hill and thought to himself that at last he was going to witness a real full-scale battle.

Yet to his surprise there was still no great bustle or any urgent movement. The steamer could not moor on the opposite bank as it was too shallow, though it could get very close. However, this did mean that rafts had to be used just to get from the bank to the ship, and this meant a lot of pushing and pulling for the bullock carts. The elephants had to come across on their own, lifting up their trunks as they crossed the deepest part of the river in the middle. The tents and the greatcoats they had been carrying all had to be loaded onto the steamer separately. Then on the western side they had to be loaded back up on the elephants, made firm and fastened.

It all took time even though the first line of infantry began moving forward before all the unloading was complete. The whole process had started very early in the cool of the morning, but the sun was rising fast and it got hotter and hotter. MacAlistair could see that there was no hurry.

On the other side of Darabad, the detachment of the 68th regiment escorting the 12-pounder cannon from Jaunpur had crossed the River Soane the night before, once the steamer, which had been holding them up, had been neutralised. They were now about twelve miles away from the western outskirts of the town – but it was of course in those very western outskirts that the Hamid Mansion was situated. Coordination was now the vital factor for the sepoy officers. Whilst they were all competent soldiers who had deserved their respective promotions to Subadar, Jemadar, and Havildar, they were not quite so used to taking strategic decisions as opposed to immediate tactical ones.

Contact between the Havildar-major at the River Soane escorting the 12-pounder gun and the two Subadars of the 66th and 68th regiments had of course been easy. Couriers could cover the distance between them within about an hour. The same was equally true of contact with the officers in command on the Rajiv Hill who were even closer. The two senior officers were clear about the position – they had half their forces watching the movements of Reith-Davies and the arriving relief force coming from the Syed Ghat, and the other half keeping up a barrage against the zenana house ready for a final assault. It was easy for them to send another courier back to the River Soane to call for the urgent arrival of the 12-pounder cannon. It was not so easy to decide how the cannon should be deployed once it arrived.

In the end the two officers decided to call another council of war with the Nawab. This decision was a significant moment. It was typical of the relationship between the mutineering soldiers of the Bengal army on the one hand and the current native political leadership in the areas under their control on the other. It illustrated the fact that most of the mutineering regiments had no political agenda or initiative of any kind. Here in Darabad it meant that 'power' in their interaction began for the first time to flow away from the sepoy officers towards the otherwise militarily inexperienced Saridar Khan. Psychological domination, that nebulous immeasurable factor, began to swing away from the hitherto overbearing military men.

Nevertheless until this moment the necessary orders had been issued. The 12-pounder was lumbering down the road to Darabad as fast as it could go. The British force at the Syed Ghat had still not yet advanced – and in any case it was known to be commanded by the same young man who had failed to break through to the besieged fort only a week or so ago. A messenger was sent to the da Costa house requesting a meeting for a discussion on some strategic matters.. The two senior subadars together with a couple more junior officers strolled up to the maidan.

Meanwhile, Conrad had remained for almost three days hidden in the da Costa house. The inspection of the zenana quarters by the two Jemadars had passed in an atmosphere of acute embarrassment on the part of the two sepoy officers. Sunitra had taken full charge of the situation from the moment that the old lady had opened the door, The elderly woman had started the softening up process immediately by giving the two men and the soldiers behind them a freezing look of great contempt. She stood aside for the two officers but stepped quickly back into the doorway and turned her back on the soldiers outside making it quite clear that they could not enter.

The two young officers moved into the heavily scented room and were clearly very embarrassed to be intruding into another man's zenana. They kept their eyes away from the lovely face of Sunitra, who had deliberately raised her veil.

"Gentlemen, I understand that you wish to search the zenana in case some young man is hiding here. I find it quite extraordinary but please go ahead and go into any of my rooms. I and my two companions will remain here. Please do your work as quickly as possible."

The two officers mumbled their thanks and went round the other rooms in the zenana. In all the rooms Sunitra had had the time to arrange for intimate articles of female clothing to be left all over the place. The two men really had no chance. Everything

– class – caste – the cultural taboo of invading the women's quarters – meant that they simply could not wait to get out of there as quickly as possible. Conrad, suffering with his feet forced into the tiny slippers and himself uncomfortable in the heavily feminine atmosphere, was not aware of how impossible the task was for the two native officers. Accordingly, his heart was pounding with fearful anticipation as the two men passed from one room to the other. But even in this extremity he could not after all keep his eyes closed all the time and he was as aware of Sunitra's beauty and charm as he had been of Marietta's. Meanwhile, Sunitra herself was not the least bit afraid and as the two men shuffled back into the room indicating that they had finished, looking daggers at them she said –

"Well – are you finished looking at all my intimate things? Are you proposing now to examine me? No? Well then, if you are satisfied that I am not sheltering some strange man in my rooms , please go."

And they did!

That same evening Sunitra arranged for servants to go out and purchase clothes suitable for a high-caste Indian boy of Conrad's age and size. Saridar Khan was out of his depth in this situation. He wanted to make a friend of this 12-year-old English boy, but he really had no idea how to do it. Furthermore his motivation was so mixed as to be incomprehensible to him. Did he intend to hold the boy as a sort of hostage? Did he perhaps simply like the lad and want to preserve his life in what was a dangerous situation? What about the hope that by saving the boy's life from the mutineers, he might be able to avoid the otherwise inevitable retribution from the avenging British? Then finally what about his lack of any sons of his own despite all those wives? He never knew, he never worked it out.

Meanwhile, however, Conrad remained for three days in a little room and watched through the window the comings and goings in the maidan. He ate his meals alone, but at 4.00pm every afternoon without fail he went to the Nawab's reception room and they had tea together with English-style cakes and polite and somewhat stilted conversation, during which Conrad managed to say 'sir' in almost every sentence. Despite his moments of fear and despite his beating by the boys, Conrad never really believed that he was in any real danger. He knew nothing of the massacre at Cawnpore. He was unaware that in their frenzy and uncertainty, the desperate sepoys, in many ways victims rather than perpetrators, were denying their own culture in deliberately slaughtering the children of their oppressors when they could be found. So it was that, unaware of any danger, Conrad made every effort to behave as a well-brought up English boy would behave at any afternoon tea party. He knew that he should not slurp his tea, that he should converse quietly and politely, that he should not wriggle about on his chair or be inattentive. He spent the rest of his time, when not in his little room, exploring all over the da Costa house, noting all the little hiding places where he could hear and not be seen.

It was now the 19th August and Conrad was up and about like everyone else.

At the Syed Ghat the Relief force was at last on the move. All the guns and stores, together with the elephants and the bullock carts, were now across the River. Dr MacAlistair again carefully wrote down in his journal what he himself witnessed as the battle in and around the town of Darabad began.

"Our combined party, comprising about 280 British regulars together with a further 80 or so Sikh volunteers who had joined the force from Dinapore, began to advance up the road leading to Darabad at about 10.00am. The four cannons were limbered up and moved forward with the first line of infantry. In front of them went some skirmishers and scouts and it was they who received the first shots from the advanced enemy pickets. They were all hidden in the woods on either side of the road.

Our young Captain made no attempt to start any complicated flanking movements but simply moved steadily on with the front line. The muskets firing from the woods on either side were fairly useless as they were over 200 yards away, but clearly they had to be dealt with before we could risk going past them.. As the front line moved on, the cannon were dragged ahead, were unlimbered and immediately started firing point blank into the woods on each side. I saw, with some glee and excitement, groups of sepoy soldiers running back from the woods on the right and up the hill towards where the line of waiting sepoys could be seen on the ridge firing down at us.

Then to my surprise from the woods on the left I saw a loose order of sepoys moving out and down the hill towards our own rearguard; this despite the fact that on the right side the sepoys were fleeing back in confusion. It showed how in battle conditions one group of men can react in panic, while in exactly the same circumstances not even far away, complete calm and order can continue to exist in another group.

This party of advancing enemy closed on the rear of our column still moving up the hill behind us, causing a lot of confusion and even some loss of baggage. The elephants carrying the tents and the greatcoats were stampeded and there was a great deal of uproar and a lot of shooting from our rearguard. The noise was considerable and caused me some concern, but I saw that the men around me and also our two officers ignored it all, keeping their eyes in front leaving it to the rearguard to deal with.

I soon realised that most of the noise was coming from the trumpeting of the elephants who were getting in a panic from all the shooting, as they so often do. I really do not understand why the military here still use them. In the past when battles were man to man at close quarters, and where even muskets had little effect unless the combatants were close, they might well have been useful if only to terrify the enemy by their size. However, now, with cannon and above all the deadly rifle, accurate at up to 1000 yards, they are really not worth bringing anywhere near a battlefield anymore. I saw one of them shake himself loose of his mahout, throw off all his baggage and come rushing forward to where we, having got rid of the enemy on our flanks, were now moving forward up the hill. Never looking where it was going, it caught the trail of one of our 9-pounders and upset the whole lot – gun – drivers – bullocks – ammunition; everyone yelling at the beast adding to the uproar.

However, that episode aside, the front line continued steadily to advance up the low incline of the hill towards the enemy. Once the rearguard had dealt with the sepoy flanking party which had caused such pandemonium, the guns which had moved up were again unlimbered and began sending shells up at the line of sepoys holding the top of the ridge. I don't know what damage that short bombardment did, but the next thing

I saw was what I had always heard about – the sight of a line of redcoats with fixed bayonets charging at the enemy, yelling at the top of their voices. Impossible, of course, if the enemy had had rifles like the Lee-Enfield. However, with only the old Brown Bess musket and facing the terror of cold steel I did not wonder that I then saw a whole line of men rising in front of us and running back down the road on the other side as fast as they could go.

I was amazed to find when I too reached the top of the hill, where the men had halted, that I had to treat only a few men for injuries. There were only three deaths and I found on examining them that only one had died of a bullet wound – the other two had died of a mixture of heat exhaustion and sunstroke.

However, when we reached the top of the hill we saw that the sepoys were not just running away in panic. They were in fact running back to where a sort of mud breastwork had been constructed across the road. This extended to about 50 yards on each side of the road, going right up to some woods on my right, but ending in the middle of cultivated fields on my left. We had already advanced about a further mile by this time and so these breastworks were only about two miles from the outskirts of the town which could now be seen shimmering in the distance. I came up to where the young Dinapore captain was looking at the defences through his spyglass. After a few minutes he turned to our own captain and said –

"Well, Garner, there is no way we can storm them there with another frontal assault – we simply could not afford the casualties that would cause. Fortunately we have plenty of time and I think we could mount a flank attack on our left through the fields from the south. We will have to keep them occupied on our front as well."

"Could we afford a feint on our right as well."

"Not really – we just don't have enough men."

Meanwhile I watched as all our men, previously keyed up for their charge and in a state of nervous tension with their eyes alight with the fire of battle, flopped down to take a rest in the shade of a clump of trees at the side of the road. Suddenly, in a matter of seconds, they looked exhausted.. My first battle – and I wondered if other battles were like this – moments of extreme tension, uproar and excitement, interspersed with periods of extraordinary calm and quiet when you can even hear the birds singing. The officers continued to confer – after all there was no urgency.

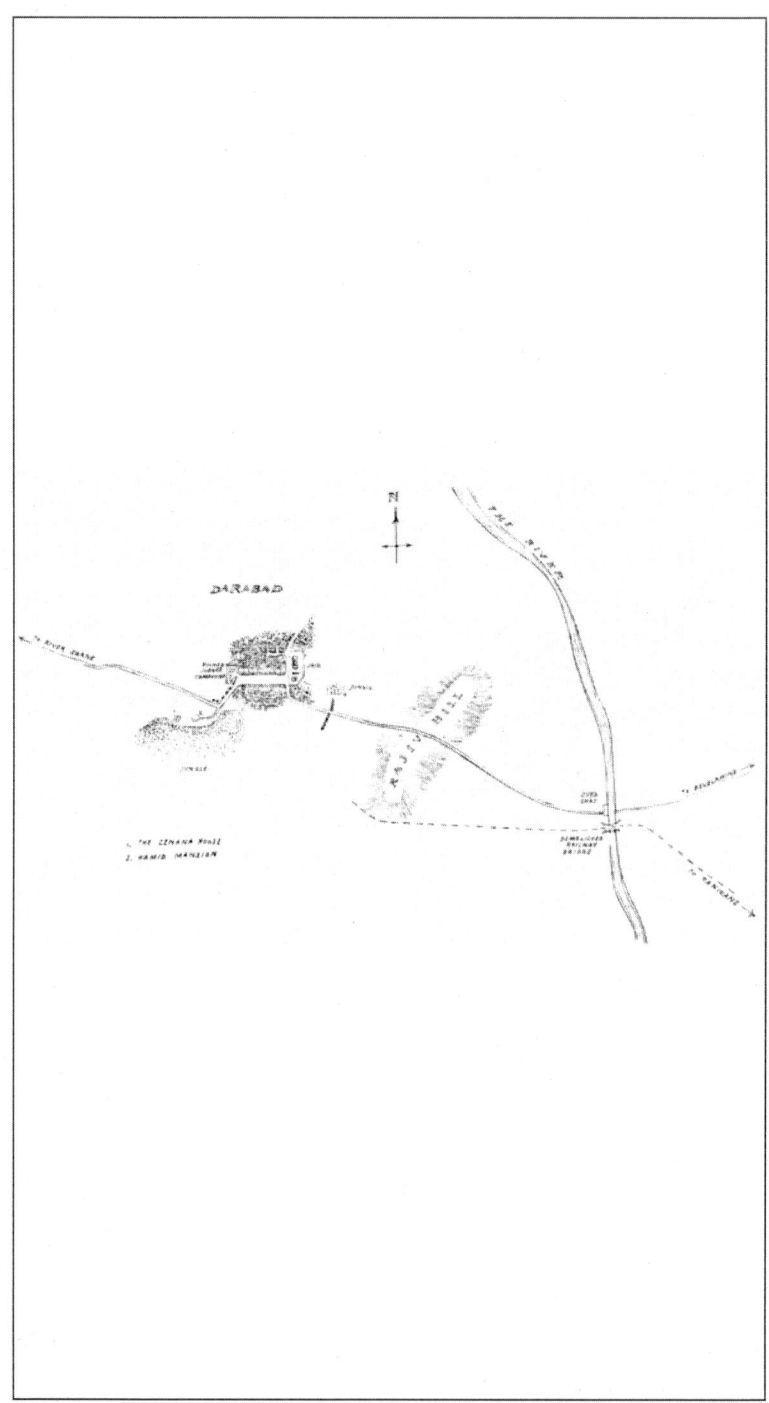

When the Sepoy officers arrived at the da Costa house, Saridar Khan was already seated in what had become the audience room. This was where the polite daily teas had been served. Unnoticed by anyone Conrad was perched in a niche behind a rather tasteless statue in the hall outside, curious to hear all that was going on if he could. The atmosphere in the meeting was quite different from all the previous meetings between the Nawab and the sepoy officers. A subtle change had taken place. The Nawab sat with a confidence he had never felt before. The fact that he was here entirely of his own accord; that he had been acting, however muddled his motivations, entirely on his own initiative, seemed to give him a new confidence based on his own character rather than on any inherited wealth or position. His little defiance in the matter of the young English boy also appeared to have given him even more resolve. He may not understand much of what was going on around him, but by God he was not going to be browbeaten anymore by these pesky Brahmins.

The change was reflected in the sepoy officers. They sensed the difference in the Nawab, and they were conscious that they themselves really should have acted more decisively and not convened this advisory council at all. For the first time they were sitting up straight in the Nawab's presence and not lounging.

"Your Excellency, we have arrived at the critical point of this siege. The 12-pounder cannon, purchased through the good offices of Haidar Presaud, is now only a few miles away and approaching the town fast. It should arrive within two more hours at the most."

"Well Subadar, that seems satisfactory. I am told that it will reduce the feringhi fort into rubble within an hour. So why this conference?"

"Your Excellency, a small British relief force has meanwhile arrived at the Syed Ghat and is attempting to advance on the town from the east."

This news took the edge off Saridar's new-found confidence for a moment. He had not even been told that for the past two days Reith-Davies and a force from Dinapore had been holding the Syed Ghat.

"Hmm – well Subadar – you had little difficulty holding them a week ago – are they now that much more numerous?"

"No, sir, but they do have cannon, 9-pounders. I am sure that we can hold them. This council is really being held to decide where and how to deploy our own approaching big gun."

"What's the problem?"

"Do we first train the cannon on the zenana house and reduce it to ruins, capture the fort and then hurry across the town and use it in defence against the force moving against us from the Syed Ghat? Alternatively, do we just ignore the fort – after all it can do us no harm – and take the cannon through the town immediately, in order to blast the force coming from the east, after which we can bring it back and take the fort at leisure."

The discussion, which the two senior officers had been unable to resolve between themselves, ran on for over half an hour. The Nawab said nothing, largely because he had no idea what to say or what it was all about. Conrad in his little corner perch outside, unaware of how important this discussion could be for his family, got bored and slipped out of his niche and quietly padded back to his room.

Form a purely military point of view there was really no doubt that the approaching cannon should be pushed through the town as fast as possible while the breastworks holding the road from the Syed Ghat were still strongly held. Once properly sited it might well be able to turn the tide against the approaching relief force. It would prevent any flank attack through the open fields, while in any contest with the 9-pounders now reduced to only three due to the panicking elephants, it could well force them to move back out of range. But a series of considerations caused the sepoy officers to make their final tragic decision to use the gun first against the fort.

To begin with, the cannon was after all approaching down the road which went right past the Hamid Mansion. Then, it would seem that the British force now facing the breastworks appeared to have stopped. Above all there was the psychological factor.

These men had been trying to defeat the irritating little fort for weeks and they were determined to finish it off – come what may. So it was decided that the cannon would first go into action against the zenana house the moment it arrived. The current force defending against the British on the road to the Syed Ghat, at odds of over four to one, should be more than sufficient to hold on until the fort was captured. Accordingly the force of about 400 men currently held in reserve in the town would be deployed at the Hamid Mansion to join the men already there for the final assault once the fort was reduced to rubble.

It was George Grant who first noticed the build-up of the enemy among the trees and in and around the Hamid Mansion. He immediately drew the attention of Baldur Singh to this and both men watched carefully as the morning wore on. It soon became clear that some sort of assault was again being prepared. But they had beaten off assaults before. The garrison, whose mood swings had been so violent, were now in a state of almost feverish excitement and this applied as much to the phlegmatic Ghurkas as to the more volatile Europeans.

That morning they had already heard the roar of Reith-Davies' guns on the other side of the town when they had opened up against the sepoy line on the Rajiv Hill. Once again a relief was being attempted and this time it was not just the sound of muskets and rifle fire – there was also artillery. GG and the Sikh commander stood together watching every movement as more and more soldiers arrived to join those already present surrounding the fort.

"Well Jemadar sahib, what do you make of this build-up," said Arthur Drummond as he came up to the two men together with John Tate who was already standing beside them carefully looking out with his powerful spy-glass.

"I believe that they are going to make one more final effort to take the fort before the relief force breaks through. Mind you I don't see that anything has changed to make this assault any more likely to be a success than all the others they have tried," replied Baldour Singh

The judge nodded in agreement and then added –

"You know, I really can't see why they are so obsessed with this one little spot."

"Because they are unthinking simpletons totally under the thumb of some bloody Brahmins who have persuaded them that if they don't wipe us out they are going to lose caste, or be dishonoured in their religion or something equally silly." said GG.

"Hmm! I'm not sure it's quite as simple as that Grant," said John, speaking directly to GG for the first time since Conrad's disappearance. "It seems certain that the immediate and deliberate killing of their officers, once any mutiny began, was carried out by the tiny minority of leaders and instigators of each regiment with the clear intention of committing the waverers in the ranks. Once that had happened the majority, desperate and in a panic had to go along with the minority."

"But that doesn't answer – why this little fort?"

"Because it's here – that's all. One way or another, whether we like it or not we have become a symbol."

"Then why did we...."

But at this point all conversation ceased, for a great shout of triumph rose from the four or five hundred sepoys now massed around the Hamid Mansion and in the trees. Out came John's spyglass; but it was not really necessary. Trundling down the road leading to the River Soane came a column of sepoy cavalry led by a Havildar-major with a pennant proudly fluttering from his raised lance – the British colours of the 68th regiment – and behind them slowly coming into sight a line of bullock carts. There was no need for any spyglass. In plain view, leading the column was a great cart drawn by a team of eight strong oxen, on which was the unmistakeable and ominous shape of a large cannon.

"Oh my God it's a monster", said John.

"Ah yes, I'm afraid it's a 12-pounder," muttered the Jemadar. "It will take them almost two hours to have it properly unlimbered and sited. But once set up, they are going to pulverise this place. I'm afraid the building doesn't have a chance."

"What do you suggest," said GG. "What about a sortie just before they finish setting it up with a view to getting to it and spiking the damn thing. We did it with the tunnel, surely we...."

"Grant, sahib, look at the five or so hundred men poised ready for an assault. Your suggestion of running across 300 yards in the open is just a form of suicide. Our only chance now is a continued defence in the hope that the relief force will break through in time. Let me tell you how I propose to deal with it all."

By now the remaining male Europeans, except for Dr. Henty already working to get his hospital room ready, were gathered round the little group together with the Ghurka sergeant and the two Sikh havildars. They all listened carefully as Baldur Singh explained exactly what his plan was. He set out what he believed was going to happen once the bombardment began and exactly what he was proposing to do about it. Everyone understood perfectly and they each went off with the grim determination to explain it to the women, while Baldur Singh explained the plan to the rest of the men and directed them as to exactly what each was to do when the signal was given.

The whole garrison worked cleaning up their rifles, building up spare ammunition to be ready at hand, filling whatever they could find with water and putting them down by their side. They watched grimly as the bullocks turned into the Hamid grounds and slowly but surely the cannon was taken down placed on its base and turned to face the little building.

Back in the da Costa house, Saridar Khan, the Nawab of Jagpur, fated to be the last in his house of Timurid ancestors due to the lack of any son, sat on after the sepoy officers departed contemplating his situation. He was caught between two implacable forces. On the one hand the sepoy mutineers who deep down despised him and who were using him only for their own desperate purposes. On the other, the British who would surely now focus their vengeance on him despite all his protestations if they won the coming battle.

He needed to act, to do something. He could no longer

remain simply sitting in this house waiting for whatever might transpire. It now felt as much of a trap as had his isolated palace at Jagpur. Every decision he had made, from the moment that that blasted man Haidar Presaud had clattered into his court-yard with the men of the 68th regiment, had turned out to be wrong. Now even his sheltering of the feringhi boy looked as if it could rebound on him. If the British attempt at relief failed and the fort fell, sooner or later the boy would be discovered and his already shaky relationship with the officers of the mutineering regiments would collapse. If, however, the British succeeded and the sepoys were defeated, then, coupled as it would be to his voluntary return to the siege, it would appear as if he had been holding the boy to be used as a hostage.

The sound of the gunfire and the growl of the British cannon to the east of the town on the road from the Syed Ghat seemed to be getting closer all the time. No sound came from the west, but Saridar knew that the 12-pounder was on its way and would soon open up. One way or another it was going to be the day of decision. He could not afford to hesitate any more. In the end it was his warlike Mongol Timurid ancestors who prevailed over the soft living of his forbears of the latter centuries. The defer-ence shown to him by the sepoy officers only an hour ago; the admiration of the lovely Sunitra who had been thrilled by his atypical decisive action over the English boy; the stirring of a sort of ancestral martial pride; and a recklessness that began to effect him as he took stock of the very few options remaining to him; all combined to make up his mind in a fashion that would have been unthinkable only a few weeks ago.

He sent for the mahout and for Conrad.

"Mahout – is the howdah in which we first arrived still avail-able?"

"Certainly, Your Excellency. I can have it ready and in place within an hour."

"Then do it at once. I intend going down to be present at the final assault on the zenana house of the Hamid mansion. No, no don't be anxious I will not be making any attempt to intervene. I understand perfectly well that the state elephant is not and never was a fighting animal. But I wish to be present in state for the final assault."

"Your Excellency I...."

"Ah. Master Tate – come in, come in."

"Good morning sir" said Conrad as he knocked and then walked straight in. He was fully dressed in the high quality Indian clothes purchased by Sunitra – but without any headgear. He had already been three days in the house and went about the premises with a new confidence and a complete lack of any of the fear that he had experienced during the two days that he had been on the run. He no longer even felt any shyness towards the roly-poly figure of the Nawab with whom he had been enjoying all those polite teas in the afternoons.. Saridar Khan himself never had the slightest idea how to talk to a young boy and so had always talked to him as if he was an adult and an equal.

"Look, old man, those shots that you can hear are the sounds of a battle going on at the Syed Ghat on the River. Have you heard them?"

"Yes, sir. I thought they were another attack on the fort. I couldn't tell what direction the gunfire was coming from."

"Hm – well as it happens there is indeed going to be another assault. I am going down there on the elephant. I'm afraid, old fellow, as the sepoys now have a large cannon, it looks as if the fort will fall today. . I hope that there will be no unnecessary killing once the fort is taken and I want to be there to try and control things and prevent any...er...er...whatever. Most of the garrison will survive the bombardment I'm sure."

"Yes, sir."

Conrad was not such a child that he did not realise perfectly well that they were talking about the survival of his family. But at the same time it was unreal. Somehow, he did not equate what was about to happen at the fort, perhaps even to his own family with all the blood and gore which he had coped with more than adequately when helping Dr. Henty.

"Listen, old chap, would you like to accompany me on the elephant. There will just be you and me and of course the mahout. You never know but you might perhaps be of some help when the fort falls."

The idea did not come out of the blue – it was in the Nawab's mind all along. But even he did not quite know why. He felt for a start that he could not leave the boy alone in the house. Sooner or later one of the servants was going to disclose his presence to the soldiers and with passions inflamed as they were that could result in a nasty death. At the same time, while he had no idea what was going to transpire at the Hamid Mansion, he did have a vague feeling that his presence and that of the boy might prevent a massacre. Finally there was something dramatic – traditional – glorious – in his going forth in full regalia on the state elephant. He would have his rifle with him and riding behind him would be his enemy's son, also fully and ceremonially attired, looking as if he was the son he himself had never had.

For his part Conrad never thought of the extraordinary anomaly of his joining this portly gentleman at the fall of the fort – his father's fort. He had never been on an elephant before, though he had seen many and he was excited at the idea. He was aware also of the danger in remaining in the house alone and without the protection of the Nawab. Although he had understood every word that the Nawab had said, it failed to cross his mind that he would be 'witnessing' the destruction of the very building in which his parents and his sister were sheltering. Somehow the polite teas and the formal stilted English conversations had contrived to cover over the memory of the pain, blood and squalor of the siege.

"Yes, sir – that would be super."

And so for the next forty minutes the household prepared for the solemn departure of the state elephant of Jagpur with the great carpet and the howdah fixed on its back. A splendid white turban was wound onto Conrad's head and Saridar Khan then fixed one of his own jewelled aigrettes on the front. The elephant knelt and His Excellency Saridar Khan, the Nawab of Jagpur, mounted and sat, hunting rifle in hand, behind the mahout with Conrad Tate clambering up and sitting behind. On the mahout's command the animal lumbered up and with the sound of gunfire now coming from both sides, it began a stately walk down the maidan and towards the Hamid Mansion.

At the bottom of the Rajiv Hill, Reith-Davies and Garner looked carefully at the breastworks which were preventing a move into the town ahead of them. The position held by the two regiments was strong. A direct frontal assault was almost out of the question even against muskets. The three cannon had been roaring away while the bulk of the men rested. A certain amount of damage was undoubtedly being done by the cannonade, but merely reducing the defences to rubble would not solve the problem of the difficulty of a direct frontal assault. Dr. MacAlistair stood behind the two officers as they calmly discussed the situation as if they were in a military seminar arguing out the problem in front of a training officer. His journal which he wrote up that night and which eventually formed part of the official report set it out as a non-professional would have seen it.

"I had no difficulty in following exactly what these two young Englishmen were pointing out to each other. Our total force was rather small in view of the numbers against us and it was accordingly dangerous to split it up. Nevertheless, a flank attack was going to be necessary. On the right the breastworks ended in a dense wood and attempting to attack through there would be a long and laborious task. On our left the breastworks ended in the middle of open fields. However, these fields were crisscrossed by muddy lines of tiny irrigation canals – all easily splashed through but with no cover of any kind.

I could see that it was going to be a careful matter of working out the exact range of the Brown Bess muskets wielded by the sepoys. The two young men worked it out to their own satisfaction – then explained it all to the Sergeant who understood at once. The movement to the left was to be completely open, indeed to be well-advertised. The men deputed for this movement were to continue moving round in the fields keeping as far as possible beyond the 200 yard effective range, making a great deal of noise and kneeling and firing their rifles as they advanced. At a point which the two officers had already decided upon, they were to stop and get ready for a charge. A small detachment of skirmishers, the best sharp-shooters in the regiment, were to move out simultaneously on the right in order to keep the enemy's heads down on that side, and to keep the sepoys in the woods in their position..

Meanwhile the bulk of the force was to remain in its present position about 300 yards away down the road, lying low. Even I could see immediately that the plan was that the actual final main assault would come where at first it seemed impossible – right down the main road – the very frontal assault which the two officers had started by rejecting.

The first move now began. A detachment of my own regiment – the 5th Fusileers – numbering about 150 men moved off as arranged to the left and began splashing across the little irrigation canals. This immediately resulted in a furious but rather useless firing from the breastworks in front. I could see the sepoy officers shouting and yelling at their men to move across to their right to face the flanking movement openly taking place in front of them. At the same time our skirmishers began moving out to the right toward the woods and began peppering the enemy in front of them. This resulted in a slight movement of the enemy to their left as well as their major move to their right to face the 5th Fusileers advancing across the fields.

I had by then dealt with the few wounds and the one major amputation resulting from the first attack. Only three men had been killed so far, but nowhere is Jack Pandy more at home on the battlefield than when sheltering behind defences himself and potting out with his musket at the enemy in the open. Accordingly it looked as if he could have gone on defending for hours if not days. But all the time, as the 5th Fusileers advanced across the fields on the left and the skirmishers moved forward firing as they went on the right, the sepoys continued to shuffle to each side weakening their centre. They seemed to be unconscious of the Dinapore men hugging the ground behind the guns right in front of them. By now the breastworks across the road had been reduced by those cannon to rubble.

Then, suddenly, right by my side where I had crept to get a better view, in a sort of high-pitched squeak, Captain Reith-Davies jumped up and shouted –

"Up and at-em men. We've got them – we've got them."

With an ear-splitting yell the men from Dinapore, together with the volunteer Sikhs, reinforced by some of our men as well, rose as one man *with their terrible bayonets fixed and glinting in the sun. They charged down the road in front of the cannons, which only then stopped firing for the first time. They ran straight down the road right at the few men now holding the centre of the defence works. It was going to be costly this time. I immediately saw men falling as they charged forward. I should really at this stage have gone back to get my operating station ready, but I could not move away from the spectacle before me. Within seconds I saw the sepoys in the centre rise from their positions and turn and run even before the first line of redcoats reached them.*

Meanwhile when the main party of the 5th Fusileers on the left saw the charge down the main road, they knelt and fired one volley en masse at the crowded sepoys now on their front. Then with their own wicked bayonets flashing in the sun they too rose and with another yell began charging, though with much more difficulty and a good deal slower than those on the road. This second charge might have been suicidal if the sepoys on their front had not seen the centre giving way and the British soldiers already over the breastworks. Within only seconds more the whole sepoy line was fleeing back in complete disarray towards the town behind them.

At this point I saw no more, as the first wounded were brought in and I became up to my ears in blood and guts, doing what I was there for in the first place."

This was the point at which Dr. MacAlistair's report ended. Reith-Davies and Garner met again on the far side of the breast-works, as the men – adrenalin still pumping – finished the bayonet slaughter of the few sepoys left vainly trying to defend their position. The bulk of the rebels were streaming back down the road to Darabad, but there seemed to be no point in chasing after them at this stage until the cannon could be brought up and the baggage moved forward. There was no cavalry available to cut down the fleeing enemy and in any case militarily the day was already clearly won. There was no way that the sepoy officers could organise any sort of rally. The battle was over.

All the yelling and the fury ceased and a silence came over the battlefield. Wounded men were being taken back to the medical station now working at full stretch. The men – still all in good order – sank to the ground once again looking exhausted with passions momentarily spent.

Then, in the sudden hush came the sound of a great deep 'boom'. The unmistakeable sound of a heavy siege gun firing about a mile or so away on the other side of the town. The 'boom' of the gun was followed immediately by the immediately recognisable sound of crashing masonry. Reith-Davies jumped up and shouted out –

"My God – they've got a cannon and they're pounding the fort....There's no time to lose. We've got to move on now....now!"

At the fort, the 12-pounder had been slowly placed onto its base. With a lot of excited pushing and pulling it was carefully pointed and loaded. The elevation was as low as possible and aimed directly at the building. Water was available to cool the barrel. The gunners were ready. The fort itself was maintaining a steady fire with the Ghurkas firing from the roof, and the Sikhs and the Europeans from above the brick walls on the first floor and the lower ground floor.

Then, as the sepoy gunners could be seen getting ready for the first shot from the cannon, the Ghurkas sidled back along the roof as arranged and clambered down the ladder into the billiard room and on down the spiral staircase to the deep and dank lower floor. The moment they got down, Baldur Singh called out –

"Second Party down!"

The Sikhs and the remaining Europeans on the first floor now stood back from their first floor loopholes and began filtering down the spiral staircase after the Ghurkas, following to the letter the Jemadar's plan. The roof and the first floor veranda, so full of men only a few moments before, were now totally abandoned just as the first great roar of the cannon went off and the great shot smashed straight into the front of the little building.

Baldur Singh had been right – not one of the unmortared brick walls remained standing. Every single one of them crumbled into a useless great pile of bricks, leaving not a loophole above them but a great big gap between each pillar. But already the great gun had been reloaded and a second shot went crashing into the pillars holding up the roof. Masonry began falling down into the billiard room. Shot after shot now slammed into the little fort – no one on the roof could have lasted a moment as the ceiling fell down in great mounds of rubble onto the veranda and into the billiard room. But as the wily Baldur had worked out, the collapsing roof and pillars completely blocked the spiral staircase leading down to the lower floor.

More shots crashed in onto the fort but all they achieved was more piles of rubble above. There was no way that the great cannon could be positioned to fire downwards, it was already at its lowest elevation. All the makeshift walls of the lower ground floor had also of course collapsed – but down there, the depth of the floor below the window openings was sufficient to give some cover to the men now shoulder to shoulder ready to fire and sell their lives dearly once the inevitable assault was mounted. Choking with the brick dust flying all over the place, and scarcely able to see more than 50 feet away from them, the garrison waited grimly for the final charge.

Slowly and with the calm dignity of thirty years of great occasions, the state elephant of Jagpur lumbered step by digni-fied step down past the ruins of the judge's compound and on towards the Hamid Mansion. The great roar of the cannon had already burst out several times as the elephant moved on with the howdah swaying from side to side on the carpet draped over its back. What was it all about? Did it represent something symbolic? What did the corpulent rather soft man sitting proudly, even arrogantly, on the back of this symbol of power think he was doing? Was this only a symbol of old India collapsing in a ludicrous delusion of majesty?

And what of the boy sitting behind, resplendent in silk robes and with a fabulous jewelled turban on his head. Seated on the back of an elephant for the first time in his life, Conrad couldn't contain his excitement. On the cusp of puberty – thirteen, even fourteen when he was helping Dr. Henty in the middle of the blood and shattered limbs of the hospital, yet scarcely even eleven as he sat behind Saridar Khan. There he sat, childishly oblivious to the irony of his being there at all, on his way to the destruction of the building which was sheltering his family.

As shot after shot slammed into the zenana house, demolishing the upper storey completely and reducing the flimsy brick walls to dust, the elephant finally arrived at the fork in the road leading to the Hamid Mansion. The fort itself was no longer visible, completely obscured by the swirling dust of the shattered stone and the collapsed bricks and with the smoke from the cannon hanging heavily in between. The four or five hundred men standing ready for the final assault gave a great cheer as the elephant turned the corner and came up to the mansion. Saridar Khan, the Nawab of Jagpur, stood up proudly as the elephant knelt at the command of the mahout. As the soldiers lifted their muskets into the air and gave a great 'huzzah', he raised his hand high in acknowledgement of the acclamation. Then at that precise moment a shot rang out from the jungle to the side.

On the road to the Syed Ghat, neither Reith-Davies nor Captain Garner had hesitated for a moment. There was no need for any elaborate discussions. Only one thing now mattered – the relief force had to storm through the town and get to the other side immediately and without any more careful manoeuvring. The men had already charged, they had just taken a prepared fortress-like position in a frontal assault. They now had to get up and do the whole thing all over again.

For the two officers it was easy. They were fired with dreams of heroism and glory. Educated in the classical tradition, with schoolboy memories of the Greek heroes, it was understandable that they should lift their swords and cry out – "Forward men – forward to the rescue!"

But what was it that made these undersized, unhealthy, runts of the industrial slums that constituted the bulk of the British regular army, ignore their exhaustion, jump up and with bayonets still fixed and levelled, trot after these two privileged men with whom they had absolutely nothing in common. Training? Fear of the brutal lash? Tribal pride? Or was it above all, the atavistic requirement to stand shoulder to shoulder with your comrades!

It was a mystery as deep as finding the motives for the symbolic, quixotic gesture of the Nawab. Whatever the reasoning the entire force – the 5th Fusileers and the men of the Dinapore garrison together with the Sikh volunteers rose as one man and with another yell of triumph began trotting forward in two distinct groups. The Dinapore detachment followed Reith-Davies in a direct drive down the road towards the houses on each side just ahead of them. The 5th Fusileers followed their young captain across the fields heading straight for the woods south of the town beyond which lay the Hamid Mansion.

Dr. MacAlistair was no longer in any position to prepare any report. Left on the road, with a small rearguard protecting the elephants and the cannon, he was fully occupied with the wounded. If the sepoy officers could have had the chance to rally their men, they might have been able somehow to delay the drive through the town, or the dash across the fields. But they never had the chance. It was one of those constants of warfare that once broken, armies often simply melted away. A battle could slog on with the issue in doubt right up the moment that suddenly one side broke. Then, once broken and streaming away in panic, the victory to the other side would be complete. On one side would be an army – on the other side a rabble of fleeing men.

And so it was at the Battle of Darabad. The 66th and the 68th Bengal infantry just melted away. Reith-Davies and his men simply raced through the town, along the maidan and out the other side meeting no resistance. Garner and his men crashed through the suburbs. They arrived almost simultaneously at the moment that the sepoys waiting to assault the fort had shouted out in honour of the smiling Saridar Khan, who had raised his hand in acknowledgement of his army – at last his very own army. An anonymous British soldier knelt and raised his Lee-Enfield rifle. One shot rang out and Saridar Khan already in the act of stepping down from the kneeling elephant lurched forward and toppled onto the ground below him – dead. As if on a signal a roar of rifle fire tore into the sepoys who had failed to react to the arrival of the victorious little army. Finally with yet another yell, the scum of the industrial north raised their rifles and led by Captain Garner they ran forward with their fixed bayonets, overran the cannon from which the gunners had already fled and chased on after the fleeing sepoys.

The smoke began to clear – the dust settled – the sounds of the slaughter as the relief force chased off the enemy began to fade. From under the rubble of the zenana house the first to creep out from the gaps in the lower storey was GG. He walked slowly forward towards the Hamid mansion. From there, also walking slowly but towards the zenana house, holstering his pistol, came Reith-Davies.

Standing halfway between them in the midst of the settling dust as they approached each other, stood Conrad. He stood there, tears streaming down his face for the first time since leaving the fort, trailing in his right hand the remnants of a bedraggled turban with a costly jewelled aigrette still pinned onto it.

EPILOGUE

So far as the British people were concerned, news of the Mutiny first reached England on the 27th June, over six weeks after the actual outbreak in Meerut. Letters, even official reports, took at least five weeks, but usually even longer, to go to and from India at this time. George Grant wrote regularly to his mother, and in the last letter she received he did indeed refer to the rumours of the outbreak at Meerut. But from the moment the sepoy regiments at Dinapore and Revelkhind mutinied, no more letters arrived and she had only the Press and the official reports on which to rely in finding out what might have happened to her son.

Once the Times first announced the news, nothing else could be thought of throughout Victorian England. Every family of all classes had ties with India and hunger for news of the Mutiny became the dominant consideration of the British public. The agony of not knowing what was happening was so great that in August the Times in a special editorial included the following sentence –

'The storm is terrible, but it's surrounding darkness is even more awful than the occasional flash of lightening.'

It was this agonising suspense, coupled to the exotic and dramatic nature of the background in which the events were taking place, which so fired the imagination of the British public. Meanwhile, the hysterical Press fed into this imagination, drip by drip, 'horror' stories of the most ferocious and lurid type. The stories all included an undercurrent of very specific violent sexuality, which quite clearly appealed to a dark unrecognised streak in the Victorian psyche. No other war, no other crisis throughout the whole of the nineteenth century had such a long-lasting effect on the mind and attitude of the British people.

As the crisis lessened and it became clear that British India would be saved, the issue of retribution arose. The demand for revenge was stoked by the popular press, which claimed that there was unanimous support for such a policy. But that was not true. In fact the whole issue fell onto a society that was irredeemably split on all aspects of the mutiny and the role of the British in India. It only needs the difference between a father and a son, commenting on the events, to illustrate this.

The mutiny broke out at the height of the evangelical movement which started in the thirties and forties. James Mill in his book on British India written in 1818 and published in the twenties excoriated Hinduism. He scornfully derided the religion as false and corrupt – "a system in the highest degree absurd, mean and degrading". Inspired by this sort of assessment the East India Company, who for one hundred years had carefully kept the missionaries out of all areas under their control, began in the thirties and forties to pursue a reform agenda, encouraging Christian missionaries to pour into the country and thus adding to the alarm of the Bengal soldiery.

As against this, John Stuart Mill, James' son, writing some thirty years later, referred in articles to the Christian/Jewish God as "the most perfect conception of wickedness which the human mind could devise – a tyrant who appears to have brought the human race into existence in order to consign the majority of them to everlasting torment." He went on to write that "the malignant principle of the 'absolute truth' of a God, any God, leads necessarily to the motive for blood revenge."

So there was a great dichotomy in the public towards the policy of swift and basically lawless retribution which the avenging evangelical British commanders, such as Havelock or Neill, were visiting on the hapless Indian soldiers and those villagers caught in the crossfire. But despite the approval of the popular press there was from the very start a strong strain of opposition to this policy of revenge, but that opposition came from the secular spirit of the age and not the religious.

On the Indian side of these events there are now some historians who consider that the Great Sepoy Mutiny, which broke out in the army of the Bengal Presidency in May 1857, should be regarded as the First Indian National War of Independence. By referring to it in this way, the events that took place in that year are presented as a direct progenitor of a Second War of Independence, begun in the 1930's and which came to its glorious conclusion in August 1947.

By inference, therefore, it equates the personalities who came to lead the Sepoys, with the great figures of what they then refer to as the Second Indian War of Independence. Personalities like the Nana Sahib of Cawnpore, or the medieval figure of the Rani of Jhansi, or the vicious and cowardly sons of the old gentleman in the Red Fort at Delhi are thus by implication depicted as the ancestors of the great figures of the true War of Independence in the twentieth century, - men like Gandhi, Patel or Nehru.

It is a total travesty, and if it was not for the fact that it is espoused only by Indian academics, it would almost seem to be postulated by people determined to 'slander' the Indian people and their patient and glorious bid for freedom from the domination of a foreign power.

For the hundred years prior to the outbreak of the mutiny, and for almost one hundred years after, in all the many other episodes in British-Indian relations there was never any deliberate or wholesale violence against European children. The 'babalog' grew up in an environment where they never felt any fear of being abused or harmed by Indian people. This applied as much in the 1940's as in the 1740's. The mutiny was unique in the fact that hundreds of European children were deliberately slaughtered with some ferocity. So much so that, whilst no accurate figures are available, it is very likely that far more children under the age of ten or eleven were murdered and died during that year than 'civilian' adults.

Of course, the Victorians, being what they were, professed to be more horrified by the slaughter of European women than by the hundreds of children killed. The hysterical British Press always harped on about the suffering of the 'women'. Lurid stories of rape, hardly any one of which was ever found to be proved, appeared on a daily basis in the columns of the newspapers. They almost all ignored the children – European and Eurasian alike – who died in their hundreds.

But to equate the mindless ferocity of the desperate Sepoys, more the victims of circumstance than deliberate villains, with the calm dignity of a Mahatma Gandhi, or the cool rational pressure of a Nehru, is a total nonsense. To refer to the Sepoy revolt as the First National War of Independence, of which the Congress movement was presumably the Second, is such a slur on the modern figures of Indian independence that it would almost seem to be deliberately intended to blacken the good name of the whole Indian freedom movement.

Wars of Independence, whether independence from an internal tyranny or independence from a foreign domination are never anything but messy and likely to give rise to a considerable amount of cruelty and even horror on both sides. So it was in the American War of Independence, so it was in the French Revolution, the independence movements in the Balkans and in India in the 1940's. But rarely if ever were the children of the dominant power or class deliberately targeted as an integral part of such movements.

But they were in 1857, because that was an irrational and desperate mutiny, which while it might well have been occasioned by the stupidity and inefficiency of a ruling class was nevertheless not a War of Independence.

As one other Indian historian has put it succinctly and dryly – 'it was neither the 'First', nor was it 'National', nor was it a 'War', nor was there any element of 'Independence' at stake.